Iron

PG Forte

"May you always have walls for the winds, a roof for the rain, tea beside the fire, laughter to cheer you, those you love near you, and all your heart might desire."

Irish Blessing

I'd like to dedicate this book to the memory of my maternal grandparents:

John A. and Maureen J. Lonergan
(nee Mary Josephine Liston)

Of Counties Tipperary and Limerick, respectively.

To quote from Enya:

"Aoibhneas a bhí
Ach d'imigh sin.
Sé lean tú
Do fhear chéile.
An grá mór i do shaoil
Treoraí sé mé."

"There was blissfulness
But that is gone.
You followed
Your husband.
The great love in your lives
Will guide me."

Praise for Iron

"The author takes the reader into a past time so convincingly that the present is lost. The characters are incredibly well written and their emotions drive the story in a haunting way. Everything about this story hit the right note for me. The characters were amazing, the dialogue spot on. The story flowed along perfectly with a strong plot, deft pacing, and a command of setting that I really enjoyed. "

The Romance Studio

"I loved the setting of this story, and P. G. Forte makes it come to life so well. Both Gavin and Aislinn are well defined and intriguing characters, with many layers to their personalities... There are tears and laughter here, and the happy ever after is an unusual one. If you enjoy magic and history, this is the book for you."

Whipped Cream Reviews

Iron was selected as a Finalist for the EPIC 2011 ebook Awards in the Paranormal Erotic Romance category.

Prologue

County Clare, Ireland
Anno Domini, 1898

Gavin O'Malley was a blacksmith, as was his father and *his* father before him. His forge stood just outside the small seaside village of Kilbanning. For three generations, there was not to be found, anywhere in the region, a horse that did not owe its shoes, nor a wagon its wheels to the O'Malleys. In fact, you'd have been hard pressed to find so much as a single nail anywhere in that part of the county that had not come from the Kilbanning forge.

"'Tis honest work," Gavin would always say when asked about his craft and, being as he was a man of few words, he seldom said more.

A blacksmith's life is rarely a long one. Gavin's father and grandfather had both died from the black lung and he himself had long accepted an early death as part of his fate. There were those who said, rather, that it was something he wished for; though they didn't say it loudly or anywhere within his hearing as the smith had the muscles that went with his profession and a temper as hot as the fires he tended.

In his youth, he'd been of a far different temperament. He'd often laughed and more than often smiled and seldom it was, indeed, that you'd have found him without a song on his lips. But neither smile nor song had graced those lips in many a year, not since the love of his life, his wife Mairead, had died giving birth to their first child—a boy, who'd died along with her.

After a decent interval had passed, the old mothers of the village, having judged that the worst of the blacksmith's grief had likely subsided, decided he must surely be wanting to wed again. Then, many a pretty miss or a bright lass—

even a handsome young widow or two——longing for a husband to care for and a hearth and home of their own to tend to, was trotted round to visit him. The hope being, of course, that one of them might catch his eye and a marriage result.

O'Malley showed no interest in any of them; and, as he seemed to grow more sullen and less cordial with each visit that was paid him, he was eventually given up as a hopeless cause and a confirmed bachelor and allowed to go his own way and peace be with him, the poor man.

But 'twas often said of him, ever afterwards, that when Gavin O'Malley had laid his young wife and child to rest in the churchyard that cold, winter's day, sure he must have laid his own heart in the ground right along with them.

Chapter One

It was just past midwinter, at the tail end of yet another cold, December day when Aislinn Deirbhile rode up from Kilbanning. She halted her mount on the rutted, dirt track and surveyed the situation before her. O'Malley's forge, and the smith's cottage which was situated across the yard from it, stood all alone in a quiet hollow, just down the road from where Aislinn sat, steeped in thought. The horse on which she was riding, being of a breed perhaps more perceptive than most, was clearly as nervous as she at the prospect; he tossed his head and whinnied softly causing the silver bells on his harness to jingle.

"Milady," pleaded the small man who rode at Aislinn's side. "Will you not reconsider? Come away from this place—now, before it's too late. My people are still willing to offer you shelter, as we have done ere these months past, and ye have yet to come to any harm with us."

"Nay, Foghan." Aislinn smiled sadly at her companion. Though slight in stature, quite dwarfed, in fact, by the tall, silver-white steed upon which he sat, the spriggan's courage was that of a giant. "You and your people are true friends indeed, but my enemy is at his strongest now. None can hope to stand against Annwn's full might." She turned her gaze back toward the small, stone buildings at the end of the lane and sighed. "If there is any shelter to be had against Winter, or if I've any hope of surviving the *geasa* that have been laid upon me, I must find them here."

"But, Lady," the little man implored, his distress evident in every line of his face. "How can there be any help for you here? A *blacksmith*. A worker in *iron*. The very ether is contaminated with its foul essence! Can you not smell it on the wind? Can you not almost taste it?"

"Oh, aye." Aislinn grinned in reply. "And can *you* not imagine the look it will put on Tiernan's face when first he tracks me here? How I wish I could see it!" But just thinking

7

about Tiernan ap Annwn, her would-be husband—nay, her would-be jailer—wiped the smile from her lips in a hurry. She urged her horse forward. "Come. Let us make haste. Night is upon us."

As they picked their way between the rocks and mud of the rutted *boreen*, Eoghan continued his litany of complaints. "Are ye still after putting your faith in that oracle you consulted this past Samhain? You canna be serous. You know as well as I that most of what occurs in the realm of the Fae is well outside the druid's ken."

"Indeed, my friend." Aislinn inclined her head. "But, as I am banished from the Realm 'til Summer's return, 'twas for information pertaining to *this* dimension that I sought out the Oracle of Death; as well as for advice on how I might best survive in *this* world."

"Sure and that Druid must have imbibed a cup too much of the *nawglan*," Eoghan said in tones of disgust. "To have bid you find shelter with a blacksmith."

Aislinn sighed. "Ah, my friend, can you not at least enjoy the irony with me? Is not the plan elegant in its subtlety? Sure and 'tis the last thing Tiernan will be expecting me to do; and once I am safe behind yon walls even you must admit I will be beyond his reach for as long as I choose to stay there."

"Aye, Lady." Eoghan's voice was grim. "And beyond the reach of any help such as I or mine might wish to offer you, as well. But why talk ye of choosing? Methinks you will not *be* safe once you are locked behind the walls of such a place. My Lord Tiernan is not the only one whose plans may be thwarted thus. That same iron you trust now to keep your too-ardent suitor *out*, may very well serve to keep you *in.*"

"I'm not unmindful of the risk, Eoghan. But, think you, how much trouble is one mortal man likely to present me? In any case, I'm sure and I'd rather take my chances with one such as he than fall prey to Tiernan's tender mercies. I fear my actions these past months have not increased his lordship's affection for me."

Eoghan chuckled. "Nay. 'Tis not likely he took it well—all his great plans laid bare aforetime and himself made to look foolish before both courts. Have a care, Lady. Even an you make it past this winter, there is still likely to be a reckoning between ye."

"I know it," she said as she sighed again. "But, hush, my friend. No more talk now. Even in this desolate place, the Night may have ears."

The sound of their horses' hooves, clattering against the cobbles, echoed loudly on the still, evening air as they entered the smith's yard. Light spilled out onto the stones when the cottage door swung open and a man appeared in the doorway. Even with his face in shadow, Aislinn's sight was such she could still detect the frown on his visage as he looked them over. His gaze swept her with barely a pause, seemed hardly to touch at all on Eoghan, who had cloaked his true form, and lingered longest on the horses.

He was an exceedingly well formed man, she observed; eyeing him back with interest for, after all, this was the man, or so the druid insisted, on whom her safety—nay, her very life—might well depend. She estimated his age at about three dozen summers, maybe a couple less. He stood well over six foot; strong and fit and fairly muscled, with hair dark as a raven's wing and thick, straight brows which almost met above an equally straight nose. Several days' worth of stubble darkened his cheeks and softened the angles of his jaw. She thought his face would have been quite pleasing, overall, were it not for the scowl that sat too comfortably upon his features, as though it had found a permanent home there.

"Well, then?" he asked, at last, and something about the deep timbre of his voice caused a shiver to run down Aislinn's spine. "And what would you two be wanting?"

"Is it Mr. O'Malley to whom I'm speaking?" she inquired, still trying to determine, in the failing light, whether his eyes were as deep a blue as she suspected. "Mr. Gavin O'Malley? The blacksmith?"

"Aye. 'Tis my name," he said. "Might I know yours?"

"Milady," Eoghan whispered urgently as Aislinn threw him her reins and slid to the ground. "Have a care!"

"It is well," she replied, amused by the spriggan's concern. Did he think her so far gone in her fear as to forget herself and make a present of her name to the whole outdoors? Still shaking her head at his foolishness, she turned toward the mortal and smiled. "My name need not concern you, for now, sir smith. But, lo, the day grows late. Will you not invite me indoors that we might discuss our business in greater comfort?"

The smith folded his arms across his broad chest. "If we have any business to discuss, you and I, sure and we can do it here. But, as you say, 'tis late, and I am past wanting my supper. So, if your business has aught to do with shoeing your horses, you'd best come back on the morrow. For they're decent looking creatures and 'tis not a job I'd wish to hurry."

At this, Eoghan uttered a muffled oath and the two *coomlaen* stamped restlessly. It was all Aislinn could do to keep from laughing at the suggestion. "Nay, it has naught to do with that." She took a step closer, subtly altering her appearance, as she did. "But, are you so cruel hearted, then, you'd deny a lady the chance to warm herself at your hearth this bitter eve?"

The blacksmith's eyes widened as he looked her over once again. "By the saints," he said, his voice suddenly thick with concern. "Are you addled, lass? To be dressed as you are, and out on a night like this? Sure and it's a wonder you've not caught your death already."

"Might I not come in then?" she inquired again.

He nodded, still frowning. "Aye, to be sure. In with ye. Quick now, before your very feet freeze to the stones."

Eoghan heaved a worried sigh as Aislinn flashed him one last glance. "*Slán agat,*" he whispered for her ears alone. "Farewell, Milady. And may your trip succeed with ye."

"*Slán leat,* my friend," she replied just as softly,

lifting her hand in farewell. "And the same to you. *Go raibh míle maith agat.*" *May you have a thousand good things.* Then she turned her smile once again on the bemused blacksmith and took his arm and, together, they entered the cottage.

*****

What madness is this? Gavin wondered, shaking his head like a man trying to awaken himself from a dream. *Am I possessed, then? Or fallen into a dream?*

It might well be a dream, he thought, given the woman's appearance, for she was like none he'd ever seen in waking life. Tall and slim, she wore a filmy green gown that well displayed her narrow waist and ample breasts but was far more suitable for a summer's day than the depths of winter. She had waves of bright hair that rippled down her back, eyes like a gray mist, and a voice whose spell you'd be glad to fall under, time and again. As for the rest of her—no, he'd not think on that.

He watched, bemused, as the creature boldly made herself at home in his cottage, tossing off the light cloak that was all she'd worn against the cold; going directly to his hearth and seating herself there beside his fire. She moved with confidence and grace and, indeed, there was such an air of nobility about her he was surprised when she chose the low *sugan* chair with its slatted back and seat of woven rope. He'd half expected her to claim the padded, wooden armchair for herself for it was larger and more comfortable looking, its leather coverings secured in place with rows of nails he'd fashioned himself.

"So, what is this business—?" he'd started to ask when a clatter of hooves on the stones outside reclaimed his attention. He turned in time to see the lady's companion riding out past his gate, with her horse tied behind. Starlight shimmered on the horses' white flanks, and the bells on their harnesses jingled softly as they jogged along.

"Hi," Gavin called out to the man, though it seemed a great effort to speak at all. "Where the devil are you going

11

then? Hi! *Hi!* Come back here."

The rider made him no answer, but the look he gave, turning briefly in his saddle to gaze sternly over his shoulder at the smith, was chill and unearthly and Gavin felt his blood run cold. The rider's eyes were pale, his face even paler, and his long, white hair outshone the moon. Gavin found himself suddenly speechless, marveling that he had not remarked the man's strange appearance before; and he was reminded, all at once, of a daydream he'd had as a boy, whilst out walking in the woods one evening. Just such horses and riders he'd thought he'd seen then, through the shadows and the mist and the twilight; and though his father had pronounced it nonsense, his mother and grandmother had been sore troubled by his story.

Now, he stood in the doorway struck dumb by the sight, leaning out into his yard with one hand on the door and the other on the lintel, quite unable to gather the pieces of his thoughts together, 'til the woman at his hearth called out, "Hurry, now. Come inside and latch the door before the Night crowds in on us."

Barely aware of what he was about, Gavin stepped back into the cottage and closed the door behind him. The heavy clank of the latch as it dropped into place seemed to clear his head a little, but the green-clad woman shuddered at the sound.

"The windows too," she urged impatiently, rubbing her hands up and down her arms as though she'd only now realized she was cold. "Lock them. Hurry."

Gavin frowned. "I'll thank ye to leave me the task of deciding for myself how my own household is to be run," he replied, much annoyed, for he was not used to being ordered about in his own home. "As it happens, the windows have already been latched. Now, as to this business—"

"Truly? All of them? With iron locks and iron hinges?"

"Aye, iron, what else would they be made of, woman? What would you be expecting to find in a

12

blacksmith's house, then—tin?"

At that, the woman laughed; a sound as soft as a summer breeze lofting through green branches and just as sure to lift the hearts of those that heard it. Gavin had to shake himself awake again. "Ah, no," she said, smiling at him. "The tinker's art would in no wise serve me tonight. But this..." She looked around her, seemingly pleased. "Four walls with iron bound. This will do quite nicely." She nodded at the hearth. "Now, you, sir, have a care, for I judge your supper is just about burnt."

"Ah, the devil," Gavin cursed as he rushed forward immediately to pull his bacon from the fire before the rashers were ruined. The rest of the meal he'd removed from the heat before he'd gone to the door so that all of it was ready now to eat; though most of it was colder than he'd have liked and the rest of it was overdone. He frowned at the woman who was the cause of all his troubles tonight and grudgingly asked, "I don't suppose you'd be wanting some, now would ya?"

"Aye, I would indeed," she said getting up at once and seating herself at his table. "And I thank you most kindly for the hospitality."

Gavin stared after her, caught between annoyance, displeasure and surprise, and thought seriously about telling her there was not enough to share. But, he couldn't do it. Giving up, he went and took down his seldom used second set of dishes and placed them on the table before her. He apportioned out the food between them, poured out two cups of tea and then sat himself across from her, frowning at his half-empty plate. In truth, there was not enough to share. He'd not thought he'd be feeding two when he'd started cooking and he was feeling hard put upon now, forced to make do with half of what he'd planned to eat.

"So, if it's not shoes for your horses, what business *is it* that brings you here?" he asked at last, as he shoveled food into his mouth. "And what is it I'm to call you, then? For I must call ye something."

She gazed at him a moment before answering, as

though determining what to say. "I am called Aislinn Deirbhile and that's a name you might use for me, if you wish. I've come here seeking shelter."

So, it is a dream then, Gavin mused, 'dream' being the literal meaning of her given name. Then the rest of her statement caught his ear. Putting down his fork, he stared at her perplexed. "Shelter, is it? For what?"

"Why, for myself, of course." An amused smile glimmered on her lips. "And thank you most kindly once again, for I'm feeling quite comfortable here already."

"You can save your thanks for him as will earn it," Gavin advised her as he went back to his meal. "'Twill not be me, for 'tis not an inn I'm running"

"No," she agreed as she glanced around. "'Tis surely not that. But, in truth, an inn would not suit me half as well."

"And your staying here does not suit me at all," he replied. "So, whether you will or no, you'll have to seek your shelter elsewhere. As soon as your man returns from wherever it is he's gone, I'll be turning the two of you out."

"Very well," she murmured, acquiescing so readily that Gavin felt immediately suspicious. "'Til Eoghan comes back then. And you'll swear you'll not make me go beforehand?"

He frowned. "He is just down in the village, is he not, perhaps keeping himself warm while he gives us time to conclude our business?"

Aislinn's eyes gleamed when she raised them to meet his and the look on her face was like that of a cat playing with a mouse. "He will journey much farther than that tonight."

"But, he'll be back for you soon, will he not?" Gavin prodded. "Very shortly?"

"Shortly? Oh, aye. As he reckons it, he and I may hope to see each other very shortly indeed."

"Within the hour?"

At that, her mouth pursed into a reluctant moue. "Nay. He will not return here quite as soon as that. Nor anytime this evening."

Gavin stared at her in confusion. "What is it you're saying, then? Sure and you're not telling me he's off and left ye?" he asked, bringing his fist down hard on the table when she nodded. "Bloody hell, woman, what are ye about? I've no patience with your games and I tell you plain, I'll not have ye staying here tonight!"

"'Tis no game," said she, sighing grimly, the playful gleam dying out of her eyes. "And, I assure you, had I any other choice, I would not be imposing upon your kindness in this fashion. But, come now, surely you're too much of a gentleman to cast me out into the cold. There must be some way to persuade you?"

"None that I can think of." Crossing his arms, Gavin glared at her. First his supper disturbed and now this. The woman was surely daft. Too much a gentleman, was he now? Bah. If he thought it would do any good he'd attempt to scare her out of *that* notion and maybe convince her she'd best leave on her own. But he didn't want to be responsible for whatever misfortune might befall the creature if he chased her off into the night, ill-equipped as she was for the cold.

As it was, he supposed, he would have to harness up his jennet and drive her around to his neighbors himself, going door to door until he found one with a room to spare. It would be something of a rarity at this time of year when all the folk as what could would be coming back home for the holidays.

"Have you no wish for riches, then?" she asked with a cunning smile. "Or the promise of a long life?"

Gavin snorted. "And how is it you're in a position to offer me either one? Nay. Even if you could keep such a promise I'd refuse it, for I've life and money enough for my needs. But if you've the gold to pay for a room, why offer it to me? I've yet to meet the innkeeper who would turn away a paying customer."

"Have I not told you already? I've no wish to go to an inn. But if neither gold nor long life interest ye, sure and there must be another form of payment 'twould better suit?" Her smile turned sly as she added, "Or are you that rarest of creatures—a truly happy man, with no wants or needs to speak of? If that be so, you're the first such I've ever met."

"Happy?" Gavin spoke the word as if it were one he'd heard so long ago he barely remembered its meaning, which was not so far from the truth of it. He shook his head. "Nay, though my wants and needs are few, I'd not call myself a happy man."

"Well, then, whatever it is you're craving, name it and if it's aught I have to offer, it will be yours."

Gavin stared at her, dumbstruck. He wondered if she'd any idea how her words sounded to him, or how another man might choose to interpret them. "And what have ye got, lass, that you'd be willing to offer in trade?" he asked, mockingly. "Or is it yourself you're offerin'?"

To his surprise, Aislinn's lips curved upward in a craven smile. "Och, is that what you're wanting, then? Why didn't you say so sooner and have done with it? Shall I share your bed tonight, sir smith, in exchange for the hospitality of your house? Is that a bargain you'd be willing to make with me?"

Her words caught Gavin off-guard—as did the heat that blazed in her eyes as her gaze swept over him. It's not that he wasn't tempted, indeed he was. His dick, which had been making a nuisance of itself since first he'd glimpsed her, sitting like a queen upon her fine, white steed, throbbed heavily now, as though demanding that he release it from his breeches so that it might bury itself between her legs.

Never before had a woman affected him so fiercely. And never before had one offered herself to him so freely, excepting upon his wedding night. But, thinking about that—about Mairead and all the suffering she'd endured because of him—damped his ardor right down. No. He'd no wish to go down that road ever again.

He shook his head. "Nay, I'll not make that bargain."

Aislinn's eyes widened. "And why will you not?" she

asked, clearly affronted. "Do I not appeal to you then?" She glanced around the small room. "Or is it that you think so highly of your accommodations you do not count it a fair trade? Whichever the case, I assure you it can be redressed. And I can promise ye a night such as you'll not soon forget."

"I've no doubt," he said with an unpleasant smirk, for the conversation was not at all improving his mood. "But 'twould be a sin to indulge in such pleasures, in case ye don't know it. If ye care to imperil your own soul, that's your concern, but I've yet a hope of seeing Heaven when I die. And I've no wish to put that hope into jeopardy for the likes of ye."

If he thought to shame her with talk of sin, he was once again surprised. For upon hearing his words, she put back her head and roared with laughter. Gavin watched her, feeling even more sour and out-of-sorts, for his dick was once again clamoring for attention. Her laughter held all the sweet, wild beauty of a summer storm and seeing her thus had him wanting her now even more than before.

Nay, he told his rebellious part. *Ye know what's always come of that. I'll take her round and get her settled elsewhere—let her be someone else's ticket into Hell. Sure and there must be someone in the parish who can better afford it than I.*

But who? That was the question now, wasn't it?

"Ah, me," Aislinn sighed, wiping tears from her eyes. "It seems I am now even more in your debt, sir smith. For sure and I've not laughed so hard in months." She smiled at him again, her eyes twice as bright, her face rosy and flushed, her voice even more seductive. "So, a sin, am I? Sure and I've a mind to give ye a night such as I offered ye just to pay ye back for that bit of impertinence. But, very well, I'll not tempt ye any further, for now. Come, though, there must be something you'd be willing to accept?" She cocked her head to the side and gazed at him. "A horse, perhaps? That wouldn't be a sin, now would it? Though, I suppose, the horse might view it differently. The Sons of Mil have always loved horses, have they not? And I saw how you were eyeing Eoghan's steeds. Would such a thing please ye? Or maybe more than one? Perhaps it's your own stables you're wanting?"

"Oh, aye, 'twould be just the thing. And would I also be getting the land to go with it then?"

"Well, and why ever not?" The slyness crept back into Aislinn's eyes. "For what's the use of one, without the other? Is it a bargain?"

"A landed blacksmith," Gavin mocked. "Whoever heard of such a thing? No! You silly wench, even if I believed you capable of delivering such a gift I'd not accept it from ye. I'll not be indebted to you nor to anyone for my station in life. I'm a blacksmith, I've always been a blacksmith and so I'll stay. Now, hurry and eat your supper and I'll drive ye round 'til I've found someone who'd be willing to take in a stranger. Daft as ye are, there must still be some such in the county who'll think it their Christian duty to give you aid. Perhaps the priest would have room for ye."

In truth, it was not just the lack of available rooms in the village that worried Gavin. For, despite his words to her, he doubted anyone in their right mind would take in such a one as she—a stranger lacking all good sense—even given her assets and attributes and her apparent willingness to share them with all and sundry.

Worse yet, and more wounding to his pride, was the fact that who among his dour neighbors would believe he'd no connection with the lass? Even though they knew him from the cradle and he'd spent his whole life among them, would any of them ever believe him when he swore that she had no claim on him, but had come on a whim, seeking shelter? Would he believe such a story if it were told to him? *Not bloody likely.*

Aislinn's face had gone pale. "Nay, I'll not leave this house tonight." Her voice low and insistent, sounded close to breaking. Gavin's heart was filled, suddenly, with misgiving. "And you must not unbolt the door again 'til morning. You *will* promise me this. And if you cannot think of aught right now that you would take in payment then I shall leave you ample time to think on it and I'll return in a year and a day to meet your price."

"What's all this then?" Gavin asked, more touched than he cared to admit. "Are ye in trouble, lass? Is that what this is about? Is there someone after you?"

Aislinn nodded. "Aye, that there is. And if he were to catch me..." A shudder ran through her. Her face seemed about to crumple but then she steeled herself. Her expression hardened. "I'll not go with him," she answered proudly. "I'll not kneel at his feet nor be his slave. I'd rather end myself than grant him any part of what he wishes."

"Whist," Gavin whispered, soothing her as he might a jumpy horse he was trying to shoe. "Calm yourself now. Sure and it will not come to that. You're safe for the present. The windows and door are all bolted fast and I'll not be letting anyone else in. You'll come to no harm here."

"Your word on it, sir," Aislinn insisted. "You must give me your promise."

Gavin nodded. "All right then, lass, 'tis a promise. Though I'm not happy to be forced to it, you may stay the night. For, I'll not be handing ye over to a ruffian without knowing the whole of your story. You've my word on that." No sooner were the words out of his mouth when a tingling feeling swept over him, a warm sensation of surety. "Saints, what a strange thing," he muttered, mostly to himself, as he looked around, baffled. "What was that, do you suppose?"

She looked at him in surprise. "What? Have ye never before sworn an oath then?"

"Indeed I have," he replied bitterly, recalling some of the vows he'd made. "And ne'er felt naught like that. But, tell me," he continued, "This man who is after you, why come here to evade him? You're not from these parts. Have you no family you could go to?"

She shook her head sadly. "None who'd be likely to take me in if I went to them now and none who could do me any good, even an they were willing. 'Twas a blacksmith I was needing, at least 'tis what the druid told me."

"Druids! Oh, saints preserve us," Gavin said as he quickly crossed himself. "So, that's the way of it, is it? You're a witch then? Consorting with heathens and fortune tellers and all manner of devil? Tell me then, is it a demon who hunts you, looking to take your soul in exchange for your sins? Or is it something even worse?"

"Sins again!" Aislinn scowled at him. "Hark at yourself—warding off evil with ancient gestures you scarce comprehend while you prattle on about sinners and saints— and all of them mortals like yourself. If you'd even half the sense of your forebears you'd know me for what I am, for I fancy you've seen my kind before. You've the look of one who's been gifted with the sight."

Gavin stared at her for an instant, uncomprehending. *I fancy you've seen my kind before.* What the devil did she mean by that? he wondered. And then, too late, understanding dawned. "Fae," he whispered, his heart lurching between fury and fear—for surely that's what she was. "You're one of the Gentry then, aren't ya? You're one of the *Daoine Sidhe*." His glance fell on the plates of food on the table before them and he staggered to his feet. "And, oh, dear God, I've eaten with ye. Curse me for a fool! Oh, Holy Mary, help me. Am I still myself, even? Is it yet tonight? Or will I wake in a minute to find I've aged a thousand years and everyone I've ever known has turned to dust?"

Aislinn's expression was unreadable as she stared back at him for all of a second, and it was the longest second of Gavin's entire life. Then a smile broke over her face. "Ridiculous man!" she laughed, the sparkle in her eyes bright enough to put diamonds to shame. "Why, sure and it is *your own food* you've been eating. And in your own kitchen too. If you take any harm from it, 'tis naught to do with me. 'Twill be your own fault for being such a terrible, poor cook. Now, sit back down again," she urged. "Do. And I'll promise not to let *you* come to any harm here tonight as well. Or, at least, not much harm."

Reluctantly, Gavin resumed his seat. He studied her more closely and, now that he knew her nature, he found it hard to understand how he could have missed seeing the sparkling shimmers of light that seemed to attend her every movement, or the coldness that seemed to lurk behind those bright eyes. And he remembered once more the dreams-that-were-not-dreams he'd had as a child; all the stories he'd learned at his grandmother's knee; all her warnings about the dangers of consorting with the Fair Folk.

"Beautiful they may be to gaze upon, Gavin, my boy, but you keep your distance from them just the same; for they're perilous breed, they are. Completely heartless. And they'll steal your soul away as soon as look at ye."

"You should have told me from the start how it was," he said at last, as annoyed with himself as much as with her. For, despite his *Maimeó's* warnings, he was thinking that perhaps he *should* have taken the fae up on one of her many offers. After all, it was not every day a man found himself in the position of having one of the gentle folk freely offering gifts out of hand and here he'd gone and pissed the opportunity away.

"Sure and I said nothing to you that wasn't true," Aislinn protested, still smiling.

"No, ye would not, would ye?" Gavin replied for even *he* knew that the fae, though always willing to trick a man into mischief, could not utter an outright lie. "But, tell me now, is it another of your kind who's after ye?"

"Another fae, aye. But *not* my kind. Tiernan ap Annwn is of the *Unseelie Court—the Sluagh Sidhe*—one of those who deal in fear, darkness and coercion, and whose kind holds sway in Winter and Dead of Night."

Gavin sighed heavily. It was not every day a man found himself caught in the middle of a Fae war, either. "Well, I've promised you safety here tonight, though I wouldna done it had I known what you are, and I'll not go back on my word, but this argument is between your two courts. It has nothing to do with me and I want naught to do with it. So, I'll have your promise now that you'll leave come morning."

Aislinn looked searchingly at him, but Gavin's mind was made up and he would not be bent. Finally she nodded. "Very well. I'll promise that unless you change your mind before the dawn comes, I'll leave here in the morning. Will that satisfy you?"

"Aye," Gavin answered, relieved, having felt the tingling surety of her own oath as it washed over him. "Aye, Fae, it does."

Chapter Two

It was in the darkest part of the night that it began.

Unearthly music stole through the quiet house, enchanting every living thing it touched. Through the door of his bedroom, Gavin heard it as it roused him from his sleep. *Ah, wonderful*, he thought in the instant before he recognized it for what it was: the *ceol sidhe*, the spell-songs with which the Fae lured mortal minds astray, putting them outside of time or into a trance. But even as he realized the music for what it was, he knew he was lost to it. It was too beautiful, too powerful to struggle against. Though a part of him fought to stay unaffected, its magic called to something deep within him, to a hunger too long ignored, a need too long unsatisfied. And he knew he had no will to resist its pull.

"Who can that be?" Gavin muttered as he sat up in bed and rubbed the sleep from his eyes, for he was certain that it had been the sound of someone lightly tapping on his bedroom door that had awakened him.

It seemed an odd question to be asking, though. Surely, he must know the identity of whoever was knocking on his own bedroom door. But his thoughts were muddled and hard to hold onto, as though his mind was still mostly asleep. Reluctantly, he threw back the bedcovers. The night air, as it hit him, sent a shiver up his spine and the boards beneath his feet were like ice as he shuffled across them, but when he opened his door it wasn't the cold that caused the tremors to run through him.

"Saints preserve us," he whispered, staring in shock at the wife he'd not seen in he knew not how many years. "Is it a dream I'm having?" With her dark hair gleaming about her shoulders and the merry sparkle in her blue eyes he could never have mistaken her for anyone else. "Sure and you are not really here?"

"Och, such questions," she chided as she glided toward him, and the chill seemed to fade away as she drew near. "Do you always doubt the evidence of your own eyes then?" She looked every bit as beautiful and full of life as she had in the days when she'd first caught his eye. A wave of possessiveness washed over him as he drank in the sight of her dressed in only a sheer, white nightdress that molded to her body revealing almost more than it concealed and he felt his cock harden. "Touch me, why don't you?" she suggested, her voice sweetly mocking. "And find out for yourself whether or not I'm here."

Gavin didn't wait to be asked twice. He took hold of her arms and pulled her across the threshold with hands that shook. "How can this be?" he muttered as his eyes roved over her face, searching fearfully for any sign of the reproach he could still recall having seen there for too much of their brief marriage. But the eyes that gazed back at him now were clear and bright, not clouded with pain or grief, and the smile on her face spoke only of her love for him. He felt his heart, which for all these years had sat like a lead weight in his chest, come stuttering back to life. Groaning, he swept her into a tight embrace. "Oh, Mairead, my little love. What miracle is this?"

"Hush," she murmured as she melted against him, warm and convincingly tangible in his arms. "No more talk now. For surely only a fool would think to question a miracle. And, after all, is not this the season for them?"

He lowered his mouth to hers. "Aye. 'Tis indeed. 'Tis the most blessed season of the whole bloody, beautiful year." And it seemed to him it must really be so for her lips met his gladly and she kissed him back eagerly as she had in the days when first they'd courted—before he'd married her and all their troubles began.

To be kissed by her at all was a miracle, as he'd often had occasion to remark during the course of their marriage. But to be kissed thus, with her entire body pressed against his, and her mouth as hot and demanding as his own, was doubly so and it set all his senses ablaze. With his mind bemused, he could not recall if she'd ever kissed him in this way before. But with his body on fire for her, as it was tonight, he didn't much care—for she was kissing him like this now and that was all that mattered. And his need for her, so long denied, exploded within him

"Let me love you," he begged as he released her enough to draw her toward the bed. "For the love of God, Mairead, lie with me. Let me bed you tonight."

"Oh, aye," she breathed in response. "'Tis what I want as well."

Looking at her, he could tell that she meant what she said and his heart rejoiced. She was flushed and trembling, and excitement fairly gleamed in her eyes. And if those eyes seemed now to be a shade more gray than he'd remembered, what cared he for that? The wanton look they held, one of lust and need and reckless desire—that's all he cared about. To see that look now, and to know he'd put it there, that it was for him she trembled and ached and yearned, was everything he'd ever wanted in a wife.

And yet, he never had seen such a look in her eyes, had he? Not 'til tonight.

That thought fell clear into his mind, rimmed with such pain and grief and loss that he lost his breath. Eyes swimming with tears of remorse, he sat down on the bed and pulled her against him. "I'm sorry," he said brokenly. "I'm so sorry, Mairead."

"Whist," she answered, stroking gentle fingers through his hair. "Why do you sorrow so? What is it that grieves ye?"

"Everything," he said, gazing up at her with troubled eyes. "I'm sorry for all the hurt I caused you. For being such a miserable husband to you. For letting you die. 'Twas my fault. 'Twas all my fault."

A small frown creased her brow. "Nay, sure and it could not have been so—not as you're remembering it."

"Aye," he insisted. "It was. I know."

"Stop," she commanded quietly, framing his face in her hands and smiling at him. "Hear you this. Even if things were truly as you remember them—with all the hurt and the pain you're imagining now--it is of no import and best forgotten. For, as sure as I'm standing here looking in your eyes, I can see that such a thing was ne'er what you'd intended. Was it?"

He shook his head. "Nay. Never."

"Well, then, 'tis in the past, why think on it now? Why borrow trouble from a day gone by? Rather, why not show me how you wish things might have been?" Then she leaned down and kissed him again, her tongue tickling his lips 'til he opened to her and then licking inside, teasing and tasting, until he could not but respond.

He pulled her onto his lap, letting his hands coast over her body, loving every inch of her. As he cupped her breast he felt her nipple peak beneath his palm and thoughts of suckling there, of laving each rosy tip with his tongue drove all else from his mind.

"Ah, the beauties," he murmured, wrenching his mouth from hers and gazing at the twin swells that threatened to spill from the top of her nightdress. "Right, then, let's see them."

Taking hold of the frail fabric at the front of the gown, he tore it open, exposing her to his sight. She gasped a little in surprise as he filled his hands and then his mouth with her. "By the saints," he whispered, pausing for a moment to gaze up at her face. "Sure and you've never tasted so sweet to me as you do tonight. I canna get enough of you."

"Is that so?" She chuckled, low and amused, as she clasped his head in her hand and pulled him back against her chest. "Well, glad am I to know it."

"I can scarce believe it still," he murmured while his lips caressed one ruby tip. "Have you truly come back to me? Is it to be like this between us then? Forever?" He felt her grow still and raised his eyes again to her face. "Mairead?"

She looked like she was struggling within herself. "I cannot promise you forever," she said at last.

He nodded and, stretching up, he pressed a chaste kiss

against the side of her head. "'Tis too soon for that, I suppose. For, here you are—an angel returned to Earth—and I've yet to win Heaven even once."

"But...I might, perhaps, stay through the winter," she whispered, her breath warm and sweet against his neck. He shivered as her tongue traced the shell of his ear. "Could I not? Through the worst of it, at least? Through Twelfth Night, if nothing else. Or maybe a little beyond that...'til Spring, even...if you're willing?"

"Willing, aye," he said, dipping his head once more to nip at her shoulder. "I should say that I am. But one winter hardly seems enough. Say, rather, that you'll stay 'til the end of the world and I'll gladly forsake Heaven for ye. Or, just let me love you like this 'til we're both naught but dust and I'll be content." His hands growing bolder, he pushed aside the ruined remnants of her gown, sliding between her bare legs, searching for that spot he well remembered, where her silken folds and sweet honey lay hidden.

She halted their search saying, "Stop, now. Not yet. Before we go any further you must first promise you'll not turn me out aforetime; that I may safely stay here with you while Winter's strength is at its peak."

"Yerra. Does Winter have peaks too then?" he teased, clasping her waist and biting gently down on the tip of one breast. "What care I for those, when you've these peaks with which to torment me? Surely you'd not deny me them?"

"Ridiculous man," she laughed as she swatted his arm. "And, aye, indeed I *will* deny thee, an it comes to that. Swear to me now or I'll torment thee further by taking my peaks and I away from you entirely."

She'd started to get up, as though to make good on her threat, when he stopped her. "Nay, Fair Torment. Not this time." And he rolled, suddenly, pinning her beneath him; laughing when her eyes went wide and she gasped in surprise. "How now, my lass, what say ye to that?"

"I'd say you're a fair hand at torment yourself," she said as her eyes—surely more gray than blue—snapped angrily. She pushed at his shoulders and bucked her hips but though his body greatly appreciated her efforts to move him off of her, he declined to be so moved. Finally, she gave up and lay still, glaring at him. "Enough of this nonsense. Will you do as I ask, or no?"

Gavin grinned at her. "Aye, Beauty, though it seems to me you're in no position to make such demands, I will. I'll do whatever it is you wish. But, first...you must tell me, my darling girl...what is it you're wanting me to do for you again? For, with all of your wriggling around, I fear the matter has been driven completely from my head and I forget my own name with you here to distract me."

"Swear only that I may stay here 'til Winter's power has ebbed entirely," she answered quickly, scarcely seeming to breathe while she awaited his answer.

He shrugged. "Have I not already said it? But, aye, I swear. Are ye content now?"

"And you'll not change your mind on the morrow? Nor recant any of the promises you make tonight?"

"Is it faithless you think me?" he asked, his good mood dissolving. "What have I ever done to merit such distrust from ye then? I'm not a man to go back on my word—and well you should know it."

"Swear," she repeated, gray eyes gleaming like a cat's in the dark.

"Fine, then" he answered, angered and hurt by her lack of faith in him. "An it will make you happy, I swear to all that you ask. I'll be constant as the bloody damn stars— and as distant, too, an it pleases ye. But, come what may, whate'er else befalls us, so long as I live you'll come to no harm here. On pain of death I swear it."

And, as the warm wave of a vow truly made washed over him, he saw her smile with smug satisfaction. "It is well."

"Oh, it is, is it?" he growled, rolling off her to lie on his back, certain he was facing yet another night when his needs would go unmet and he must lie awake, in torment.

There was something about the triumph gleaming in her eyes that struck him as soulless and uncaring and far too cold. "I think not."

"What ails ye now?" she asked as she repositioned herself so that she was lying partially atop him with her arms folded on his chest. She cocked her head to the side and gazed down at him curiously. "Why so unhappy?" But he looked away, refusing to satisfy her with an answer.

'Tis always the same, he thought glumly, *and you'd think I'd have learned it by now*. Ever and again she'd inflame his lust for her in such a fashion and then refuse to let him satisfy it; or else she'd allow it but so grudgingly he could take very little pleasure in the act.

"Ah," she breathed softly, sitting up. "I see now how it is with ye. How very like a man." And then her fingers were moving swiftly along his chest, unfastening the long row of buttons down the front of his undergarment. "Poor Gavin. Did ye really think I'd use you so shamefully then?"

He ignored her until she moved once more, this time to straddle his legs. "Stop it," he groaned. "What mischief are ye up to now?" Then he gasped because her hand had closed tight on his rigid shaft.

"Ah, the darling," she crowed as she pulled it free of his clothing. Her eyes were gleaming excitedly as she looked upon him; her hand stroked slowly up and down the length of his cock as if taking his measure. "Look at him then. I'd known you were a well built man, Gavin O'Malley, but I'd not expected *this*."

Heart flooding with despair, Gavin nodded. "Aye. So you've said." For Mairead had made similar complaints about his size in the past. Still, she continued to fondle him and he continued to watch, mesmerized, unwilling to utter a word of complaint lest she stop; until she bent her head toward the weeping tip, when he groaned again, "Mairead, don't!"

"Why, and what's this now?" she teased, raising her head to smile mockingly at him. "Would ye prove yourself so soon a liar? Did ye not just promise I'd come to no harm here? And do you not know that if I doona have a taste of ye soon I shall think myself most grievously harmed indeed?"

"Aye?" he said angrily, his heart pounding in his chest. "Well, torture me much more like you've been doing tonight, woman, and I'll surely die of it and then my life will be ended and likewise my vow."

She grinned at that; and tightened her fingers around him until his cock jerked in her hand. "Torture, is it? Well, sure and I'll have to put a swift end to your torment, then, for to have your vow so quickly concluded would not suit me at all."

For a second time she lowered her head to him and as she twirled her tongue around the head of his cock, licking at the milky fluid that pearled up from the slit, his heart beat even faster than before. But though the blood thrummed loudly in his ears and his body wanted nothing more than to let her to continue with what she was doing, years of anger and guilt and confusion and hurt won out over the lust he was feeling and made him cry out, "Hold."

"How now?" she asked as she paused again, looking greatly annoyed.

"Was it not ye who always told me that to do such would be a great sin?" he demanded crossly, though he'd cared little about such sins then and even less now. For, as he'd told her himself, *if the Good Lord had meant for us to live like saints He'd not have given us Confession with which to redeem ourselves.*

"Sins again, is it?" For a moment she looked perplexed then her face cleared. "Perhaps you were dreaming? For sure and 'tis not *I* who would ever say such a thing to thee."

"Perhaps it *was* a dream," he said and, recalling nights when he thought he'd go mad if he could not feel the touch of her hand on his flesh, he groaned, "I wish it had *all* been no more than a dream."

And she answered softly, "Then think of it as such."

This time, when her mouth closed over him, he made no further protest nor moved again to stop her. And when his eyes would close he forced them to stay open because the sight of her lips as they milked his cock was not one he wanted to miss.

The heat of her mouth engulfed him, sending sensations sweeter than any he'd ever known racing over his flesh. His hips jerked convulsively as he thrust himself into her mouth, again and again; crying out as the first wave of ecstasy broke over him and his seed poured out in a hot gush of fluid that she swallowed down eagerly.

"Holy Mother of God," he moaned when he could speak again. He was frowning a little and shaking a lot as she crawled up beside him. "Mairead...you, you've changed."

"Have I?" she replied, smiling slyly. "You do not seem to mind."

He shook his head. "'Tis a change for the better, in my opinion. I'll not lie about that. But, even so, 'tis still a mite...confusing."

"No doubt." She nodded. She gazed at him thoughtfully for a moment and then asked, "And why was it sinful, what we've just done?"

He sighed, not wanting to remind her; not wanting to be reminded of it himself, if it came to that. "Because of the spilling of my seed where it will bear no fruit."

"Ah." Her gray eyes were glimmering as she pulled him down on top of her, whispering in his ear, "Well, that's easily remedied, is it not? Quick now, let us atone for our sins by spilling some more--this time in the proper channel."

"'Tis not so easy as that, I fear," he said, but she was kissing him by then and as she'd lost her torn nightgown, at some point, and was now entirely naked and entirely his, he quickly determined this was no time for conversation.

His cock was ready for her again sooner than he would have thought possible. Experience told him he would need to move slowly, gently, carefully; to not thrust too deep or too hard if he wished to avoid hurting her. But when she dug her nails hard into his shoulders and urged him on crying, "More, more, give me all of it now, do, please," his restraint left him. He pounded into her much harder than he'd planned; intoxicated by the feel of her slick flesh as it tightened around him; shouting aloud when his release tore through him. It wasn't until afterwards, when his heart began to slow and his mind to clear, when he heard her soft cries and felt her body convulsing beneath him that he realized what he'd done.

No! Despair seized him and he sat up as quickly as he could. *Not again.* "Please, don't," he begged as he pulled her into his arms. Shivering spasms continued to rock her and the thought that he'd hurt her again left his heart torn with anguish. *God help me, 'tis true. I'm a beast, a monster. I'm every foul thing she's ever called me.* "Don't, Mairead, please. Don't cry, my love. I didn't mean to do it—truly, I didn't. I never thought to hurt you like that again."

*****

Aislinn started in surprise. "What's this now?" she asked as she pushed Gavin away, startled out of her post-coital bliss by the realization that the arms that held her were quaking and the man himself was close to tears. Frowning, she gazed up into his face. "What ails ye, man? Who's hurt?"

"You are...aren't you?" He hung his head, looking even more piteous. "I thought surely I must have—Did I not...did I really not hurt you then?"

"Hush, now, of course you did not. Why ever would you think such a thing?"

He met her gaze cautiously, his expression by turns hopeful and confused. "Because always before it seemed...that is, whenever I, we...is that not how you remember it too, Mairead? Did it not always seem so?"

She gazed at him blankly, wondering what answer she could give him because, of course, she did not recall any of the events to which he referred; and could not even imagine the source of his present unhappiness. She was saved the trouble of answering, however, when his face convulsed and he swept her back into a fierce embrace.

"Nay," he whispered brokenly. "'Tis better so. Do not remember it thus. Do not you ever remember those awful, black days, I pray you. Let's leave them behind us and never look on them again."

"Hush, now," she repeated, pushing away again and gazing into his face once more. The tortured look in his eyes was painful to see and it was clear that either his mind or her glamour was sure to break soon under the weight of it. "Hark to me, Gavin O'Malley," she commanded softly. Humming a faint tune, she laid her fingers against his brow and willed him to sleep. "There's naught here to give ye distress. Let go the shadows of the past and let peace find thee. Sleep now," she urged as his eyes closed and his arms fell limp and he slumped against her. "And sweet visions be upon thee."

She settled him on his back, with his arms crossed over his chest and the covers pulled up around him then she lay down beside him and resumed her true form. Propping her head on her hand she gazed at him curiously. "What is it that weighs so heavy on your spirit?" she wondered aloud, tracing one finger down the slope of his nose and over his lips. "Who was she, Gavin? What is it she did to you? For it's sure I am that you never could have treated her as shamefully as you seem to think."

But the sleeping man made no answer and, touched though she'd been by his sorrow, Fae emotion is a fleeting thing, for the most part, and the feeling was already fading. "Ah, well," she murmured, stretching her arms above her head and yawning widely. "I promised ye a night you'd not soon forget and I trust I've given it to you."

Leaning over him, she kissed him lightly, just once, on the lips then she lay back down and curled up beside him and closed her eyes. She was tired tonight—weary and worn out—but at peace with herself and her situation, content with the night's work and more relieved in general than she'd been in many a long month.

'Tis nice, she thought as sleep crept up to claim her,

and she snuggled closer to the warm weight of the blacksmith at her back, *very nice, for once, to fall asleep and not be afraid of what the morning may bring.*

Chapter Three

Something was different.

As the soft, gray light of a winter's morning crept through his bedroom window Gavin stirred; but even before he'd come completely awake, he felt it. He could not tell whether the 'it' in question was something within the room itself, in the wide world outside it, or even an indefinable change that had occurred only within the recesses of his own heart and mind, but something, this morning, was definitely different.

But, whatever the cause, the result was a lightening in his mood such as he'd not felt in many a year and, remembering that today was Christmas Eve, why, it was almost enough to make him believe, once again, in the magic of the season. Perhaps it was an aftereffect of the strange dreams he'd had? Though they'd already begun to fade away, as dreams will do, enough stray wisps still clung to his mind to bring a smile to his face. *Such sweet, sweet dreams.* He stretched, and felt the pleasant ache of muscles that had no earthly reason for being sore. *Odd, that.* Then something shifted beside him in the bed. And he knew.

No, surely such things are not possible? His heart pounded fiercely as the thought that he'd *not* been dreaming, that his wife might *actually* have returned to him—in the flesh, so to speak—took hold. It was...well, he didn't quite know *what* it was. Disturbing, he supposed, to say the very least.

Not knowing what to expect, how he should feel, nor even what he might say to her, he steeled himself, sent up a silent prayer for guidance, then turned round to face her. The reality was far worse than anything he'd imagined.

"Oh, bloody hell." Bolting upright, Gavin stared in horror at the woman lying asleep in his bed, at riotous gold curls fanned out across his pillow and a sweet flower-like face that was *not* his wife's. "What's *this* now?"

Gold-tipped lashes fluttered and slumberous gray eyes opened. "And a very pleasant good morning to ye as well," the fae replied, lips curling up in a sensuous smile as she reached a hand toward his face. "But, tell me, must ye always scowl so?" Cool fingers stroked his cheek. "Methinks ye'd be much more attractive an ye smiled."

"Explain yourself, Fae," Gavin snarled, jerking his head back, away from her touch. "What is it you think you're doing here?"

Her eyebrows rose. "Well, I *thought* I was sleeping...'til some fool woke me with his blathering. What is it that ails ye *this* time?"

"You're what ails me!" Gavin fisted his hands in his hair to keep them from her throat. "You're a bloody, fekkin' pox upon my life."

"Nonsense. From what I've seen of your life so far, I'm sure I could only bring improvement to it." Yawning, she sat up in bed, and pouted at him. "Can ye really not think of anything nicer to say to me than that of a morning?" But Gavin barely heard her for as she came erect the bedcovers slipped to her waist and his mouth went dry at the sight of all that lush, naked, female flesh so close at hand.

He scrambled off the bed, hoping to put some distance between them before the temptation to touch her became too much to deny. "For the love of God, woman, clothe yourself."

That brought a lazy smile back to her lips. "Well, and I would, to be sure, had my gown not met with such a tragic mishap last night. But 'twas quite torn from my trembling flesh, as I recall it, and so roughly, too. And, even if I knew, now, where the remnants of it had been flung, I'm sure 'tis un-wearable and altogether beyond repair."

Gavin groaned, remembering all too vividly the event to which she referred. "I'd thought 'twas but a dream."

She shook her head. "Nay. Though I'll warrant it was as pleasant for you as any dream might be, 'twas all quite real. But, speaking of such, will you not come back to bed?

For, as I look upon you standing there it occurs to me that we might yet have some business we could attend to, you and I."

"I will not," he replied scowling at her. "And there is *no* business we have with one another. I want nothing whatsoever to do with ye."

"I think there be some parts of *you* as would disagree with some parts of *that*," she said, her eyes growing darker as her gaze traveled the length of him. "One part, for a certainty. And a very substantial part it is, too, I must say."

Looking down at himself, Gavin was appalled to discover that all his buttons were undone and his cock, hard as a post, was jutting outward; head bobbing as it strained toward her, as eager as a dog for a stroke. "'Tis of no matter what *some parts* of me may appear to want," he replied stiffly. "For 'tis not *those parts* as rules my actions." And, so saying, he stuffed his turgid flesh back where it belonged and buttoned his underclothes back up. "And I'll thank ye to be putting your eyes back in your head now," he told her, blushing as her sigh of regret caused his cock to give another eager leap; a movement she could not miss seeing with her eyes still fastened on his bulging member. "And leave off looking at me as though I'm a Christmas goose and you're behind for dinner. Have ye no shame at all?"

"Shame?" She repeated the word doubtfully, glancing up at him with thoughtful eyes. "Oh, a very little I'm sure, from time to time, an the situation warrants it. But none that pertains to matters of the flesh. And..." she purred, smiling again as she tossed off the covers and stood, pirouetting before him in all her naked glory, "As pertains to my *own* flesh, certainly not. For I canna see anything there for to give me shame. Can you?"

"Nay, that I cannot," he admitted grudgingly, quite unable to tear his eyes away from her, and quite unable to move as she advanced upon him.

She slid her arms around his neck. "Very well then. But, if you truly will not be persuaded to come back to bed and fuck me once again, would you not at least satisfy another of my hungers? Will ye not make breakfast for me? For I find that I'm feeling quite famished this morning, having eaten only a very light supper, and all this talk of geese and dinner is not helping matters at all."

Gavin closed his eyes but, even so, he had to swallow hard before he could speak. "Why are you here? You were supposed to be gone ere daybreak. We had a bargain."

"Aye," she whispered softly. "That we did. And are ye sure ye will not let me show you how very grateful I am to you for your kind reprieve?"

Gavin caught his breath in a ragged sigh when she ran her tongue along the rim of his ear. "Stop your teasing, woman. To what reprieve would you be referring? I never did any such thing."

"Sure and you did. For did ye not give me your promise, last night, that I might stay the winter? And right glad am I that you did for, otherwise, I'd have been forced to leave your pleasant company and make my own way in the cold, cruel world."

"'Twas not to *you* that promise was given," he growled. "And well you know it."

"Not to me?" Aislinn leaned in closer, chuckling softly as she trailed kisses all along his jaw. "Oh, aye, *mo chroí*, it was indeed."

Mo chroí. My heart. He ground his teeth, seething at her use of any such endearment for him. Taking her by the shoulders, he held her away from him. "You tricked me with your foul, faery magic. I thought you were *my wife*."

Aislinn nodded. "I may have used a wee bit of glamour to alter your perception and my own appearance, but I only did what was necessary and I'd hardly call it foul. Certainly you didn't seem to find it so last night?"

"I care not for what you think about it, witch. You should not have done it. And you cannot hold me to promises I did not intend to make."

"Oh, but indeed, I can." She gazed at him with deadly calm. "And indeed I will." Her voice, though soft overall, had a flint-like edge to it. "Have a care, mortal. *On pain of death*, you swore it—-do you not recall? 'Twas not *I* who told you to say such a thing, 'twas your own words, born in your own foolish heart. And if you find yourself betrayed now, 'tis yourself ye should be blaming. For 'twas your heart betrayed you—not I."

"Nay. 'Twas *you* who betrayed me." Thrusting her away from him, he pulled a spare shirt from his cupboard and threw it at her. "Here. Put it on." Then he took his own clothes from the chair where he'd thrown them the night before and began to dress; repeating once again, "You tricked me. 'Twas the music—I recall it now. That's how 'twas done. You used your bloody magic—your bloody, fae treachery, I should say—against me."

"So what if I did?" she said as she buttoned the shirt around her. "I'm as grateful to ye now as I'd have been had ye'd made the promise of your own free will, and more than willing to show my gratitude, as I've already said. But I had to have that promise from ye...'twas a matter of great importance to me."

"And what of *me*, ye heartless creature? Or think ye the welfare of my very *soul* is of no importance then?"

She rolled her eyes. "Och. What nonsense is this? Sure and your *soul* was never in danger. An ye do not break your vow, how should you or it come to any harm?"

"Devil's hag. What would ye be after knowing of the kind of harm that might befall a man *or* his soul?" he demanded as he left the room, with her scurrying to keep up. "Being as you've no soul of your own, I care naught for your opinions on the subject; so you can keep your thoughts to your bloody self." He shoved his feet hastily into his boots, took his jacket from its hook and headed for the door. "And, as for your gratitude, ye can damn well keep that too."

"Wait!" she called after him in alarm. "Where is it you're going?"

"Off to see the priest," he answered as he wrenched the door open. "To make my confession and have it from *his* lips how damned my soul might be—thanks to you."

Then he slammed the door behind him and was gone.

*****

As the latch fell back into place with a fell sounding thump Aislinn huffed out an uneasy breath. It was as Eoghan had said, the iron barred the door in both directions; and she could not pass through unaided. If the smith did not return...but, no, angry though he might be with her, she could hardly believe he'd forsake hearth and home over such a thing.

"And it's not as if ye did not enjoy yourself either," she muttered as she turned her back to the door and, resolving to put all thoughts of the blacksmith from her mind, she went off to see about getting her own breakfast.

She could scrounge up very little: just a bit of bread, some cheese and an apple. With all his cooking utensils made of iron, she found herself unable to do so much as boil a cup of water for tea. Still, a meager breakfast seemed a small sacrifice considering this was the first morning she'd drawn an easy breath in months—not since she'd learned of Tiernan's intentions toward her, in fact.

She was safe from the arrogant bastard now, however, and she had Gavin to thank for that. Though she could not regret what she'd done, still it pained her, just a little, that Gavin—or any mortal, for that matter—should feel himself ill-treated by a fae of the *Seelie* Court, for such was not their reputation. Perhaps, she could have tried something else; something that might have been less hurtful to him. And, if she'd had more time to consider the matter, perhaps she would have. But time had been against her and she'd been left with very little choice. She *would* make it up to him, however. He would have her gratitude whether he wanted it or no.

And so, determined to find a way to make amends with the smith, she next turned her attention to her wardrobe—a subject that appeared to be of some importance to him.

40

She had been forced to travel light and so she had only the one dress with her. Now that her chemise was in tatters on Gavin's bedroom floor, even that one dress would not do. She poked and peered into the various dressers and cupboards without success. Finally, she looked inside a cedar chest he'd had shoved into one corner of his bedroom; there she unearthed a bundle of women's clothing and a small sewing kit.

She took out one of the dresses—a simple wool gown in a soft bluish gray—and held it up against her as she studied her reflection in the looking glass. It was just as she expected: the hems would have to be let down, since she was taller than the original owner, and the waist would have to be taken in; but it would do.

Tossing the dress aside, she looked at herself in the glass. And, here, too, she saw what she'd expected. Sidhe flesh is relatively impervious to the ravages of such things as time or stress or weather, or even the normal wear and tear that humans took for granted. Aislinn looked the same now as she had for the past three hundred summers, give or take a few.

She shrugged out of the shirt Gavin had lent her and let her eyes roam over her body. As she fondled her breasts, she remembered the way his eyes had glazed over as he looked at them this morning and she smiled. She wished she'd tried just a little harder to talk him back into bed. Like all her kind she had very lusty appetites when it came to sex and yet she'd had precious little opportunity for that while she'd been on the run from Tiernan.

And now...now she was stuck in this little cottage, for the next few weeks, with only the blacksmith for company. She was going to need a little something more than her memories of last night to carry her through until such time as she could talk Gavin back into bed. "Stubborn, impossible man," she growled, crossing the room in a few quick strides and throwing herself face down on his bed. "Why could you not have made the best of things? Why, oh, why could you not have given in to me this morning? We both know it was what you wanted." She'd wanted it too.

She wanted it still.

Burying her nose in his pillows, she breathed in deeply, searching out the scent of him there; a tangy scent of musk and sweat and smoke. A scent that called up images of naked bodies twisting and grinding against one another, skin shiny and slick in the firelight, as they brought each other to the brink of ecstasy and then over it, trembling together in the aftermath.

Groaning, she rolled onto her back, covering her face with the pillow, closing her eyes to better remember the magnificent sight of his proud rod rising out of his ridiculous underwear to greet her. Why couldn't he think a little *more* with his cock, like other men seemed to? It was a far less complicated portion of his anatomy than...well, than whatever it *was* that passed for a mind with him, and probably a good deal larger, as well.

Just remembering her pleased surprise when she discovered its prodigious size last night had her growing wet all over again. Clearly, the smith had been created with the pleasure of women in mind. She'd not had nearly enough of him last night and none at all this morning and she was feeling the lack. Spreading her legs wide, she slipped one hand down over her mons to stroke the hard nub of her clit, already swollen, already aching. As she did, she let her mind recall how Gavin's fingers had felt there last night, trembling, hesitant, oh-so-eager. And, oh, how she longed to feel them again now, too. Her own fingers, strumming her flesh with such steady efficiency, were too practiced, too intimately acquainted with her needs; she knew, perhaps too well, the quickest way to bring herself to climax.

It was a skill that had stood her in good stead whenever a lack of suitable partners had presented itself, but sometimes the quickest route to satisfaction was not always the best...and rarely was it the most enjoyable.

Still thinking about last night, she let her other hand

caress her breasts; plucking and squeezing nipples already tender from all the attention he'd paid them. "Oh, gods," she moaned, remembering how he'd suckled her; strong hands spanning her back, holding her tight against his face, so tight it was a wonder she'd been able to draw breath. Strong hands—aye, that's what she looked for in a lover—coupled with a gentle touch. But not *too* gentle.

She bit down on her lip as she felt the tension inside her start to crest. Cream flooded her pussy and delicious slow spasms took hold, rocking her over and over and over again.

"Ah, me," she sighed as her body finally stilled and she stretched out, relaxed and happy, in the now-warm bedding. "That felt good." She pushed the pillow away from her face, swiping at sweaty, stray strands of hair that clung to her face. Her fingers smelled of sex.

Smiling, she coasted her hands back down the length of her body, once again enjoying the smoothness of her own skin as it curved over each peak, each valley, each hollow, each mound. She plunged her fingers into her hot depths and then brought them to her lips so that she might taste her own essence. As she licked at the wet digits and sucked them into her mouth she tried to imagine she was Gavin; tried to experience herself from his perspective. What would he think, she wondered, when he tasted her juices for the very first time?

...you've never tasted so sweet to me as you do tonight.

Words from the night before wafted through her brain. His words. And there were others, too.

You've changed. 'Tis a change for the better, but still...

Frowning, she sat up again. A new thought had just occurred to her. He must have known. Oh, maybe not the whole of it, and maybe not consciously, but she was suddenly sure that, on some level at least, some tiny part of him had known, all along, that something was different, and was glad for it.

Which made all his protests that *she* was neither who nor what he wanted ring even more hollow.

"Well, then, Gavin O'Malley," she growled, eyes narrowing as she thought about it. "If that be true, methinks the next few weeks will likely be most entertaining for us both. But, I wonder what it is you think you're up to?"

*****

Morning Mass was drawing to a close when Gavin slipped inside the small stone building that housed Saint Ita's Church. He was breathing hard, having run most of the way there beneath a cloud-covered sky that looked to be full of snow, and with the tools he'd forgotten to remove from his jacket pockets the day before slapping against his thighs with every step he took. The temperatures had dropped overnight and the fields he'd passed were gray and white and furred with frost. While he'd wanted to vent his rage by tearing up the path as fast as he could, he'd had to watch his footing since the rutted mud within the boreen had frozen into uneven ridges and black ice had accumulated in all the boggy places where water tended to gather. As a result, his thoughts were still chaotic and wild as he paced in the vestibule, waiting for the service to end and the faithful to depart.

Confession—that's what he needed; absolution for everything he'd done last night and everything he'd only thought of doing so far today.

The moment he'd seen Aislinn asleep in his bed this morning—and realized what her presence there must mean—his temper had ignited. But each memory, as it surfaced, fanned the flames higher, until he'd felt himself ready to explode. Though he'd never yet laid a hand on a woman in anger, it was all he could do to contain the impulse to seize hold of the creature. The urge to throw her down upon the bed—or the floor, or up against the nearest wall—and unleash both his lust and his fury on her flesh had been nigh impossible to ignore.

Her all-too-willing flesh. And, aye, wasn't *that* the problem, then? For it was not just the flames of his temper she stoked, but those of a more sexual nature, as well.

Had she shown the least bit of reluctance, the smallest hint of fear or uncertainty, sure and he wouldn't have found his urges as hard to manage. But though Mairead had oftentimes lamented his too-animal nature, he'd never in his entire life felt less civilized than he had this morning.

Excepting, perhaps, last night...but no, he'd not think about that now.

When finally he went forward to greet Father Cullen, Gavin had yet to catch his breath and his thoughts were still in a muddle.

"A good morning to ye, Gavin," the old priest said cheerfully. *"Beannachtaí na Nollag!* And may all the blessings of the Season be upon ye."

Gavin nodded impatiently. "Thank ye, Father, but I'm needing for you to hear my confession."

Father's eyebrows rose in surprise. "What? Now?"

Gavin nodded again. "Aye."

"Oh, very well," the old man sighed as he motioned him toward the confessional booth. "'Tis right glad I am that it's only you who's asking, For 'tis sure Mrs. Hogan has my breakfast already laid out for me in the rectory, and with some of t'others my food would likely be cold by the time they were halfway through their list. But you, now—" He broke off and peered at him. "Good Lord, man, you're all over crimson and shaking like a leaf. Are ye ill?"

Gavin groaned. "Aye. I think I must be." Just the mere mention of breakfast had been enough to call up Aislinn's image, her lush curves pressed against him, her arms twined 'round his neck and, oh, he had something he wanted to feed her, all right. Not, perhaps, what she'd had in mind when she mentioned breakfast...although, on the other hand, perhaps it was. She'd certainly seemed to have enjoyed the snack she'd made of him last night. He groaned again. "I think I've a fever."

"Well, let's be swift then," the priest said, pulling open the door to the central chamber and waving Gavin

45

toward the curtained partition at one side. "Go on in, and tell me what it is you've done."

Gavin sighed in trepidation as he settled himself on the kneeler. "Bless me, Father, for I have sinned," he recited in slow, lugubrious tones; reluctant, now that it came down to it, to get to the point.

"Yes, yes, lad," Father Cullen interrupted. "We've already established that much, I think. Go on."

"I scarcely know where to begin," Gavin muttered, loathe to bring up his involvement with the fae. On the one hand, he seemed to recall having heard that one must never tell of one's dealings with such creatures, for to do so would allow them to rescind their gifts to you. And, on the other, how the devil was a man to explain that he had a renegade fae holed up in his house? *I left a fae alone in my house? What the bloody hell was I thinking?* It would serve him right if he got home and found the whole forge had disappeared behind a cloud of invisibility. Again he groaned. "'Tis a right fool, I am. Ne'er should I have left the house this morning."

"Not if you've a fever," Father Cullen agreed. "Have ye been round to see the doctor?"

"I've not." *No doctor could cure what ails me*, Gavin thought, *not with a mountain of saltpeter.*

"Well, you should do so then. Now, tell me about these sins of yours."

"Last night," Gavin began, and felt himself blushing as visions of last night rose before his mind's eye. Furious though he was with the fae for having used him in so shameful a manner, was he really ready to repent his part in it? After a moment he mumbled, his voice barely audible, "I've been having impure thoughts."

"Well, and I don't doubt it," the old priest sighed. "It's nigh on eight years since Mairead's passing, is it not? Tell me, is it one of the girls from the village who's troubling your thoughts in this fashion?"

"What's that?" Gavin asked, scandalized by the suggestion. "One of the—? Nay! 'Twas my wife, of

46

course...or, so it appeared. That is to say, it wasn't really *her*, at all, if you take my meaning. Being as she's dead it couldn't have been. But, you see, I thought, until I awoke this morning, as it was."

"I don't quite follow that," Father Cullen replied. "But, my son, while sure and it's a shame your wife was taken so young, the Good Lord gave her to ye, for that short space of time, to be your helpmate. I very much doubt that he'd take it too much amiss that you're feeling the loss of His gift to you. Perhaps 'tis a sign you should be thinking of marrying again?"

Gavin shook his head. "Nay. I can never marry again. When Mairead lay dying she—" He stopped short as an idea hit him. "Do you think I should then?"

"Well, now, 'tis not for me to say. That's a matter that's best prayed over. Saint Paul, of course, would have said 'tis better to stay single. But, on t'other hand, as the Good Lord Himself said of Adam, 'tis not good for man to be alone. Now, do you have aught else to confess, or are ye done?"

"I don't know," Gavin answered absently. "I can't recall." A terrible plan was taking form in his mind—breathtaking in its possibilities, but surely too unnatural to be anything but sinful. Perhaps, after all, there *was* something he wanted from the Fae; something that only one such as she could give him. "Tell me, Father, if a man swore never to allow another woman to take his wife's place, would it be a sin if 'twere the woman herself, by all appearances, with whom he replaced her?"

"Lad, perhaps we should be leaving the philosophical questions for a time when you're feeling less ill? Now, do ye repent these sins you've confessed?"

"Aye," Gavin sighed, his mind racing. He crossed himself automatically, barely listening as the priest recited the prayer of absolution.

"*Ego absolvo te a peccatis tuis in nomine Patris, et Filii, et Spiritus Sancti. Amen.*"

47

"Amen," Gavin repeated, getting slowly to his feet.

"Well, Gavin, my boy," the old priest said, getting his own feet under him and patting the smith genially on the back. "I'm off to my breakfast. I'd advise ye to go round and let Doctor Butler have a look at you. And then get yourself home. A few days rest ought to cure you of these morbid thoughts and, if not, come back to see me when you're feeling better and we'll discuss the matter further. A Happy Christmas to ye, in the meantime."

*****

The sky was still thick with fleecy gray clouds when Gavin exited the church. The soft light should have cast a soothing hush over the little town but it was Christmas Eve and the streets were bustling with shoppers, mostly women, attending to the last minute details of their holiday preparations.

Despite Father Cullen's injunctions, Gavin was in no mood to go home just yet. What awaited him there, after all, but a scantily clad fae hell-bent on destroying what was left of his principles? Before facing that, he decided, he'd best fortify himself with breakfast at the local public house; and, if breakfast failed to do the trick, perhaps he'd have a pint or two to top it off.

A fine holiday mood was upon the whole village, it seemed, and as Gavin made his way down Geashill Street he was greeted by everyone he passed. He nodded curtly in response, shoulders hunched against their scrutiny. Coming on top of Aislinn's frank appraisal this morning, the glances cast his way by an easy score of his townswomen left him feeling naked, exposed; as though the skin had been flayed from his body.

There was only one other time he could recall feeling so transparent, and that was in the days immediately following his wedding. They should have been among the happiest days of his life, instead, he'd felt certain then that anyone who looked at him must surely sense his shame, feel his self-loathing, and know the reasons for both. And, now, his rage at the fae grew hot again, for having brought back to life memories he'd been eight years burying.

He breathed a sigh of relief when he finally reached his destination—The Starry Plough. As he pushed through the pub's front door, the comforting, familiar scents of peat smoke and pipe tobacco, whiskey and beer rose up to greet him like old friends from whom he'd long been absent. The dim room was filled with a noisy crowd—mostly husbands of the shopping women—all singing and talking together cheerfully as they passed their time while waiting to assist their better halves in the carrying home of their purchases.

Gavin returned their calls of *Dia Dhuit, Fáilte* and *Nollaig shona duit* while he ordered his meal, then retired to a small table in the corner, hoping to escape further notice. But he'd no sooner started in on his breakfast when that hope died aborning.

"Well, now, if it's not young Gavin O'Malley," a cheerful voice addressed him as the spry older man to whom the voice belonged sat himself down at Gavin's table. "A very merry Christmas to ye, Gavin."

"*Nollaig shona*, John," Gavin replied tiredly. John MacNamara was an incorrigible busybody with sharp eyes, keen ears, a long memory and an even longer tongue. Nobody knew how old he was—he'd been Auld John to all and sundry for as long as anyone now living in Kilbanning could recall—but, it was often said if there was anything worth knowing about anyone in the county, Auld John was the one who'd know it. *"And glad he'll be to share it wit' ye, as long as ye can spare the several days time you'll be needing to listen to the telling of it."*

"'Tis not often we see you in here," the old man continued. "What is it brings you up to town on this fine day? Not come into sudden riches have ye?"

Caught off-guard by the question, Gavin frowned suspiciously over the rim of his tea cup. But Auld John's face gave away nothing. "Nay," he answered shortly as he resumed eating. "That I've not."

The old man nodded thoughtfully, then asked, "So what think ye of the weather we had last evening? Not much of a night to be on the road, wouldn't you say?"

"A mite cold to be out and about," Gavin agreed as he swallowed a bite of smoked haddock and washed it down with more tea.

"Aye, 'tis true, that. But, would you be after guessing then, at what I did see while I was out walking my dog last evening just after supper?"

His mouth full, Gavin shook his head.

"Sure and if it wasn't a wee, small man astride such a beautiful white horse as ever you've seen, going right along the road ahead of me."

At that, Gavin all but choked on his eggs. "Was it now?" he asked, as he called for a pint. "And where might they have been headed then?"

Eyes blue as Bantry Bay gleamed with mischief as Auld John smiled. "Now that I couldna say, for no sooner had I set eyes on the beasties then a mist did come up, convenient like, to hide them from my sight. Always assuming I wasn't imagining the whole t'ing, of course. But 'tis *where* they were coming from—ah, now, that I thought 'twould be of interest t'thee."

"Which would be where?" Gavin asked, though he imagined he already knew what the answer must be.

"Why, up the road from your own forge, if you can believe it. That was the strangest part, I thought. For whoever did hear of a fae having dealings with a blacksmith?"

Gavin shoved the last of his breakfast into his mouth, nodding his thanks to the barmaid as she deposited his pint on the table in front of him. But, finally, he had to ask. "And why not a blacksmith then? If such creatures do indeed exist, and ride horses such as those you describe, why wouldn't they be in need of a blacksmith's services now and again?"

At that, John's eyes grew wide. "What's that you say, man? You cannot be talking about shoeing such creatures, can ye? Yerra, 'tis a scurrilous thought, that. Surely your *seanmháthair* must have told you something about such things? Nary a fae can abide the black metal—not at all. They canna pass, unaided, through a door that's closed with an iron bolt, nor endure for an instant the touch of it against their skin, and their steeds be just the same."

Well, that explains some things, doesn't it? Gavin pondered the idea as he drank heavily from his pint glass. *So that's why she was so insistent about the latches.* But why, he wondered, should the old man have thought to mention Gavin's grandmother in connection with the fae?

As if in answer to his unspoken question, Auld John shook his head and asked, "You did know your Ma was an O'Brien on her mother's side, did ye not? Well do I remember the day when she upped and announced that she was marrying your Da. Oh, it near to broke her own grandmother's heart, when she did so. For now, *she* was only an O'Brien by marriage, y'see. Not that you'd know it to hear her carry on about the tragedy it was, her only granddaughter turning her back on her heritage, and on her own people. Quite proud she was of the connection, ye see."

"What connection might that be?" Gavin asked.

Auld John clucked his tongue as though shocked by his ignorance. "Do ye really not know of this, lad? Sure and many of the old families are said to have fae blood running through their veins. My own people, so they do say, are descended from one of the merrow, for that matter. But the O'Briens, now, *they* claim as their ancestor no less than a Faery *Queen*, don't ya know? A lady by the name of Aoibheal, if I'm remembering correctly. But, I suppose it was your da kept you from hearing the old stories, yeah? Ah, he was a good man, your father, but not one given to believin' in aught he'd not seen with his own two eyes."

"Aye, that he was," Gavin admitted grudgingly. *Superstitious nonsense*, his father had called his grandmother's tales. *"Don't you be taking none of these airy-faery notions into your head now, boyo,"* he'd told him time and again.

Gavin emptied his glass, glancing up in surprise when the barmaid returned with a second pint and a shot of whiskey. She smiled sympathetically as she placed them on the table in front of him. "Sure and you'll be needing it," she said, upon observing his surprise. "If you're after listening to himself and his stories." Then she turned to the old man and placed a fresh pint down in front of him as well. "For pity's sake, John, give the man some peace. 'Tis Christmas Eve, can ye not see he just wants to be left alone to eat his breakfast?"

"Looks like he's done that," Auld John replied with a nod towards the empty dishes. "Now, why don't you be minding your own business, like a good lass, and clear the lad's plates away?"

The woman cast one last, apologetic look at Gavin as she picked up the dishes he'd emptied. Auld John waited until she'd walked away, then he turned his crafty smile on the smith once more. "And wouldn't you be after telling me what it was the Fae wanted with you last night? For sure and I can see there's a story in it."

Determined to keep his own counsel, at least for the present, Gavin tossed back his whiskey and shook his head. "I wouldn't be after knowing it myself this morning," he replied, forcing a small smile. "And that be the truth of it. But, if e'er I do figure it out, sure and you'll be the first person I'll likely be telling it to."

Chapter Four

By mid-afternoon the crowd in The Starry Plough was growing thin.

Their shopping completed, the women of Kilbanning began arriving at the pub to collect their men. Gavin watched as his neighbors departed, one after the other, heading for home to make Christmas for themselves and their families. There was nothing unusual in this, of course, the same routine had been followed for as far back as anyone could recall. It was tradition. It was all part of village life; part of the life he had always assumed would be his; the life he thought he was getting, as a matter of course, when he married Mairead. And the feeling that he'd been cheated out of so much—out of the every day things he'd deserved and expected and ought to have had—left such a bitter taste in his mouth that an ocean of porter couldn't have washed it away.

When those who were left behind, mostly emigrants home for the holiday, were grown too jovial with drink and began to press Gavin to join them in song, he decided he'd had enough. Arms laden with the burdens he'd somehow managed to accumulate, seasonal gifts his neighbors would normally have dropped off at the forge had they not found him so conveniently at hand, he headed for home.

Stray sunbeams piercing the gloomy gray sky lit up the landscape like visions of heaven. They did nothing to lighten his mood, however. Neither did the sight of the horseman stopped in the middle of the road just where it crested the hill overlooking the forge. The stranger's aristocratic features were set in a sneer as he gazed down at Gavin's demesne, causing an upwelling of territorial pride and anger in the smith's heart.

"Can I help ye then?" Gavin asked as he came to a swaggering stop several feet from the stranger. If truth be told, between the drink and the bitterness besetting his spirits, he was spoiling for a fight; and the idea of wiping the boreen with this arrogant-looking young prick seemed all too appealing.

The horseman turned to him, a look of cold surprise on his face. Gavin was surprised, as well, and none too pleased. *Bless my soul, if it's not another bloody, damned Fae. 'Tis a fekkin' plague of t'em, is what it is.* This one had the look of a hunter, though, and coming so close on Aislinn's heels it didn't take a genius to figure out it must be he from whom she was running.

Not my kind, Aislinn had said of the fae that was in pursuit of her, and now that he'd had a look at him Gavin was much inclined to agree; the two were as different as day and night. As he took in the wintry expression in the stranger's eyes, the cruel curl of his mouth, he felt the hackles rise on his neck. His temper flared hotter, burning off the effects of the alcohol, leaving him clear-headed, alert and murderously calm. *How now, you cheeky devil?* he thought angrily. *You think you can just ride up to my door, bold as you please, and take her away from me, is that it? Well, think again.*

Even without the promise she'd wrung from him and despite the anger he still harbored toward her; without knowing anything beyond what his senses had already told him about either fae, or anything at all about the argument between them, Gavin knew he'd not be handing Aislinn over to this brigand. Not without a fight.

But what weapons did he have with which to fight against one such as this? Despite the somewhat effete cast to the fae's features, Gavin could sense the power that lay coiled inside him, as cold and deadly as any serpent.

"I'm looking for someone," the stranger drawled at last. He had a voice like dry leaves scuttling across bare rock.

His mind racing as he searched for a solution, Gavin let his face relax into a drunken leer in an attempt to buy himself some time. "Lookin', is it? Well, sure and I'd say you'd *found* someone. Or amn't I someone then?"

The stranger shook his head impatiently. "I'm seeking

a *particular* someone. A woman. A young lady, in fact. Tall, with long, blonde hair, quite fair to look upon, she's to be my bride. I thought to meet up with her hereabouts, but she seems to have...gone astray."

"Yerra," Gavin shook his head sorrowfully. "'Tis a turrible t'ing that, young ladies goin' astray. Have ye searched down in Cork for her? That's usually where they end up, you see, on the streets o' Cork City."

"'Tis not what I meant," the fae replied, staring down his nose at the smith. "I believe she passed through here quite recently. Perhaps you might have seen her?"

"What's that?" Gavin feigned horror. "Me? Keeping company with some harlot outta Cork? Are ye daft, man? Who's been telling such lies? You'll have the missus down on me poor head if you go about spreading such stories as that!"

"Enough of your nonsense," the stranger uttered in frosty tones. "Silence!"

Gavin fell dumb as the interdiction hit him. Like a cold hand it wrapped around his neck stealing his speech, almost stealing his air entirely. His heart labored as he struggled to breathe. Meanwhile, the stranger's horse tossed its head and stamped impatiently, teeth snapping as it extended his neck in Gavin's direction.

"Now, tell me," the fae demanded, attempting to fix Gavin with his steely gaze, as he urged his restless mount forward. "Have ye or have ye not seen, or heard tell of, the woman I seek?"

It took all the willpower Gavin possessed to keep from answering; or to keep his eyes from meeting that fell gaze, but he knew he was as good as lost if he did. So he focused his attention on the stranger's horse, instead. With an Irishman's appreciation for horseflesh, he couldn't help but be impressed, even despite the danger he was in. It was a beautiful creature, with eyes of coal, a dappled gray coat that shone with the same dull gleam as pewter, deadly white teeth, and those hooves—black as iron and probably just as heavy—ripe to cut a man down with a single kick, he didn't doubt. Suddenly, Auld John's words came back to him: *"Nary a fae can abide the black metal—and their steeds be just the same."* And Gavin knew he had just one chance to save himself.

"I see how 'tis now," he muttered, nodding like a simpleton, though it was a battle to say anything that was not in answer to the fae's question. He dropped his packages carefully on the dried grass at the side of the road, hands fumbling slightly as the dug into his jacket pockets. But as they closed around his all-but-forgotten tools, he felt the pressure from the fae's spell ease. "Sure and your beastie must have a stone stuck in his hoof, to put him in so foul a mood. But, 'tis your lucky day, for I've just the thing for it." And, so saying, he held up the implements of his trade—hoof parers and cleaning knife. The gray reared in alarm. Eyes flashing, whinnying fearfully, it stamped and twisted as it tried to back away from the smith.

"Put those away, you fool!" the fae ordered, savagely working the reins while his horse continued to pivot and buck in its efforts to distance itself from the iron.

"Now, now," Gavin soothed, keeping an eye out for those hooves as he moved closer to the frightened animal. "It must be hurting him turrible to put him in such a state. But 'twill be all right. Just hold him still, can't you?" Reaching out, he quickly swiped the tip of the parers along the horse's flank, as though he were striking a match. The response was every bit as immediate and inflammatory.

The horse let out a scream of pain, as though it had been burnt; its hind legs shot out in a vicious kick that had Gavin jumping back to stay out of range, and that nearly unseated its rider. Then it bolted down the road, while the fae, howling furiously, tried in vain to halt its flight.

"Yerra," Gavin jeered after them. "Off with ye then." Laughing softly, he watched the pair disappeared from view. "And a good riddance to ye both." Then he pocketed his tools, collected his parcels and resumed his journey.

*****

Since several of the windows in the cottage faced the road, Gavin had hoped Aislinn might have been looking out one of them, so to have observed his victory over her enemy. But, when he let himself in he found her seated by the fireside singing softly to herself as she sewed, seemingly unaware of anything that had transpired outside of the room.

He stared at her for a moment, entranced not just by her song but by the cozy, domestic picture she made. Though the fire had burned low, the room had never seemed so warm or welcoming to him. By comparison, his usual existence seemed colorless and drab.

When she glanced up at him, the look in her eyes had him wondering if she hadn't read his mind. Was she mocking him again? Surely the glow on her cheeks was suspiciously rosy, but when she smiled it was with such disarming sweetness Gavin couldn't help but smile back.

"What's all this?" she inquired, laying aside the green gown she was repairing and nodding at the bundles in Gavin's arms.

"Why, I've brought home the Christmas," he replied, feeling suddenly expansive as he deposited his bounty on the table and shrugged out of his jacket. "Come and see."

His neighbors had done him proud this year. He'd been gifted with both a Barm Brak cake *and* a loaf of brown bread, a jug of ale, several hand-sized mince pies, one sack of oranges, one of turnips and another of potatoes, and a dressed goose all ready to be roasted for tomorrow's dinner.

The fae eyed the food greedily. "But is it all for tomorrow then? Can we not eat at least some of it now?"

"Now?" Gavin glanced at her, askance. "Why, today's a Fast Day. Don't you be knowing anything about church law? You shouldna have more than one full meal today."

"Indeed?" the fae replied waspishly. "Well, and if ever I should feel myself bound to abide by the rules of *your* religion I do hope I shall recall that. But, at present, I feel no

57

such compunction. Besides, you've already left me here to fast for most of the day, as it is. Do ye really mean to starve me then?"

Gavin frowned. "And, if you do starve, how would that be my doing? Are ye so helpless then, you could not have fed yourself? Or is it that you think I exist to be your servant? If you wanted to eat, why did ye not cook yourself something afore now?" Aislinn's lips tightened and she looked away as though reluctant to answer. Gavin glanced toward his hearth where all the implements anyone would need to fix a meal stood ready, most of them made by his own hand, or that of his da. All of them of iron. And, finally, understanding dawned. "Ah-ha. You couldn't, could ye?"

Aislinn hesitated for a moment then finally shook her head.

"'Tis because of the iron, isn't it?"

She nodded, even more reluctantly.

Crossing his arms over his chest, Gavin allowed himself a small gloat at the fae's expense. "Well, now, my fine lass, this *is* a pretty mess you've made for yourself, is it not? Perhaps you should ha' given a little more thought to what you were about afore you forced yourself upon me and made me take you in."

"I did think about it. I knew exactly what I was facing coming here."

Gavin grimaced. "Having met your intended, I canna say as I'm surprised. I believe I'd sooner take a chance at starving, too, rather than find myself fallen into his clutches."

Aislinn's mouth tilted in a rueful smile. "Aye. 'Tis what I thought as well."

"Ah, well," Gavin sighed, unbending just a little. "I suppose a spot of tea wouldna be out of place. Especially when I've a heathen such as yourself as a houseguest." As the insult registered, anger flashed in Aislinn's eyes. Gavin smiled mockingly and allowed his own gaze to rove openly over her figure, feeling certain that her treatment of him this past twenty-four hours more than justified any insolence he cared to show her. But insolence soon turned to incredulity. "Sweet Saint Joseph. Woman, where the devil did you get that dress you're wearing?"

"'Twas in the chest in your bedroom," Aislinn replied, sounding puzzled by the question. "You did seem offended by my nakedness this morning, and I thought it more fitting that I find something other than your shirt to wear. Did I do wrong?"

"Nay," Gavin muttered, looking away. It was just that he remembered the garment too well and had thought never to see it again—one of the reasons he'd stored it out of sight, rather than giving it away. It was the dress Mairead had been wearing the day she'd informed him he was to be a father. He remembered how her breasts, swollen by her condition in a way he'd found endlessly fascinating, had filled the bodice to the straining point. He'd wanted to fill his hands with them, to draw their distended nipples through his fingers and marvel at the sweet globes in all their ripe fullness. But she'd waved him away when he tried to embrace her, insisting she was too uncomfortably sore to endure his touch. And also insisting that, until such time as she could conceive again, there was now neither reason nor need for the two of them to lie together. Gavin had never been certain which had given her more joy—the thought of the babe growing inside her, or the fact that she'd finally found an excuse to avoid his bed.

"You're not pleased," Aislinn said quietly.

Gavin shook his head. "'Tis not that. I'm just surprised to see it. And I wouldna thought it would fit you so well as it does."

"Well, I did have to let the hem down."

"Aye, that you'd have had to do," he sighed, as he hung the kettle on the hook over the fire. "She was just a little slip of a thing as wore it." Small but spirited, or so Mairead had seemed to him at one time; with eyes of the brightest blue, a smile he thought would surely one day break his heart. And an unexpected coldness that seemed to grow worse each day they were together, and which was what finally ended up doing to him what her smile could not. He took the dishes down from their shelves and the silverware from their drawer and stacked them on the table. "Well, now," he said, after clearing his throat to dislodge the lump that had formed there. "If dishware isn't a problem for you, why don't you see about setting the table for us?"

*****

As Gavin moved about the kitchen preparing their meal, Aislinn studied him surreptitiously. He was not at all what she'd been expecting.

Despite what both he and Eoghan seemed to think, she'd not come here on a whim. She'd pondered long and hard before allowing herself to be guided by the Oracle's advice; putting off the decision until it was almost too late, as Tiernan's arrival today attested.

It wasn't merely the proximity of so much iron that had her worried. The thought of placing her fate into the hands of any mortal man seemed to her to be the height of foolishness. Watching from the window this afternoon as Gavin confronted Tiernan, it seemed clear to her that she'd been right to be worried. For it had seemed obvious that, by coming here, she'd doomed not only herself, but the smith as well.

How could any mortal mind withstand Tiernan's compulsion spell? Until today, had anyone asked, she would have acclaimed it be impossible. And, yet, Gavin had done just that, not only standing up to one of the Lords of Annwn—and while Winter's might was at its crest no less— but then going on to best him, turning Tiernan's own steed against him and driving them both away.

He must have had the luck that favors fools and drunkards on his side today, she thought, humming a cheerful tune as she set the table, all but laughing aloud when she imagined Tiernan's fury over his defeat. *For if I'm surprised by such a turn of events, surely himself must be flabbergasted.*

Ah, but that was not so funny, was it? Her voice

faltered as she considered the matter. Tiernan would not give up—she'd known that from the start—and the angrier she made him now, the more determined he'd become and the worse it would be for her later. Would she be forced to spend her whole life hiding from him, always on the look-out, never knowing any real peace?

No, such a fate was unendurable. There had to be a way to dissuade him—but how could she, other than by altering her very nature?

"Why'd you stop?" Gavin asked, turning away from the hearth.

"Stop what?" she said, giving him a wide berth as he carried the iron kettle to the table.

"Your singing. You're a right songbird, you are, and 'tis been many a year now since these rooms have heard the sound of any woman's voice raised in song. They've missed it, I think."

"Have they?" She looked at him curiously. "And what of you? Have you missed it as well?"

"Aye." He poured the water into the tea pot and nodded thoughtfully. "I'd forgotten how nice it could be. Cheerful. It fills the emptiness, makes the place feel more home-like."

"Well, sir," she said as she took her seat at the table and reached for one of the pies. "At the moment, I fear, this songbird is far too famished to continue her singing. But, perhaps, after she's eaten, she could be persuaded to do so again, an it pleases thee."

"Aye, perhaps," Gavin murmured absently. "'Twould be nice." But he was frowning as he took his own seat, and though he poured himself a cup of tea, he didn't drink it. Instead, he reached for his pipe on the shelf behind him and, for the next couple of minutes, sat quietly smoking, seemingly deep in thought. Aislinn could feel the tension that gathered around him, like a mist, until, it seemed, he was wreathed in more than smoke.

She had no time to consider his reasons for brooding,

however; her mind was occupied with her own thoughts. It seemed just barely possible that Gavin had succeeded in throwing Tiernan off her track for now. But, at best, that meant a reprieve of several months and Tiernan would not be idle during that time—something else she could count on him for. So it behooved her to make her own plans. Staying here until summer's return would work in the short term but what she really needed was to find a way to put herself permanently beyond his reach.

After a silence of several minutes, Gavin cleared his throat. "I've a proposition for ye, Fae," he said in a voice that strove to sound casual.

She gazed at him curiously. "Is this about the bargain between us? Have you decided what you want in payment for offering me shelter last night?"

He shook his head. "Nay, I'll not be rushing that. You offered me time to think on it, if you recall, and that's just what I plan on doing. This is a different matter entirely. It concerns the next few weeks, or however long you intend to stay here. Seeing as we appear to be stuck with each other, I figure we might as well make the best of the situation."

Surprised, Aislinn folded her arms on the table and eyed him more closely. "What is it you want?"

"Nothing beyond what you've already shown yourself willing to provide," he answered with a slight shrug. "You've seemed comfortable, so far, taking on my wife's appearance, wearing her clothes, sleeping in my bed. All I'm proposing is that you continue to do so."

"Indeed? Yet, up until this point, you've not seemed pleased with my doing any of that."

"Well, perhaps I've had a change of heart."

"And what would be in it for me?" she asked softly, wondering what was behind this change and how she might capitalize on it for her own benefit.

"For one thing, you get to eat," Gavin replied dryly. "Which you do seem to favor, and which I could make very difficult for you, if I wanted."

"Could ye now?" She smiled at that, not really worried. With a bit of glamour, she could trick him into doing whatever she wanted him to, couldn't she? Just as she'd done last night. But, then again, it would be unwise to underestimate the man who'd thwarted Tiernan so easily. "You said I'd come to no harm here," she reminded him. "And I do believe that starving me would count as harm."

"Oh, I wouldn't go so far as to starve ya," he said, smiling back at her, cocky as you please. "At least I don't think I would." For a long moment they stared at each other challengingly. Finally, he shrugged. "Yerra, I've no doubt we could both succeed in making each other as miserable as may be, if we so chose. But how would that serve either of us? Instead, I'm suggesting a truce, of sorts. Go on with your impersonation of my wife and I'll treat you accordingly and give ye all the courtesy I would ha' given her, had she lived. Ye can't ask for fairer than that, can ye?"

Considering how guilt-ridden he'd seemed the night before over his treatment of that lady, Aislinn wasn't so sure about that. Nevertheless, she nodded. "A truce. For now." And then she reached into his mind for the images she'd need. They surfaced easily enough, just as they'd done the night before; and she closed her eyes as she absorbed their essence and felt her magic take hold, transforming her. She heard the startled rasp of Gavin's in-drawn breath and smiled mischievously, for she'd purposely not bothered to prepare his mind as she had done the night before, when she'd sung him into a trance.

"'Tis amazing," Gavin murmured and Aislinn opened her eyes to find him, face white with shock, staring at her as if she were a ghost; which, in a way, she supposed she was. "If I had the two of you sitting here now, I couldna tell one from the other. How is it you know what she looked like?"

"Don't you mean what she still looks like?" she corrected gently. "For she lives on in you, does she not? 'Tis your own memories of the lady that keep her alive for you. And 'tis that you're seeing now, reflected back at ye. For have ye never heard it said that no one is truly dead whilst there is yet someone alive to remember them?"

"I'd not heard that," he muttered, continuing to stare at her with so many emotions warring in his eyes she could not have said which of them predominated—not happiness, though, of that much she was certain. And it made her wonder why he was doing this when it brought him so little joy.

After a moment, he held out his hand. Wordlessly. Though whether he was daring her to take it, or ordering her to, or begging, she didn't know. She took it, all the same. And, rising, she went to him, allowing him pull her onto his lap. As she twined her arms around his neck she smiled at him. "Now, were you wanting me to sing for you, perhaps?"

But he shook his head. "'Tis not that I'm wanting right now." The look in his eyes was bleak, hungry, hopeless, as he tangled his fingers in the hair at the back of her head. "'Tis something else entirely." Then he pulled her close and slanted his mouth over hers. She stiffened for an instant, surprised as much by the suddenness of his onslaught as she was by the voraciousness of his kiss. Then his passion ignited her own and her sex throbbed so demandingly she had to press her thighs together to find some measure of relief. She tightened her arms around his neck and kissed him back, delighting in the feel of his strong arms surrounding her, the silken softness of his hair between her fingers, the hard wall of his chest as her breasts were crushed against it. Delighting, most of all, in his lack of restraint.

He was exhibiting none of the hesitation he'd shown before, and very little of the finesse she'd come to expect from her lovers. She'd taken him for a staid man well into his prime, yet he was kissing her now with all the exuberance of an untried youth. It had been several ages since she'd been with anyone like that and she found the feeling of power it gave her intoxicatingly erotic.

"I need to see you naked," he groaned as he wrenched his mouth from hers and pressed his lips to her neck. His hands molded around her breasts, thumbs chafing her nipples through the fabric. "I need to feel you, skin to skin."

"Mind the dress," she said, gasping as she felt the scrape of his teeth against her collarbone. "Don't tear it." Once had been mildly entertaining, even somewhat thrilling, but she would *not* be spending every day of the next few weeks repeatedly mending dresses!

He lifted his head and glared at her fiercely. "Do not be telling me what I cannot do. Have I not just told you I *need* this?"

She gazed back at him steadily. "I didn't say you couldn't touch me. But you'll not be *needing* to tear the dress from me just to do that, now will you?"

"Aghh," he growled, sweeping the dishes aside then lifting her onto the table. She leaned back on her elbows, her legs falling open, and when he came to his feet between them he pushed them apart even farther. He'd risen so suddenly it sent his chair clattering to the floor, but he paid it no heed. "Always with the complaints and conditions. Did ye not promise before God that ye'd give yourself to me?"

She started as his words hit her, like a cold, wet cloth across the face, cooling her ardor on the spot. Apparently, he'd forgotten she was not really his wife. Apparently, too, he'd abandoned his attempts to get at her breasts. Instead, he pushed the skirt of her dress up above her waist. She'd put on a thin cotton shift beneath the dress, to shield her skin from the scratchiness of the wool, but she hadn't bothered with any other undergarments and as he gazed at her exposed sex a low rumble of approval pearled from his throat. And just the sound of it alone made her blood burn once again.

"Aye, that's a heavenly sight, it is," he muttered admiringly, but when his eyes returned to her face an angry light burned within them. "But, for the love of God, can ye not, just this once, give yourself to me with at least a pretense of happiness?"

"Oh, indeed, I'm quite happy for you to have me, Gavin O'Malley," she said, still trying hard to shove aside the disappointment that had come with the realization that all that passion was not for her. What did that matter, after all? It was still she who would benefit from it. "Or can ye not see that for yourself? Believe me, an I were not happy—or, at the very least, willing—you'd never have gotten this far."

He gazed at her doubtfully, as though he was unsure whether to trust her words. When his focus dropped to her naked mound again there was such heat in his eyes she felt certain her flesh would scorch. She knew just how she must look to him: labia pinked and swollen with arousal, cream glistening along the folds.

"Aye," she whispered, her voice thick as she watched him watch her. "Do you see now how she weeps with longing for you?" He nodded faintly, his throat working as he swallowed, apparently mesmerized by the sight of her. But would he ever do more than just look? If he did not touch her soon—

As if in answer to her unspoken wishes, two work-roughened fingers pushed inside her slick channel. Aislinn keened with pleasure as they moved within her, gently abrading the sensitized flesh of her inner walls. Bringing his gaze back to her face, he slowly pumped his fingers in and out. She wriggled impatiently, wanting more, wishing he'd brush his thumb across her clit too, wondering if she couldn't implant that thought in his mind as well. She watched the heat climb up his cheeks and knew it mirrored her own body's response. Her breath quickened, chest heaving softly, lips parted as she panted, "Aye, Gavin, you know what it is I'm wanting. Touch me there."

His eyes darkened to black. Instead of heeding her, however, his hand abruptly withdrew from her weeping core. He undid his pants, took hold of her legs and sheathed himself in her—all so quickly she didn't even have time to protest the loss of his fingers within her.

Not that she felt like protesting as he pounded into her, his cock filling her to perfection. But good as it felt, this position did nothing for her poor, neglected clit. And she knew she would feel even better if she could grind herself against him. She arched her back hoping to bring her body into closer contact with his, but with very little effect. He had one big hand clenched around each of her thighs, holding her legs apart but curtailing her motion. She could neither rock her hips into his as she wanted to, nor wrap her legs around his buttocks and pull him closer. She felt her muscles tighten around his engorged shaft, watched the muscles in his jaw bunch in response, watched sweat bead on his brow, and knew his climax could not be far off. Hers, however, wasn't even on the horizon.

Balancing her weight on one elbow, she slid her other hand over her mound, intending to help things along. Before she could reach her goal, however, he caught hold of her hand and lifted it away.

She glared at him fiercely, but, "Don't cover yourself," he growled rocking into her even faster, almost crushing her hand in his fist. "I need to see it all."

She followed his gaze and found it directed entirely on the junction where their bodies met; on his cock, thick and corded with veins, gleaming wet with her juices, as it slid, in and out, between her swollen lips.

Aislinn could have wept with frustration, but it would have done her no good. Another instant, and she felt him stiffen. He threw back his head and grunted loud and low as he thrust himself deep within her one last time. She felt the blast of his cum as it bathed her insides. And an instant after that he was withdrawing from her body, hurriedly shoving his still-dripping cock back into his pants, righting his overturned chair and seating himself on it, all while his chest yet heaved.

She gawked at him. "Sure and you're not just going to sit there now?" she demanded after a moment, outraged by his inattention to her needs.

He slanted an uncomfortable glance in her direction, not meeting her gaze, seemingly trying hard to avert his eyes from the dripping folds between her still parted legs as well.

"'Tis all right. 'Tis over for now."

Openmouthed, she watched as he lifted a hand and patted her knee awkwardly then reached for her bunched skirts apparently intending to draw them down over her legs. Before he had a chance to do so, however, she whipped them away from him.

"Won't you at least have a taste while ye're here?" she asked, her voice dripping acid.

His mouth tightened. Color stained his cheeks when he raised his gaze to her face, but whatever he saw there changed his embarrassed frown to a look of puzzlement and then to one of surprise. "Are ye saying you want me to then?"

"Aye, 'tis exactly what I'm saying," she said, still staring at him in disbelief. "'Tis the least you can do to ease the ache you've started, don't you think?"

He blinked at her, for a moment, as though she were speaking a language he'd never heard before. Then, without another word, he pulled his chair closer to the table, slid his hands beneath her hips and lifted her to his mouth.

"Aye. Oh, aye." Aislinn groaned in relief as his tongue licked up along the center of her slit. "'Tis much better that." She welcomed the tickle of his hair against her inner thighs, the sweet suction of his mouth as he licked and sucked and licked again. But, good as it was, she soon realized it was, once again, not quite enough. Once more she slid her hand between her legs, this time making contact with her aching clit.

Gavin pulled back a little to watch her, his expression curious now; his tongue flicking out, from time to time to lave the spaces between and around her fingers as she stroked feverishly over the swollen nub until, finally, the tension broke. He inhaled sharply then hesitantly poked a finger between the fluttering lips of her sex, causing her muscles to contract even harder around it.

"What is it doing?" he whispered, sounding almost fearful.

Aislinn almost choked on her laughter. Propping herself up once again, she stared at him. "What's this then? Have ye not ever seen a woman climax before?"

He shook his head, his eyes lifting to her face once more. "Does it hurt?"

She shook her head. "No more than it hurts you to do so, I'm sure."

Gavin's tongue crept out and moistened his lips as he slanted another quick glance downward. "Will ye do it again?"

"Oh, aye," Aislinn laughed as she pushed herself off the table, sliding down to straddle his lap. "Most assuredly, I will. But, another time."

Gavin's hands closed around her waist. "Why not now?"

"Because I do not feel the need to do so," she said, stretching up to kiss him, her arms once again twining around his neck. "I'm content for now."

His lips met hers eagerly; almost as voracious as before but with an added softness. "I'm not," he whispered as he broke the kiss to nip gently along her throat.

Groaning in delight, she dug her hands into his hair and clasped him closer. "Ah, Gavin O'Malley, you're an odd one, you are. Whatever shall I do with ye?"

*****

Whatever you wish to do. The words were trembling on the tip of Gavin's tongue, and he very nearly spoke them aloud in the instant before he remembered who and what she was. He bit them back in time, shocked by the narrowness of his escape; for surely those were the very last words you would ever wish to say to a creature as dangerous and treacherous as a fae.

He continued for a moment longer, however, to lavish her throat with tiny licks and bites and kisses, unwilling to stop, unable to get enough of her taste, barely resisting the urge to mark her as his. *Fae*, his head tried again to remind him. *Woman*, his body corrected, *My woman*; insisting in no uncertain terms that he take her again.

"Perhaps we should stop now," Gavin murmured, straightening away from her, too conflicted to continue.

His wife's eyes narrowed as the woman in his arms studied his face for a moment and then, without warning, it was Aislinn whose waist his hands encircled. "Perhaps 'tis better thus?" she asked, her voice soft and slightly rueful.

"Aye, perhaps." He nodded, silently cursing himself for being a fool. *Give up this plan,* the voice of reason tried to caution him. *It'll only end in disaster for you. Sure and you're playing with fire, boyo.* But the warnings fell on deaf ears. *Aye, and what of it?* the more reckless portion of his nature responded. *Am I not a blacksmith? Do I not work with fire every day?*

He did at that. And though he had a healthy respect for the substance, he was not about to start fearing it overmuch, either. Its only purpose was to serve his needs, after all.

And, perhaps someday, if he played his cards right, the same could be said of the fae in his arms.

Chapter Five

That Christmas was the happiest Gavin had known since childhood. He was up early for Christmas Mass, leaving the house shortly before dawn, and leaving a pouting Aislinn in his bed with the promise he'd be back within a few hours time to fix breakfast for her.

While the world lay silent and cold, he made his solitary way into town, his path lit only by the stars that sparkled overhead and the Christmas candles that burned in the front window of every house he passed. And a thought occurred to him, as he walked along the empty lane, that each flame was a sign of hope for the future—and that, perhaps, he could feel an answering flicker, newly kindled in the darkness of his own heart. And he laughed at himself then, for putting on such airs and for the absurdity of his thoughts and his breath puffed out in little white clouds that melted away in the frosty air.

When he got to Saint Ita's he found a seat in the very last pew, where he'd be sure of being among the first out the door when mass ended. He didn't take Communion, although he'd made his Confession just the day before and he was sure Father Cullen would remark on that fact the next time he saw him. But too much had happened between then and now and his soul did not feel easy with the thought of it. Although he'd still have sworn to anyone who'd asked him that the woman he'd made love to the day before had been his wife, a small part of him doubted whether the Church—or Mairead herself—would choose to see things in quite the same way.

Not that he regretted his actions of the day before. To the contrary, he felt more at peace with himself that morning than he had in many a year. But his mind was so consumed with thoughts of repeating the act he barely heard a word of the service and hurried off as soon as it was over, before anyone could engage him in conversation, or take notice of his agitation.

Then it was home again, where breakfast and a sulky fae awaited him. Aislinn was wearing her own, repaired green dress and, at Gavin's request, she once again resumed her impersonation of Mairead. It was obvious she was less than happy about it, however. But Gavin was in a good and generous humor so, once the goose was cooking, he took a few minutes to tease her out of her bad mood. He sat her on his lap, just as if she were his bride in truth, and fed her pieces of orange, tickling her as she tried to eat them until she laughed and then licking at the juice as it ran down her chin, until, finally, her smile was restored. And she rewarded him with several songs while he saw to the rest of the meal.

He did nearly spoil things again, though, before the food was even on the table for he would speak mockingly of the fae and their heathen ways, and question the usefulness of a woman who couldn't even cook a decent meal for herself, just to watch her eyes smolder. And, also, to remind them both that she was *not* Mairead. But when at last he bowed his head to make his prayers—over Christmas dinner, at his own table, and with the semblance of his wife seated across from him, once again smiling at him indulgently—he was all but overcome with gratitude. Even knowing it to be an illusion, and a short-lived one at that, he still felt as though he'd been granted a taste of the life he'd once hoped would be his and he felt anew the wonder of the day.

And the prayers he said were humble and heartfelt and Aislinn was among the blessings he counted. For though he was still bemused by the strange course his life had taken, over the past few days, he was not unmindful of the fact that she was the root cause of much of his present contentment.

Finally, when dinner was over, and they were relaxing by the fire—Gavin with his pipe and both of them with pints of mulled porter—he asked her a question that had been uppermost in his mind for the past two days.

"So, tell me, lass, what is it about the iron that makes the fae dislike it so much?"

She looked surprised, as though the question had

caught her off-guard and, for a moment, it seemed she didn't know how to answer. Finally she shrugged. "It is an anathema. Even its stench—which you seem not even to notice—is repugnant to us. It binds our power so that we grow weak in its presence. Its touch is painful to us, or so I've always been told. Never having touched it myself, nor known anyone foolish enough to try, I canna say exactly how that would be. But I'm sure that it is bad for I can sense its presence and something there is about it that warns me off. Like the heat of a fire, if you get too close, will signal danger. You do not have to touch the flames, do you, to know they will hurt you? Its proximity alone provides a warning you cannot deny."

Gavin stared at her. "Its stench? Good Jesus, woman, if it's that distasteful to ye, whatever put the thought of coming here into your head?"

Aislinn shrugged again and sipped at her porter. "My need was great. And, as I've already told ye, 'twas the druid oracle I consulted who told me where to find thee. She said your hearth could ward me from Tiernan's wrath."

"What's that you say?" Gavin asked, growing alarmed at the thought that he might have been singled out. "*My* hearth? Why mine? Why not someone else's?"

"I do not know," she answered. "And it might not be just yours that would suffice. But 'twas yours she mentioned."

Gavin shook his head. "Bloody, damned druids. What have I ever done to any of them, I'd like to know, that they should be after bringing me into this mess of yours? And what is it this Tiernan fellow wants from ye, anyway, that it'd drive ye to such straits that you'd consent to hide out here, in my stinky forge?"

Aislinn's eyes flashed with amusement. "Would it be so hard for you to believe he might want me for my own sweet self? I have been told by some who've known me that I'm quite beyond compare. Do you not find me so?"

"Aye, you're a beauty, sure enough," Gavin admitted.

"And well ye know it too, I'm thinking. But, for all o' that, I'd still not be out scouring the countryside in search of one who so clearly does not wish to be found." He stopped then, as a thought occurred to him. "He does *know* you doona want him, doesn't he? For when I met up with the scoundrel yesterday he claimed you two were to be married."

Aislinn stared into the fire. "He knows what my feelings are. There has never been any doubt as to my unwillingness to marry with him. The great lengths to which he's gone to try and ensure I'd have no choice in the matter attest to that."

"So what is it he wants?" Gavin repeated, adding when she seemed reluctant to answer. "I think I've a right to know what 'tis all about, seeing as you've seen fit to stick me in the middle of it."

"Some of it, perhaps." She gazed at him speculatively for a moment then smiled. "A bargain for ye then, mortal. I'll tell ye why it is that Tiernan pursues me so ardently. And in exchange I want to know about this wife of yours, to whose memory you cling so tightly even though it does not seem to me you had much joy of each other."

Gavin scowled. "My marriage does not concern you, Fae. Nor my wife either."

"Oh, indeed?" Aislinn smiled mockingly. Spreading her arms wide to draw attention to the form she wore, she threw his own words back at him. "And yet, it does seem you've seen fit to stick me in the middle of it, does it not?"

'It does, I suppose," Gavin admitted grudgingly. "Very well, then. But I'll also be wanting to hear more about this druid witch and what she had to say. And I'll make no bargain with ye for that piece of knowledge. For, if she mentioned my name, I've a right to know what it is she said about me."

Aislinn nodded. "Agreed," she said and then fell silent, staring once more into the fire for so long of a time that Gavin was just about to prompt her and then at last she began to speak. And her voice, soft and low with a silvery sweetness, wrapped its magic around Gavin's mind. "If you're to understand my story, I must first needs tell ye a little about the fae and how our world is ordered. Soulless you have called us and heathen and you are quite right about that, I suppose, although it is in no wise as simple as you seem to think.

"For we are elementals. We draw our life from the *spirit* of the green world, rather than its flesh. We are the unfading ones who have walked these lands since the dawn of time. And when your body has returned to dust and your soul has fled to whatever place such things do go; when this forge you take such pride in has vanished from the landscape and you yourself are no longer even a memory to anyone yet living then I, Aislinn Deirbhile, shall remain, even as you see me now. Mark ye that, human, and remember it next time you think to make mock of the power your black metal holds over me and mine. For until the world doth end; until the last star falls and the sun no longer makes her daily journey 'cross the sky, I shall remain."

She paused then, and gazed at him challengingly, as though awaiting his response, but much as Gavin would have liked to have made a clever retort, he could only stare blankly back at her, too ensorcelled by her voice to speak.

After a moment, Aislinn lifted one shoulder in a small shrug. "Yet, for all of that, my people do have our weaknesses. We are bound by our nature in ways that you are not; and bound to the world itself in ways that differ from clan to clan. The Merrow, for example, care naught for the calendar as their lives are governed by the sea and the sea takes little notice of the seasons. While the Dryad's life is tied to neither earth or sea nor stars above, but only to the life of the single tree in which she makes her home. And for each tree that is cut down," she said, indicating his table and the chairs in which they both sat, "a dryad is no more."

"Is that a fact?" Gavin said, finding his voice at last, though he winced at the sound of it for it seemed too harsh, like the croaking of a raven, after her cool, liquid tones.

"Well, then, 'tis a wonder you can bear to sit on yon stool there. For sure and it must be like sitting atop the bones of one of your own kind."

Aislinn inclined her head. "And dost thou not then eat the flesh of *your* fellow creatures and clothe yourself in their skins?"

He stared at her, appalled. "I do not. For the love of God, woman, what are ye saying? Sheep and pigs and cattle—they are no more my kin than the likes of *you* are. And no more are chickens or geese."

Aislinn blinked at him for a moment, and then inclined her head again, bowing with icy courtesy. "Your pardon, sir. I keep forgetting that ye humans hold yourselves apart from the rest of creation. Perhaps with cause," she added, raising her hand to forestall his next protest. "For ye do have free will and souls which allow thee to slip the bonds that connect most of the world's creatures to each other and the earth. And not even the angels have such, or so I'm told."

"Aye," Gavin answered, rallying somewhat. "And 'tis those very same souls which do guarantee us life everlasting when we die, an we deserve it."

"It may be so," Aislinn returned politely. "I would not know." And, when Gavin opened his mouth to argue, she held up her hand once more. "Nay, friend, I'll not debate the existence of your Heaven with ye—nor any other subject of which I have no knowledge. Yet, I will say this: I have seen the shades of those of your kind who have died and are yet fated to wander the Earth. And I have wondered what became of the souls of those who have also died and yet do not wander. Sure and they must have gone somewhere, though I know not where."

"They've gone to Heaven," Gavin insisted stubbornly. "To live in eternal bliss with all their loved ones 'round them. But what does this have to do with the story ye were telling me? I've yet to hear any mention of druids or this fella as is chasing ye."

"I was endeavoring to explain it. I am of the *Daoine*

Sidhe; who are also called the *Tylwyth Teg.* Of all the Fae we, and our brethren the *Sluagh Sidhe,* are the closest to humankind for, like you, our lives are governed by the turning of the earth and by the changes of the seasons— though in very different ways.

"For with each year that passes you grow older, while we remain unchanging. Yet as we circle 'round the seasons, it is you who remain constant and pay too little attention to *Rotha Mor An tSaoil*, the Great Wheel of Life, which doth divide the year into two parts, Summer and Winter, and thus holds us in its sway.

"Though equal in length, the two seasons are not quite evenly matched. Summer's strength is derived from the life it doth contain; which arrives in a joyful burst of bud and bloom and grows ever stronger 'til the last harvest has been gathered. Winter, on the other hand, takes its power from those it strikes down; and when all that can be killed is dead and their life force spent, there is no more to be had. Which is why oftentimes Winter's queen fades early, and Winter itself makes its end in small squalls and mostly bluster.

"Tiernan is of the Winter Court. And it is for to redress what he sees as an inequity between his kind and mine that he pursues me, that I might assist him in his foul scheme to overturn this sacred balance. For my influence doth expand as Winter's contracts and I grow strong with Spring's approach. Were I to ally myself with Annwn, Winter could use my strength to enhance its own. In truth, ye should be glad for this chance to aid me, mortal, and honored to be used in such service. For, think ye, how much would ye like it were Winter to prevail for a month or two longer each year than it now does? 'Twould mean a shorter growing season for all your crops and death to many of those animals which must give birth in springtime."

"Aye," Gavin agreed. "'Twould be a hardship, I see that. But, what I do not see is why it should fall to me to prevent such a thing—nor to you, either. What is it you've done to convince the villain you'd be willing to aid him in his efforts?" he asked, drawing Aislinn's ire.

"Have I not already told ye?" she demanded. "He *knows* I am unwilling. What cares he for that? He does not *need* my acquiescence, for I'm fain to be as I must be. He just needs *me*—bound to him, held captive in the underworld, in Annwn—and then all the power that I possess will be at his disposal."

"But he said you two were to be married," Gavin protested, still not completely trusting in her story. "Was that a lie?"

Once again Aislinn sighed. "Nay, but what of it? I'm sure 'tis indeed what he wishes. For would not a marriage between us further bind me to him? I'm certain he hopes to have children by me, as well—and that I'll never allow."

"So, is it that ye doona ever want to marry or have children, lass?" Gavin asked softly, thinking of his own child, of the scant minutes he'd held his son before the babe breathed his last. "Or is it just this particular fella to whom ye object?"

She shook her head wearily. "'Tis none of it as simple as you seem to think. Did ye not understand me, mortal, when I said we fae are unfading? You worry about a life that spans the course of a few score year. My children will likely live 'til the end of time. What would ye have me do then? Give birth to slaves whose only purpose is to ensure that Winter never fades? 'Twould be better were they never born or to die at birth than to have such a life."

Gavin stared at her, startled by her words and grieved anew. The memory of his son's pale face caused his own expression to harden. *Her children would live forever? Oh, aye, there's a reason for to pity her, to be sure.* "Ye doona know of what you speak," he growled harshly. "Sure and it's clear to me you've never lost a child, or you could not say such a thing. Slavery, is it? Aye, 'tis a heavy doom to lay upon a helpless child, but where there's life there's hope. Your babes would not stay babes forever, would they? And, if they're as long-lived as you claim, they'd have ample time to fight for their freedom, once they reach adulthood and so escape the fate you fear for them. Whereas their untimely deaths would leave them defeated from the start and would leave you with naught but your loss."

*****

Aislinn gazed at him, unblinking, taking in the strain on his face, the anguish in his eyes. "I see you've experienced such things," she said; and though the words were spoken softly, she knew they held a command he could not resist. "Tell me."

"Mairead was yet but a girl when I met her," Gavin said, but slowly, in a voice that made plain his reluctance to speak of such matters. "And not much more when she passed on. We were married less than a year when she died, God rest her soul. 'Twas a difficult birth. The child was too big and had tarried too long within his mother's womb. Perhaps he was reluctant to leave it. But, whatever the reason, she labored too long with him and...I lost them both."

As he stared into space, lost in his thoughts, Aislinn slid into his mind—the better to read his memories.

"She should have had her whole life ahead of her," he said, his voice barely a whisper. "Instead she lay dying. And the thought topmost in her mind was that 'twas I who'd robbed her of her life. So on her deathbed she bade me swear that I'd never let such a thing happen again. That I'd never put another in her place, or cause another woman to suffer such agony."

He dropped his head into his hands then, looking so abjectly miserable that Aislinn, watching him, and watching as the scene unfolded in her own mind, felt anger on his behalf and sorrow—as well as surprise and disbelief. "And you did this, then? You made such a promise?" By all the stars above, she had known that humans could be rash, but this seemed beyond foolish.

Looking up again, his expression pleading for understanding, Gavin nodded. "I could hardly refuse, could I?"

"I do not see why not. It should hardly have mattered to her what you did after she was gone."

He sighed. "And yet, it seems it did."

"Well then, you should have waited her out. Surely you could have held off answering for a few minutes more? After which time she'd have been in no position to reproach you, being dead."

"She was my wife," Gavin replied through clenched teeth. "What would you have me do? Turn down her last request and let her go unhappy into the afterlife?"

"Oh, nay, far better it is for you to live on for years as you are doing now. Alone. Unhappy. With hardly any more of a life than she has." Aislinn shook her head. Humans—such little lives and yet they would throw them away over the smallest of things. "'Twas naught but jealousy that prompted her to demand such a thing of ye. She knew she couldn't keep you for herself; and clear as day it is to me that she hadn't made you happy during your marriage. No doubt she feared if you went on to find happiness with someone else you'd know it had been her fault and count yourself lucky for having been set free."

"Lucky, am I?" Slamming his fist down on the arm of his chair, he glared at her. "How dare you to speak so? If she were jealous, why would she be after caring about another woman's suffering? Or mine, for that matter. Why should she have been so worried that my heart couldn't stand the pain of another loss?"

"Is that what she told you?" Aislinn asked, wondering how he could possibly have believed such a story. "That it was of *you* she was thinking? That it was for *your* sake she wished you to spend the rest of your life alone?"

"She was an angel," he insisted. "And always thinking of others' welfare, mine included, even then. Even though 'twas I who killed her."

"Och. And how is it that her death is on your head? For sure and I do not believe you capable of any such thing."

"'Twas my wish to have a large family," Gavin

replied sadly. "Boys for to help me run the forge and carry on the family name; girls for to brighten the household with their laughter and their song and to be a comfort to me in my old age. Mairead, on the other hand, would have been content for us to live together in holy piety, rejecting the temptations of the flesh, avoiding the marriage bed altogether. But such was never the sort of life I wanted and, in my selfishness, I never concerned myself with what a dainty thing she was; I gave no thought to what sort of children a brute like myself would likely sire. The babe was too large for her to birth. Have I not already said it? That's what killed her, what killed them both. And how is that *not* my fault?"

"And so this is why you insist I keep her appearance then?" Aislinn asked, changing the subject rather than answer his question. If he wished to believe himself responsible for his wife's death, what concern was it of hers? "'Tis not an attempt to recapture the past, as I first thought, is it? 'Tis not because you wish to be reminded of your wife but, rather, because you wish to remain faithful to the promise she wrung from you that day—to take no other woman but she herself into your bed."

"'Twas you who chose to commence this masquerade," Gavin replied coolly, in a voice that made no apology for his actions. "What cause have you to object to it now?"

"I've made no objections," Aislinn answered with a careless shrug. "It matters little to me if you prefer me looking thus. 'Tis amusing, in fact. But you need hardly worry that I am taking her place when, by your own admission, I am willing to do so much that she would not."

Gavin nodded. "Aye, perhaps."

"So what was it ailed the lady that she found the marriage bed so unpleasant? For sure and it could not *all* have been sinful?"

"'Twas me she found unpleasant, I think," he said with a sigh. "Or maybe the act itself." He was silent for a long moment. "I have a question for ye, Fae," he said at last.

81

"As a woman."

"Oh?" Aislinn gazed at him coolly. "And is it as a woman you're thinking of me now? Sure and I should be honored, I suppose."

Gavin looked perplexed. "A woman—aye. And what else would ye be? For, you're certainly not a man."

"Well, before, you did say I was no more your kin than a cow or a chicken. For all I know, you view me as little more than a barnyard creature. Like one of those horses whose looks you admire, perhaps?"

"Whist," he replied, shaking his head. "Now, don't you be taking my words amiss. Of course I think of ye as a woman, lass. I'd not have otherwise taken ye to my bed, now would I?"

"And yet there are those of your kind who would not be quite so particular," she answered, smiling slyly. "I could take on other forms, too, you know, besides this one. An it pleases ye."

Gavin's face flamed. "Oh, enough now. I'll apologize for having spoken rashly, if I must, but there'll be no more of that sort of talk. Not in my house. I'd say you've more than proven yourself a woman by that bit of spite. For who else would hold a man's words against him in such a fashion?"

"So what is your question then?" Aislinn asked, feeling slightly mollified by his apology, however poorly phrased, but Gavin hemmed and hawed and seemed to be having a hard time coming to his point. "Speak!" she urged him, at last. "I pray thee."

"'Tis just...well, you've lain with me for several nights now and...and you've not seemed...repelled to any great extent. Am I wrong about that?"

"Repelled?" she repeated the word in surprise.

Gavin nodded, seemingly unable to meet her eyes. "Aye."

"By what?"

"Well, I don't know. By me. By...by my...um..." His face turned an even brighter shade of red and he gestured vaguely toward his crotch.

Aislinn hid a smile. "Is it your cock about which you're wishing to ask?"

"You said 'twas not what you expected. Yet you did not seem to find it...unseemly? Or, or too large, perhaps?"

Too large? She frowned at that, certain for a moment that he was teasing, and failing to see the point of his joke, until the self-conscious look in his eyes, the mixture of hope and trepidation there, rid her of that notion. "Have you really been with no women at all since your wife died then?" she asked, for surely such a question could only come from inexperience.

Gavin scowled. "I've said as much, have I not? And had you not tricked me I'd not have been with ye either. But what has that to do with my question?"

"And how many were there before her?"

He turned his scowl on the fireplace. "None."

"Truly?" It was too good to be true and, this time, Aislinn could not conceal her smile. It had been many long ages since she'd been with anyone this close to innocent. Her gaze traversed his body lovingly, covetously; as though seeing him anew and enchanted by the prospect. An avaricious thrill coursed through her, heating her blood, causing her pussy to throb in anticipation. Oh, the things she might teach him. Putting her glass down, she got up and went to him. "You have much to learn about women," she told him as she pushed his legs apart and knelt between them. "About their wants and needs, their likes and dislikes."

"Here now, what are you doing?" he asked, stopping her as she reached for his waistband. He looked flustered. Cross. Hopeful.

"I'm not repelled by thee, Gavin O'Malley," she answered as she shook off his hand and freed his erection. "Not by any part—least of all this."

She ran her tongue up the underside of his shaft, savoring the velvety skin, watching as his eyes grew heavy. He shuddered as her tongue traced circles on his crown, lapping at the silky drops that pearled from the slit at its top. Chest heaving, he tangled his fingers in her hair, wordlessly urging her to take more of him. But Aislinn had other ideas in mind for tonight. Releasing his cock from her mouth, she shrugged out from under his hand and sank back on her heels. "I don't wish to speak ill of your lady, since I can see it upsets ye, but it does seem to me she knew as little of men as you did of women. Perhaps, if she'd lived, you two would have been able to discover many ways in which to please each other."

"Perhaps," he replied, without much conviction.

Aislinn continued to stroke him. "For sure and a rod such as this can be the instrument of much pleasure—both given and received. Shall I show you what I mean?"

Gavin swallowed hard and nodded.

"Good then," she said as she stood and gathered her skirts up around her hips. He reached for her as she straddled his legs, his hands closing around her waist, big fingers splayed across her back, steadying her as she positioned herself so that the tip of his cock just breached her flesh. His breath shuddered out of his chest on a muttered oath, and she smiled at the sound. Resting her hands on his shoulders, she slowly raised and lowered herself over him, taking more of him inside her each time. Heat rose in his cheeks and his eyes held hers as she took him inch by inch, until the entire length of his shaft was buried within her, filling her completely.

"There now, see?" She smiled at him. "Not too large at all. In fact, I'd say you were a perfect fit, would you not agree?"

"Aye," he growled as his grip on her waist tightened. His hips jerked upward but before he could begin thrusting inside her, she stopped him.

"Stay," she cautioned, laying a hand on his arm. "Not yet."

Disbelief, bewilderment, anger, hurt, need, they all chased each other across his features leaving his face crestfallen. "Damn it all, woman, is it that you're trying to kill me then?"

Smiling, Aislinn laid her hand against his cheek. "Nay, *mo chroí,* pray do not think me so cruel as that. I know what it is you're wanting. Only have a little patience and you'll get all that and more. Can ye do that for me?"

Reluctantly, he nodded.

"Good. Now give me your hand," she said, taking hold of his wrist and positioning his hand between her legs 'til his palm cupped her mound and his fingers rested right below her clitoris, "And stroke me here."

"What, this little pearl, d'you mean?" he asked as he fingered it, his eyes intent on her face, lips curling in a small, wicked smile as she nodded. Fire raced through Aislinn's veins and she felt her sheath tighten around him. Gavin's eyes grew dark. "Ah. Ye like that, do ye? Does that feel good then?"

"Mmm," she murmured in response, unlacing the bodice of her dress to bare her breasts.

Gavin's eyes grew even darker; his gaze fastened on her chest, his tongue peeking out to wet his parted lips. As she kneaded the soft mounds, cupping them in her hands, twisting and pulling at her nipples, she felt Gavin's cock jerk inside her. A soft moan broke from his lips. The urge to fuck him hard, to feel that thick shaft slide slickly in and out, became too great to ignore.

"Would you like to suckle them now?" she asked.

In answer, the hand that was not working her clit slid up her back and pulled her against him. As his mouth closed over one nipple she surged upward. Clasping her hands together behind his neck, she began to ride him.

He gasped in surprise. Raising his head, he watched her face for a moment then the hand at her back fisted itself in her hair and tugged, forcing her back to arch, thrusting her breasts higher. Even as his mouth returned to her nipple, Aislinn unraveled. Cream pulsed from her pussy to coat his cock, a small cry broke from her lips, her thighs clamped hard around his, holding him immobile as she came.

Gavin groaned. Hands clutching at her hips, he tried to take over the rhythm she had abandoned, but clearly the position wasn't working for him. He slid his hands beneath her and pushed to his feet, holding her still impaled upon his cock. Aislinn locked her legs around his hips as he pushed her against the closest wall, holding her there with one hand still cupping her bottom and the other braced on the wall beside her head. Aislinn dug her nails into his shoulders, pressing her mouth to his neck as he pounded into her, her body welcoming each invasion, gripping him harder each time he withdrew.

His fingers, wet with her juices, slipped into the crease of her ass and his hold on her tightened, to the point, almost, of pain. Feral grunts rose up his throat and the slapping of flesh against flesh heated her blood, sending her over the edge once more even as Gavin erupted inside her.

*****

As his heart rate slowly returned to normal, Gavin became aware of his muscles quaking with reaction as he continued to hold Aislinn against the wall. He dropped his head to her shoulder and bit softly along her neck. The blistering climax had snugged his balls so tight he had to resist the urge to reach down and make sure they were still there.

"By all the saints, woman, that was... Well, I've never felt anything like it, that's for a certainty."

Laughing softly, she unlocked her legs from his waist. "Aye. 'Twas not bad, all things considered."

"Not bad?" He stared at her in surprise as he set her on her feet and quickly adjusted his trousers. Was that all she could think to say? But the flushed, satisfied look on her face drove all questions from his mind. He didn't much care what she thought of it, or of him, either. He just wanted more. Fanning his hand on her cheek he lowered his mouth to hers, kissing her for all he was worth, doubting he'd ever be satisfied until he'd devoured every last inch of her. But he didn't just want *more*, he realized with a small sense of shock, he wanted *everything*. He wanted *her*.

Aislinn...

The thought scared him so badly he wrenched his mouth away from hers, breathing hard.

"Take me to your bed now," she murmured against his chest. "And perhaps we might try it again—without so many clothes."

Without a word, Gavin lifted her into his arms and carried her from the room. Minutes later, he was lying in his bed, watching her undress, so tempted to ask her to resume her true form, to let him see her as she really was, to let him have her as she really was, but he held his tongue. The need to hold her naked body in his arms—hers, not Mairead's—was a dangerous desire, one he didn't dare even give voice to.

Still, when she climbed into bed beside him and his arms closed around her, he couldn't resist closing his eyes and trying his best to imagine it. Trying to pretend that the hair his fingers tangled in was not Mairead's shiny, brown locks but Aislinn's warm golden curls. Trying and almost succeeding...

Chapter Six

"You never did tell me what it was the druid said." Gavin's breath feathered the hair at Aislinn's neck as he lay spooned behind her. She'd been drifting on the edge of sleep, enjoying his warmth at her back and paying little attention to the intimacy with which he held her, until his words startled her awake.

It should not have been so unsettling to feel the weight of his arm at her waist, the press of his thigh between her own. But, given that she had shifted back to true form in order to sleep more comfortably, it came as something of a shock. Up until now, he'd kept his hands resolutely to himself when she was not in the guise of his wife. Was it possible he had failed to notice her transformation?

She half turned within the circle of his arm. Lying on her back, she peered at him curiously. "What made ye think of that now?"

"Why not now?" Warmth spread from his hand, which he left right where it was, splayed against her belly, while his gaze roved greedily over her face for several seconds. Then their eyes chanced to meet and her breath caught at the heat that blazed between them, at the unaccustomed longing that flared from somewhere deep within her. Her lips parted on a soft sigh. But just when she thought he'd move closer, just when she was hoping he'd erase the distance between them and press his lips to hers, he pushed away from her, opening up a space of about half a foot between them and propping himself up on one elbow. "Sure and you didn't think you could distract me so thoroughly I'd forget about that, did ye?"

More like hoped, Aislinn thought as she eyed him back. The mocking smile that curved his lips suggested it would not be so difficult to do, that she maybe almost had, and she was tempted to try again. But what good would come of such games? She knew very well why she was loath to share the details of the oracle's prophecy with him—or with anyone. Knowledge was power; in this case the power to, quite possibly, end her existence. Still, he was right about one thing. The prophecy mentioned him by name, suggesting his involvement was more than casual; suggesting that, perhaps, it was ordained for him to know the whole of it.

Gazing up at the darkened ceiling, Aislinn reluctantly cast her mind back to that night six weeks earlier, to the smell of wood smoke drifting through the ancient oak grove, firelight playing along the trunks and reflecting up into the branches, to the druid's slow, sonorous chant. And as her mind recalled the words that had been spoken then, her lips repeated them now, in unconscious imitation of the oracle's voice...

> "*Aislinn Deirbhile, you'll have much to regret*
> *if ye keep to this path where your feet have been set.*
> *For Annwn's dark hand is yet creeping close;*
> *to make you his own has been his proud boast.*
> *An he catch you afoot ere the first roses bloom,*
> *sure he'll carry you off to his palace of doom.*
> *And there, in the cold and endless night,*
> *you'll dwell until time doth put out your light.*
> *So hark to me now as I lay out your quest*
> *for 'tis wise to be foolish when truth seems a jest.*
> *If you wish e'er to return to the place you were born,*
> *better take shelter soon in a place you would scorn.*
> *For none can extinguish the Dark Fae's ire,*
> *excepting the smithie and his pyre.*
> *Hard as the iron with which he doth work;*
> *close by Kilbanning town doth he lurk.*
> *Within four walls with iron bound,*
> *Gavin O'Malley, the smith, can be found.*
> *His hearth may shield ye from the Night,*
> *from Winter's rage and Winter's might;*
> *yet iron heart may burn or break,*
> *so take care what fires ye awake!*
> *And 'ware to ye both an you remain*

beyond the peak of Summer's reign.
One chance will ye get your geis to abate,
but take that chance and ye seal three fates.
A human soul will foil Night's plot
unless you forget what you should not:
Naught but the one offered willingly,
shall ever suffice to set ye free.
When Summer's harbor is in your sights,
fain you must be to do what is right.
When Winter's might be again at its crest;
brave, to endure you a most fearsome test—
hard by the pit of the black metal forge,
face to face with the bitter scourge.
Foolish it be to inspire his wrath
and dark to me yet is the end of your path.
Yet if death and destruction should follow ye home,
then there ye shall stay and ne'er more roam..."

As Aislinn's recital drew to a close, silence settled over the room. The firelight in her mind died out and she was once again aware of the pale moonlight as it shone through Gavin' window, illuminating his face as he stared blankly, his eyes wide and unseeing, as though he, too, had been transported elsewhere.

Then he shuddered and returned to himself. "Bloody, fekkin' druids," he growled. "What's it all mean, eh?"

Aislinn shrugged. "Like all prophecies it means very little until the events it describes have begun to unfold. And so it must be, perhaps, for to speak more plainly would likely cause you to act in a way ye would otherwise not and so negate the prophecy. 'Tis a paradox," she added, helpfully.

"'Tis a right, fekkin' mess, is what it is," he sighed, rolling onto his back beside her and staring at the ceiling. "So, what's this *geis* you're under, lass? You'd not thought to mention that before."

"'Tis two of them, actually, as is oft' the case. Each one serving to complicate the other. The first is that, should Tiernan catch me outside the Summerland while Winter holds sway, he may keep me and none of my kindred can interfere to stop him. The second is that, until summer returns, the gates to the realm are closed to me and I must perforce remain here, in the outer world, friendless, powerless—afoot, as it were," she added bitterly. "Just as the oracle phrased it, like a fox that the hounds have already caught scent of."

"Whist," Gavin muttered, rolling up on his side again to frown at her, reprovingly. "Enough of that sort of talk. You're safe enough for now, at any rate—the hounds'll not be getting to you here, little fox. And powerless you most certainly are not. I've seen your magic, Fae, and felt its effects."

She smiled, touched by his attempts to comfort her. Reaching up she traced her hand along his cheek. "Enough for small bits of *glamoury*, perhaps, but naught that could serve to protect me against one such as Tiernan, especially not now—when he's still in ascendance and I've been all but promised to him."

"And who was it, anyway, that put such a curse upon ye?"

"One of the very few people who could have done so," Aislinn answered sadly. "The Summer Queen."

"The queen?" Gavin repeated. "Your own queen?"

Aislinn nodded. "Aye. Who else? For surely you know such things can only be laid upon a person by one who has authority over them?"

"But why would she do such a thing? If what you say is true, 'tis not to her advantage for him to have you."

"'Twas because Tiernan did trick her," she replied. "He convinced her I sought to take her crown for myself and in her jealousy she did think to punish me."

"And, how did he manage that, I'd like to know, if he canna lie? Or was he speaking true?"

"Nay. A crown is such a weighty thing and it comes at far too high a price. I've only always wanted a simple life. 'Tis why it galls so to be thrust into this position with the doom of the whole world riding on my decision. But, to give him credit, 'twas most cleverly done. He did but needs imply there was someone quite close to her who sought to usurp her power and as he was standing right beside her at the time it was very literally true. Had she asked him directly if 'twere I to whom he referred, he'd, of course, have had to admit 'twas not. But she does tend towards pridefulness, as everyone who doth know her is aware, and she was unwilling to admit to her ignorance of such a plot. And since there has always been a measure of competition between the two of us, she easily drew the conclusion he wished her to—that 'twas I of whom he spoke."

"Why did you not speak up, lass, and defend yourself?"

Aislinn shrugged. "Sure and I would have done so, had I been there. But you cannot imagine Tiernan would be so foolish as to have made his insinuations while I was present? I did not hear of it 'til later and, by then, the damage was already done."

"You said you were quite close to her at the time."

"I said *Tiernan* was standing close to her at the time," she corrected. "I am close to her always by virtue of being her sister."

"Her sister?"

"Aye," she answered, adding, as Gavin continued to stare at her, seemingly in shock. "'Twas *Bealtaine* and she was drunk on the first flush of new power running riotous through her veins and so not thinking clearly. 'Tis most likely she has regretted her actions by now, though it's too late to change what's been done. My one hope is that a way might be found to mitigate the curse. Though it is more likely an additional *geis* will be laid upon me—to protect the realm, even an it damns me further. Since she has no power over Tiernan, there is little else she can do to avert disaster. She cannot place any restrictions on his activities other than to ban him from the Summerland, which she has already done."

"The Summerland—is that your home?"

"It is. Though it is called by many other names as well—*Tir-nan-Og, Avalon, Hy-Brasail*—I favor the term Summerland, for that's how it has always seemed to me. 'Tis always summer there, you see. 'Tis a place peaceful and green and I love it well; but, now, if e'er I see it again 'twill likely become my prison and then my doom."

"I thought 'twas the other place you were worried about?" Gavin asked, brow furrowing in confusion. "Annwn, or whatever you called it?"

"Oh, forsooth, if I have to *choose* a place in which to end my life, why would I not pick my own home? But, anywhere you are forced to stay against your will is still a prison, is it not? If I am taken to Annwn, 'twill be a disaster for the outer world, and for the summer fae alike. My kin can do nothing to prevent it now, as the *geis* prohibits their intervention. But an I make it through this winter and return to the realm come spring, 'tis unlikely I will be allowed to leave there again and place myself at risk of capture. Yet the *geis* doth doom me if I remain within its borders once summer hath ended."

She sighed wearily as she thought about it. "Understand ye yet the cleverness of Tiernan's plan? He knows I face almost certain death if I return to the realm and if I do not return 'tis likely my kinsmen will search for me here, in the outer world, and put an end to me in order to prevent Tiernan from claiming me *next* winter. They wish me dead, for they are safer thus; whereas Tiernan merely seeks to imprison me—and offers marriage both to sweeten the deal and to further bind Summer's hands an it seeks to get me back. For, as my husband, his claim upon me will hold more weight than that of my own people. 'Tis quite a generous offer he has made me, do you not think it so? And I do not doubt he expected me to flee to him, begging for his protection, just as soon as ever the awareness of my plight did dawn upon me."

"You should have told me all of this the first night," Gavin grumbled.

"Perhaps." She studied him curiously for a moment then asked, "And what would ye have done, if I had?"

"I canna say for certain," he replied, shaking his head ruefully. "But I don't know as I would have sent the bastard away, like I did, had I known the whole of it."

"Oh? So, you think I should go to him then?"

"'Tis better, perhaps, than for you to make a martyr of yourself for the sake of those who care little enough for your welfare."

"Is it indeed?" She smiled at that—for hadn't he martyred himself for the sake of his dead wife? Perhaps they had more in common than she'd first thought. "Still, 'tis my choice to make, O'Malley. And I'll not suffer you nor anyone else to make it for me."

"And what is your choice to be then?"

"'Tis the same as it has always been. As soon as I am able to do so in safety I will return to my home to face my doom."

For the space of several heartbeats, his eyes burned into hers then he rolled onto his back again and stared at the ceiling, his expression bleak.

"Now, come, doona look so glum. For sure and it will only make me more depressed if ye do so. Summer is yet months away, after all, and the prophecy doth offer hope I might still find a way to abate my curse."

"I do not understand all this talk of death and ending," he said, after a moment. "For I thought you said the fae could not die."

"'Tis not usual for us," she agreed, propping herself up on her elbow. "Yet it can happen. Here in this dimension, where we possess both body and spirit, it is indeed possible for our bodies to be destroyed and our spirits scattered to the winds, ne'er more to take shape. In most cases, however, were we to be hurt here, we would merely transport ourselves back to the realm, even if we were badly injured. For we are but spirit on the other side and would soon regain our strength there."

"But you said you cannot return to the realm."

"So I did. But, that is just me. I was speaking now in general. Even so, this is not my chief concern. There is another way for us to be ended, however, and that, I admit, I *do* fear, for I count it as is far more likely. 'Tis a perilous thing to break a promise or disregard a *geis*. Even for humans, for I understand it extracts a price on one's soul. For the fae, however, it is deadly. Such an act doth warp our spirit and so separate us from our only source of strength. And, then...well, it would be as if one such as yourself were to stop eating. Your body would starve, would it not? It would waste away for lack of nourishment? It is something very like this that likely awaits me upon my return home."

"The devil you say!" Gavin sat up at that and stared at her horrified. "And what then, lass? What comes after? Have ye not even Heaven to hope for an ye die?"

She shook her head. "Nay, for I have no soul, remember?"

"But...how long do ye have then?"

"To be safe, I should leave the realm no later than *Mabon*. If I am still within its borders come next *Samhain* I shall begin to fade and then...'tis more than likely that by this time next year—or *Imbolg* at the latest—I shall be gone."

"Mother of God," he muttered, his face ashen. "So then all your proud talk of lasting 'til the end of time? Was it just idle boast?"

"Nay." She glared at him angrily. "Tread carefully, human. Is it a liar ye be calling me? 'Tis not a boast for what I said it is as it *should* be. And as it *will* be, an I can help it. Remember, the prophecy did say I might yet find a way to survive the doom that has been laid upon me. And I'll thank ye not to count me dead just yet."

"Oh, aye, your precious prophecy, which even you admit you canna understand. That's what you're putting your faith in, is it? Are ye so certain ye know what you're doing, lass? Wouldn't ye rather go to Annwn, instead?"

"Why, what's this? Six months in the Summerland set

against an eternity spent in the darkness of Annwn—that does not seem to ye to be the better choice? Ah, 'tis only because you haven't seen either place. 'Tis quite beautiful, my home, I assure thee."

"It must be, seeing as you're so willing to give up your very life for the sake of it."

She would have scolded him again for giving up on her too easily but his voice sounded gruff and unsteady and there was a suspicious brightness to his eyes. *Tears?* She stared at him in wonderment, both touched and amused. For surely this was something new in the world—a human feeling pity for one of the *Sidhe*.

"Would you like to see it?" she asked, sitting up in bed with her legs crossed beneath her, wanting suddenly to give something back to him, to make him smile again.

The blankets slid to her waist and Gavin quickly averted his eyes. "Eh? See what?"

"The Summerland. You need only lie back and close your eyes and I will sing ye there."

"Sing me there?" Curious eyes swung back up to her face. "Ye can do that?"

Aislinn shrugged. "Of course. It is just your mind I'd be transporting. Your body would remain here, in peaceful slumber."

"Aye, no doubt," Gavin muttered, his gaze turning suspicious. "But for how long will I slumber? That's the question, is it not?"

"A night," she answered. "No more than that. I promise ye, you'll not travel outside of time tonight. When ye wake up tomorrow morning, safe in your own bed, neither you nor the world will be more than a single day older. Will ye not trust me?"

"Might I not come to harm there? For I've heard stories."

"Not tonight," she said, leaning closer to smile temptingly at him. "If I give you my word, O'Malley, that I'll not allow you to suffer any harm tonight, will that not suffice?"

"And have ye the power to make such promises, I wonder?" he asked as he studied her expression but finally he nodded and closed his eyes. "Go on then, Fae. Do your worst."

Aislinn took a moment to gather her power, humming quietly until the air shimmered and rippled around her and time itself began to shift and there she stopped it, mindful of her promise not to take him outside time tonight. *But someday I might*, she thought, and smiled at the sleeping form before her, *someday, indeed, I might*.

And then, still smiling, she began to sing...

*****

Gavin sighed as Aislinn's voice settled over him as welcome as a soft, warm blanket on a cold night; and he'd have gladly snuggled into it, if his body did not seem too heavy to move. His mind, on the other hand, felt light as air, rising higher and higher until, at last, it broke free of the bonds that had kept it tethered within him. And then, like a caged bird suddenly set free, it took off, winging its way westward over a bleak, black sea toward a flicker of light on the horizon.

The light grew as he approached until he realized it was not a light at all, but rather the reflection cast by the rising sun upon the tall, white cliffs of an island.

Gulls swept past him, crying out a greeting; and then he was soaring above the island itself. Gentle, rolling hills stretched below him as he flew and the low, throbbing tones of *Uilleann* pipes rose up from among them, as though calling him home.

Dipping closer to the ground, he spied horses racing each other for the sheer joy of it across vast, verdant pastures. The sweet, mingled perfumes of a thousand flowers filled the air and a light mist kissed his skin as he landed in a sunny glen.

Deer, browsing amid the trees, paused in their foraging, their tails flicking as they scented him, but they showed no fear. He was aware, too, of a thronging crowd of people that seemed to exist just beyond the edges of his sight and who studied him just as curiously as the deer did. But he paid them no mind for there was a sound that tugged at his consciousness, bidding him follow it.

Aislinn...

He found her, at last, seated atop the bent branch of a willow tree that had extended itself over a clear and sparkling stream, paddling her feet in the crystalline water and singing sweetly.

She broke off as he approached and smiled in greeting. Gavin paused on the sandy bank and stared at her. Though the water appeared cool and refreshing and he was suddenly aware of a great thirst, he was loath to partake.

Laughing, Aislinn jumped down from the branch to stand before him. "'Tis quite all right, you know. The water will do naught tonight but quench your thirst. Although, on another occasion it might, indeed, do more. But did ye not believe me when I promised to protect thee here? What is it that's made ye so suspicious, O'Malley? What have the fae ever done to thee?"

"I doona know," he answered with a shrug, trying not to notice the sweet smell of sunlight on her skin and in her hair. She was dressed in a simple, diaphanous gown of shimmering white without so much as a single ornament, but even with her feet bare and her hair undone she looked more elegant, somehow, than any woman he had ever seen.

No wonder her fool of a sister was so worried, he thought, *for sure and she has the look of one who should be queen.*

"But how is it you're here?" he asked. "For I thought you were banned from the place."

"Aye," she answered, casting a sad glance at the landscape that surrounded them. "From the Summerland itself, I am still in exile. But no one can remove me from my memories of it. This is but a shadow of the place. I could have sent ye there alone, had I wished to. But without accompanying ye, I could not have guaranteed your safety. Nor could I have transported ye into the past without breaking my promise not to take ye out of time. But I thought this would do to show ye what it's like and why I'm so loath to give it up. Do you not find it beautiful?"

He nodded. "I do. But what of the other place? Will you be showing me that as well, that I might compare the two?"

"Nay," she replied with a shake of her head. "Perhaps another time. I'd not wish to trouble your sleep with such a thing. You'd not thank me for it if I did. Now, come," she said, smiling once more as she took hold of his arm. "Let me show you something of my home."

Instantly, a path appeared on the ground before their feet leading to a sumptuous pavilion that Gavin was certain had not even existed a moment previously. Bright silk brocade gleamed in the morning light and a banner flew above it.

Gavin squinted his eyes to try and make out the device traced upon the fluttering fabric until Aislinn tugged him forward. "'Tis of no import," she insisted softly as she held aside the flaps that covered the doorway and bade him enter. "Pray do not worry yourself about it further."

Inside, moss-covered stones were soft against his feet. A scattering of couches piled high with pillows furnished the large, round room and at its center stood a table set with a feast.

Silver bowls of fruit and dishes of butter, clotted cream and honey, still in the comb, stood side by side with wheels of cheese and jugs of ale, cakes and pies and fragrant brown loaves of bread—all manner of delicacies. Above a grated candle, keeping warm, was a pot Gavin was sure contained tea. He felt his mouth water as he gazed hungrily and worriedly at the tempting array. Then Aislinn laughed and, with a snap of her fingers, caused the entire table to disappear.

"Nay," she said as she turned to him. "I was not

forgetting your fears concerning our food and I'll tempt ye no further with such a display. But I thought it no harm to show ye that I can indeed provide a meal fit for any occasion, as long as it's here in my own country."

"I didn't doubt it," Gavin replied with more politeness than truth.

Aislinn merely smiled. Then her smile turned sly. "So, then, since we'll not be eating together, will ye not lie with me, O'Malley?" Her expression was like that of an angel, innocent, pure, without guile, as she cocked her head to the side and gestured toward one of the waiting couches.

Gavin inhaled sharply. Though he knew that to do such a thing here, with her, would be even more perilous for him than eating or drinking, a part of him wanted to answer, immediately and forever, *yes!* Instead, he posed his own question. "Will ye not transform yourself into Mairead for me, Fae?"

She shook her head. "Nay. That I'll not. In this, of all places, I'll be no surrogate, but only myself alone."

"Then neither will I lie with thee here," he replied, pleased with the cool, firm sound of his words though he didn't doubt she could read his mind just the same and sense the disappointment raging within him, for he wished it could be otherwise. And when she gazed into his eyes and he felt her urging him to reconsider, he was tempted to give in. But, with an effort, he closed his heart to the sweet compulsion and, abruptly, felt it cease.

"Ah, well," Aislinn murmured, taking hold of his arm once more and leading him back to the doorway. "If that's to be the way of it, I think perhaps 'tis best for you to leave now."

They pushed through the soft fabric only to find that a soft, silver rain had begun to fall, obscuring the landscape from his sight. Gavin felt a pang of loss and a cry of dismay broke from his lips. "'Tis all gone."

"Do not sorrow yourself so," Aislinn whispered in his ear. "For 'tis like the stars in the sky above. Though 'tis only at night you see them. They are always there and, day or night, they shine just as brightly. This place is a part of you now, Gavin; a place to which you might return, in your dreams, if you so wish it; a place you will remember always and, I hope, with fondness. But, sleep now," she murmured and Gavin felt his eyes fall shut and his spirit start to sink, but soft and slow like a feather drifting to earth. And he heard the amusement in her voice as she added, "And may your angels gather round thee, Gavin O'Malley, and protect thee from all temptations."

Temptations? "No use in bothering the angels over something like that," he replied as sleep crept up to claim him. "For there's hardly enough of those to be after worrying over." In fact, he thought, there was really only one.

Aislinn...

Chapter Seven

And so the weeks began to pass. December gave way to January and winter continued, even more cold and cruel than usual, as though the season itself was vexed and venting its angry frustrations upon the hapless world. Yet, to Gavin, it seemed both warmer and brighter than any January he'd ever known.

And then it was February. He continued to work long hours at his forge, just as he always had, almost every day except Sunday and sometimes Aislinn accompanied him. From her perch on the old wooden bench just inside the door, she would watch with an almost morbid fascination as he worked the hot metal. After her first visit there, however, she insisted on bringing a cushion with her for she swore she could feel the bite of the bench's iron nails right through her clothing.

"Well, you're a right delicate creature, now aren't you?" Gavin teased, watching as she once again fidgeted around in her seat, clearly unable to get comfortable, even with the pillow. She reminded him of nothing so much as the old fairy tale about the princess and the pea. "'Tis a wonder, it is, that Tiernan did not pick someone more hardy for his scheme. I canna understand it at all."

"What is it that's so confusing to you, O'Malley?" she asked crossly. "Have I not already explained it all?"

"Aye, you have," he replied with a nod. "You said he's after looking for to improve the quality of his stock, did you not? To strengthen his bloodline, as it were? Which is why I'd have been expecting him to be after the sturdiest brood mare he could find."

"*Gabhaim pardún agat*?" Aislinn's head reared back. "Sure and you did not just refer to me as...a brood mare?"

Gavin shrugged unconcernedly as he leaned on his hammer, enjoying the rage that burned like silver fire in her eyes. "Well, only in a manner of speaking, of course, but..."

"You dare?" The words fell from her mouth like ice daggers, chill and fell and Gavin was certain the look on her face would have caused a lesser man to shake in his boots.

"Now, now," he soothed, hiding his amusement behind an impassive expression. "Just because you're angry at the scoundrel, don't you be taking it out on me. 'Tis not I who's looking to do ye harm after all."

She continued to stare at him through narrowed eyes, radiating cold fury and injured dignity. After a moment, a bitter smile curved her lips. "And yet, as I recall, you did claim to think it a good match," she observed with icy courtesy. "Was it not your suggestion that I should reconsider and go to him?"

At that, Gavin allowed his smile to peek out. "Oh, aye, but that was weeks ago, lass, and you and I were not then so well acquainted as we are now. I've long since changed my mind on the subject. You're much too good for the likes of him."

"How very gratifying to hear you say so," she replied dryly. "*Go raimh maith agat.* I thank you most kindly, sir."

"*Tá failte romhat.*" Gavin flashed her a wink and went back to his work. "Think nothing of it. But, tell me this, have ye made much progress figuring out the druid's prophecy?" She was silent so long he stopped working and glanced over his shoulder at her. "Well? Have ye?"

"I hardly know what answer to make," she answered at last, her voice pensive and low. "With some parts...I think, perhaps, I have. But, with others I'm not so sure. 'Tis hard to determine what she might have meant by...well, by most of it, actually."

"Aye, 'tis a right puzzle, it is," he agreed turning away again. "But don't you be after worrying yourself sick over it now. For sure and it'll come clear eventually and you know you're safe enough here until then."

Most days, however, Aislinn did not venture outside the cottage, preferring to remain inside, close to the hearth. And, on days when she was not too annoyed with Gavin, she sometimes deigned to occupy her time tending to any small tasks that did not require the use of iron tools—the darning of socks, for instance, or the mending of shirts.

If truth be told, Gavin was just as happy to have the forge to himself. There was never any lack of work for him to do there, but it was only when Aislinn was absent that he felt himself free to work on the project he'd begun shortly after Christmas.

And, as he worked—slowly pumping the bellows, waiting for the tiny open-ended rings he'd placed in the fire to turn the proper shade of cherry-red—he pondered the situation he found himself in.

Though he'd be loath to admit it to anyone else, in his heart of hearts he no longer tried to deny that he'd grown fond of the Fae and enjoyed spending time in her company. The long winter hours passed so much more quickly with Aislinn there to tease or to talk to and when he walked back across his yard at the end of the day, he liked knowing there was someone at home with whom he could share his meals and his hearth. He liked listening to her voice while she sang for him or regaled him with stories of the faery realm. He liked waking up with her beside him in the morning and, of course, he liked having her there to lie with him at night. But the thought that it must all-too-soon come to an end—and a bad end, at that—both galled and grieved him.

He'd miss her when she was gone. He feared it would feel as though sunlight and summer had been removed from his world. It was not a loss he'd willingly accept.

Surely, it had to be a sin, even for someone without a soul, to throw her life away as Aislinn would surely be doing if she returned to the realm. And selling herself into marriage with the ice-hearted bastard who'd put her life at hazard in the first place would be little better. Since neither of those choices suited, why should there not be a third for her to consider?

Why, for example, should she not stay on here with him and continue to take the place of his wife—indefinitely?

After removing his iron from the fire, he placed the rings on his anvil and joined them together with quick taps of his hammer. Then he repeated the process with more rings, his thoughts returning to Aislinn as he once again worked the bellows.

Though he'd yet to mention his idea to her, he could think of no earthly reason why she should not accept his proposition. He hadn't deluded himself about her motives; he knew it wasn't anything more than luck, circumstance and the mad ranting of a lunatic druid that had brought her to him in the first place or kept her here now. But, on the other hand, she didn't seem noticeably unhappy with how things had turned out. Sure and he knew his cottage wasn't a palace, by any means, but nor was it a dungeon, and he flattered himself that she at least seemed to prefer his company over Tiernan's. Although, he supposed, that wasn't really saying very much since, apparently, she'd also prefer to go to her death than to live on as Tiernan's bride.

Death. Just thinking about that—about her bright spirit being extinguished, about losing another woman he'd come to care for to the grim reaper—caused a pain and a tightness in his chest that made breathing difficult. Not that he'd completely deluded himself about his own motives either. He was well aware there were several reasons why it hurt to think of Aislinn being gone and most of them were purely selfish.

If truth be told, he hadn't found it all that difficult to shun the company of women after Mairead's death. His brief taste of marriage had been neither pleasant nor sweet nor anything like he'd thought it would be. Nor was it anything he had been eager to experience any more of; which he didn't doubt was a big part of the reason he'd given in so readily to Mairead's last request.

In the years since, he'd felt little regret for the choices he'd made that day; until Aislinn came along and opened his eyes. She'd shown him how different things could be. Or, rather, she'd shown him how different they *could have been*, were it not for the promises he'd made.

And now he couldn't stop himself from thinking about it.

The plain fact of the matter was this: Aislinn represented his one hope of achieving happiness in this lifetime without risking Heaven over a broken vow. Only she could give him back what he'd so foolishly promised away; what he'd wanted, needed and longed for all his life: A wife who would happily share his bed. A home filled with laughter and song. And children.

Children who he could know for a certainty he would not be having to put into the ground before him.

If Aislinn left here, come summer, to go to her doom, it wasn't just her own life and future she'd be throwing away but his, as well. And he could think of no earthly reason why he should sit back and allow such a thing to occur. Not when he had it within his power to stop it.

It was selfish, perhaps, and he doubted she'd thank him for interfering in her affairs—at least not at first. But he wasn't looking for thanks, and as for it being selfish or unfair, he didn't give a damn.

He paused the bellows again and used his tongs to remove the new links from the fire. When they'd been joined to the ones he'd made before, he plunged the whole length of them into a bucket of water to cool the metal down. Then he took them up and examined the welds, grunting in satisfaction at a job well done. It was not the strongest or heaviest of chains, but then again, he hadn't intended it to be.

He was counting on the substance from which it was made to compensate for whatever it lacked in strength. He was counting on the iron to do the trick.

*****

As the shadows lengthened in the yard outside, stretching like a cold, dark hand toward the cottage door, Aislinn huddled closer to the hearth, suppressing a shiver. It was the time of day she disliked the most, not quite yet night but still close enough; and too soon to hope for Gavin's return.

She knew it was illogical to long for him the way she did. If Tiernan came back and tried again to claim her, there was little the smith could do to deter him; it was the metal that shielded her from her enemy, not the man. But all the same, Gavin had proved to be unexpectedly resourceful in rebuffing Tiernan and she just felt safer, somehow, in his presence.

So, entirely too often she found herself watching the clock; wishing she could hurry it along; anxious for the moment when he'd come through the door. Even though she knew full well that, within minutes of his arrival, she'd likely find herself growing annoyed with him, over one thing or another, and wondering why she'd been so impatient for him to get there.

His manners left much to be desired and his teasing frequently struck her as being in poor taste. Still, she had to admit there was something surprisingly engaging about the man. She found him amusing, entertaining, arousing, even endearing...albeit in a primitive sort of way. And he was certainly easy on the eyes, especially of late; for his smiles seemed less of a rarity now than they'd been when first she met him.

For her own peace of mind she wished she could dismiss the sense of security she felt when he was around as being due to nothing more than the fact that having him there—to talk to, to argue with—kept her mind from fretting over her plight. But she knew the reality wasn't so simple.

Mere distraction could not account for the way she felt on those occasions when she found herself lying awake in the black belly of the night with the Winter wind howling and prowling around the house like a pack of ravenous beasts. Even with Gavin sound asleep beside her, she still found comfort in his stolid form; in the arm or the leg he'd, more often than not, have thrown over her as he slept. And it mattered not, at those times, that—but for the iron that warded the house—Tiernan could easily force himself inside, freezing Gavin where he lay, killing him before he had a chance to stir and snatching her from his unresisting arms. Snug in the smith's warm embrace, Aislinn knew she was safe and she would slip back to sleep unconcerned.

She was grateful to Gavin for that measure of peace. But gratitude was not an emotion in which she could afford to indulge.

If the oracle was to be believed, it would take a human soul, willingly offered, to defeat Aislinn's enemy, restore her freedom and, perhaps, safeguard her life. Though Aislinn was not yet clear on how this was to be accomplished, she had no doubts left as to *whose* soul the prophecy must refer. As Gavin himself had observed, he was not the only blacksmith in the land and yet she had been sent here—to *this* forge, to *this* man. And, locked safely away within his cottage, as she was, she'd had very little opportunity to come into contact with anyone else.

So it must be his soul, then, that was doomed to bear the cost of her salvation.

The thought saddened her, for it did seem as though Gavin was being most cruelly used by Fate. But, on the other hand, could not the same be said about she herself? Despite the affection she felt toward the man, she could not let her heart rule her head; she could not let concern for Gavin's welfare interfere with her goals.

It was not just herself she was saving, after all. She was also saving her people, their future, the world itself. When weighed on such a scale as that, the wants and the wishes of one man, or one fae, counted for very little.

*****

"You've grown very quiet these past weeks," Gavin remarked later that night as they lay in bed. "Is there aught troubling ye, lass?"

Aislinn gazed at him wearily. With so much afflicting her, where did she begin? She was still clothed in the guise of his dead wife, for one thing—a condition of her residency she'd begun to find most irksome—for although the transformation took very little magic to maintain, the seemingly endless winter had sapped her strength. Practically any expenditure of energy felt like too much effort.

Then there was the winter itself—the first she'd ever truly experienced, by virtue of the fact that it was the first she'd ever spent outside the realm. As such, she found that the season weighed very heavy on her spirit; as did the knowledge that it was also likely to be her last.

She sighed. "In truth, I did not think you required much from me in the way of conversation as long as I saw to it that your *other* needs were met." And, casting her gaze down the length of his body, she eyed his groin, just in case he'd failed to take her meaning.

A frown creased Gavin's brow and though the room was unlit she could see well enough in the dark that the blush that stained his cheeks was visible to her. "Oh, and was it only *my* needs with which you were concerned then? And here I was, foolishly thinking you were enjoying yourself as well. Was I wrong about that?"

Aislinn shrugged. "I've made no complaints, have I? But, there's still much you do not know about pleasing a woman, and as you seemed little inclined to change, I see no benefit to be gained from discussing the matter."

He fell silent at that and Aislinn closed her eyes, hoping that might be the end of it. Why had he chosen now to turn so talkative? Now, when the wind was rattling the window frames again and her nerves felt frayed because of it. She wished he would just hold her close and let her go to sleep. Or that he'd fall asleep himself, and let his snoring drown out the wind. Or, better still, that he'd let her weave an enchantment 'round the cottage; and put them both out of time until winter was over and spring was once again on the verge.

"Do not be so hard on me, lass," Gavin murmured, his voice low and rueful. "For you know I've not had your experience in such matters. And if you will not tell me what it is that's lacking, or what else you might be wishing for, well then how am I to know it?"

She opened her eyes again and studied his pained expression, his troubled eyes. "What's that you're saying? 'Tis my fault too, I suppose?"

"Come now, you do not really think me that selfish of a man, do ye?" he asked quietly as he stroked his hand down her arm. "Sure and you must know by now that I would happily give ye all the pleasure you could ask for, an I knew how to do so. Will ye not show me what it is you're wanting, or how I might do better by you?"

"I would, but...to do such a thing as you're asking...that might take some time." As she spoke, Aislinn kept her eyes downcast, for an idea had occurred to her and she did not want him to read her intentions in her gaze. "For 'tis more to be learned than can be accomplished in a single night, you know."

"Yerra. As bad as that, am I then?" he joked with an uneasy laugh. "Here and I'd hoped I hadn't been serving you quite so poorly all this time."

Aislinn rolled her eyes. "Whist now, you ridiculous man," she said, shoving at his shoulders until he rolled obligingly onto his back. Straddling his hips, she sat astride him. "I'll have no more of your nonsense. And, I'll thank ye very much not to be putting words into my mouth, O'Malley, for well you're knowing that I meant no such thing. 'Tis experience you're lacking, for the most part, as you yourself have observed. And that cannot be rushed. However, if you're as willing as you say you are, and will not begrudge me whatever time it takes to teach ye, then I'd be more than pleased to aid you in rectifying the situation. Are you willing then?"

"I am, aye." Gavin's hands closed on her hips. "More than willing."

"Ah, and aren't you the darling one to be so amenable?" As Aislinn bent to kiss him, she silently gathered her power around her. "Well, then, Gavin O'Malley, since you've consented to put yourself into my hands, I'll promise you this: I will make you into such a lover that no mortal woman shall e'er again be able to resist ye."

"And what about you, Fae?" he asked her. "Might I not become such as you'd not be able to resist as well?"

"You aim high, human," she replied teasingly as she sat up again and smiled at him, holding his gaze with hers while the room grew incrementally warmer and brighter and time bent to her will and slowed to a halt around them. "But, if that be truly your goal, who knows what you might not achieve? Though, much will depend on how diligently you apply yourself to your lessons and on how apt a pupil you prove yourself to be."

"I will do my best not to disappoint," he promised and she rewarded him with another kiss.

"As shall I, *mo chroí*. As shall I."

*****

It wasn't that Gavin didn't notice the changes taking place in the atmosphere around him. He noticed them, all right. But, just as it had the first night, the *ceol sidhe* quickly caught him in its snare and as the unearthly, inaudible music flowed through him, it demolished his resistance, silencing whatever protests he might have made and sweeping his reluctance away on a wave of ecstasy. What cared he, what sort of spell she was casting? All he could think of, all he could focus on, all he cared about was *Her*.

Her. Not as Aislinn, nor Mairead, nor any one person, but, rather, as *All-Women-in-One*, for so she seemed to him; and altogether more beautiful, more magical, more awe-inspiring, than anything he'd ever dreamed. Suddenly, pleasing this divine, this exquisite, this wondrous creature seemed his entire reason for being.

"Only tell me," he begged her. "What is it you want from me? I'll do anything you ask."

"Will you worship me with your body?" she asked, smiling down at him. "Will you lavish me with your kisses and show me, with your every word and deed, how completely you crave and desire me; how desperately you long to possess me?"

"Gladly," he answered as he toppled her down and rolled her beneath him, intent on making her his own.

"Wait," she said, holding him off when he would have plunged inside her. "Before all else you must first inflame me to that very same level of passion I have just described until I, too, am desperate with yearning, aching for completion, longing for you—only you. And only then may you seek your own satisfaction."

Gavin shook his head. "'Tis not possible. You could ne'er be made to feel as I do—nor would you want to. I must have you or die. Can any woman say the same?"

Aislinn's eyes gleamed cat-like in the dark. "Why ever not? Do you really think we are so different, you and I?"

He shrugged. "It would seem so."

"Show me anyway," she insisted. "For 'tis how I want to feel."

"I tell you, 'tis impossible."

"Try."

Groaning, Gavin lowered his mouth to hers. But where he wanted to ravish, to devour, to lay claim to her, he held back. Instead, he kissed her tenderly, tentatively, almost reluctantly. For he knew, better than she perhaps, how passion was likely to burn hotter where needs went unmet.

And, if it was that she wanted to feel, then so be it.

When he felt her start to respond, he broke away from her mouth; ignoring her softly moaned protest; feathering kisses along her jawbone; nipping at her earlobe. And all the while he whispered, in words both frank and sweet, of everything he wished to do to her, all the ways he wanted her; recounting to her every form of pleasure he could imagine the both of them enjoying.

She gasped softly, as though surprised by the litany that welled from his mouth. He was surprised by it as well and wondered if it was not some spell of hers that had drawn the words forth. For most were things he'd never before spoken of aloud, and some were things he hadn't even known were in his mind, until he heard himself give voice to them. But, once they were said, he knew them to be true and the knowledge caused such an anguish within him he nearly cried out in his grief.

God have mercy on my soul. What has the Fae done to me?

Before they'd met, his needs had been simple, his regrets few. Now, he might never know such peace again. For, without her, he'd have little to no chance of ever experiencing even half of what he now knew he wanted; he'd be alone, always alone. And his life, from here on out, would be naught but an endless longing for all that he would never know, all that he would never have, all that would never be again.

Aislinn...

Anguish gave way to anger, causing him to be more rough with her than he'd originally intended as he slid slowly down along her body, leaving kisses and tiny bites in his wake; barely resisting the urge to leave his mark upon her flesh as painfully and permanently as possible.

"*Aiii*," she cried softly when, after he'd pried her legs apart, he'd paused to sink his teeth into her inner thigh. Propping herself up on her elbows, she glared at him. "Here now, what's all this about? Did I tell you to be so rough?"

He gazed at her challengingly. "You did say, did you not, that you were wishing to ache as I do; to know the pain of longing I feel for you?" He glanced back at her thigh, at the redness he'd left there and, feeling a slight pang of remorse, took a moment to lave the soreness with his tongue. "In truth, I think I've been too soft on you. For it's sure and I've not yet caused you anything like the kind of hurt you've asked to feel."

Her eyes were dark, unfathomable, as she stared at him; and her voice held a note of caution as she asked, "Is that so?"

"Aye, Fae, it is." He spread her legs wider, inhaling the sweet aroma that wafted from her sex, feasting his eyes on the plump, pink folds. His cock throbbed demandingly, but he ignored it.

"All the same, I'll bid you remember, sir, 'twas not *I* who grieved you so."

At that, he glanced up again. "Oh, no? Are you sure about that, lass?"

"Why? What is it you're saying now, that you're not?" she replied looking startled. "Is it by virtue of my present appearance then, that you're so confused? Have you, perhaps, forgotten who I am?"

"Nay, I could ne'er forget you, Fae, nor all the pain you've caused me since e'er we met."

"Pain, is it?" she gazed at him affronted. "Are you sure 'tis not pleasure you're meaning? Am I to get no thanks for that then?"

"Aye, I've had pleasure from you as well. And I have thanked ye for it, have I not, many times over? But 'tis both the pain and the pleasure I'm thinking of tonight for it does often seem the one does not come without t'other. Now, enough of this talk." And, dropping his gaze once more, he flicked a finger at the button of flesh at the top of her sex. "Tell me then, is it this bit here that you're wanting me to stroke?"

"Gavin, cease!" The words emerged from her lips in a breathy gasp as she tried to close her legs against him, succeeding only in clenching them more snugly around his shoulders. The action sent a thrill of desire arrowing through him and it was all he could do to keep from groaning aloud.

Instead, he grinned at her. "How now, lass? Is aught amiss with ye? Sure and I could never have missed my mark? Or is it someplace else you're wanting attention?" Worry and want warred in her eyes and when her tongue peeked out to wet her lips he felt his cock grow even harder.

"Is this how you think to please me?" she asked at last. "'Tis not the sort of treatment I was expecting from ye tonight."

"Is it not?" For an instant, Gavin gave serious thought

to treating her to even worse—anything to distract her, to keep her from guessing his true feelings, or to keep himself from spontaneously confessing to his need for her—but, in the end, he relented. He had no real wish to cause her pain and, after all, such behavior would hardly help his cause or persuade her to join her life with his. "Well, then, mayhap this will better suit you," he suggested as he pushed her legs apart and bent his mouth to her.

Using the soft rasp of his tongue on her body's most secretive spot, he smiled to himself in satisfaction when her legs fell open wider, all on their own, granting him even greater access. He licked harder, sucking greedily at her flesh when he felt her nether lips begin to swell. Then her legs started to quiver, her hips to buck and strain, as though she were wordlessly begging for his attentions. Finally, her climax took her and she cried out as her sex released its fragrant dew.

Gavin lapped blissfully at the silky fluid, convinced he could never get enough; a surfeit would not satisfy him. He was sure he could drown in the taste of her and still not be satcd.

When at last she sighed in release, her body limp and still, he glanced up at her. The flushed contentment on her face was a stark contrast to the hunger raging inside him, worse now than even before. "Now, *a muirnín,*" he pleaded, his voice shaking as he struggled to maintain control; barely noticing the endearment that slipped from his lips, though it was not a term he could recall ever having used before, not even with Mairead. "I must have you now."

If Aislinn noticed his slip, she also gave no sign, just nodded and smiled in invitation. "So, come and take me then." He didn't wait to be asked twice, but surged upward, ready to plunge inside her, 'til her next words stopped him. "Your actions have earned you a bit of a reward, I'd say."

A bit? "I'll not be satisfied with mere trifles from you," he warned, his cock poised at her entry. "Or with having you only once or twice." He wanted a lifetime with her and he meant to get it, one way or another, whether fairly or not.

Her eyes widened. "Nor I you. I assure you, this 'twill not be the last time—not by a long shot."

Gavin nodded. Content for now with her assurances, he thrust into her, sheathing himself to the hilt. She cried out once again and he froze. Memories rising from out of his past turned his muscles to stone. Guilt churned like acid in his gut. He glanced at her face, afraid he'd hurt her.

But heat blazed in her cheeks and in her eyes and she slapped his arm lightly. "Oh, pray, do not stop, you silly man," she said, replying impatiently to his unasked question. "Can you not see that I'm fine? Get on with it, do. Sure and you must know by now, 'tis how I like it?"

Gavin needed no further encouragement. He brushed a quick kiss across her lips, withdrew and then thrust again, plunging deep into her hot, slick body, settling quickly into a fast paced rhythm. He felt the tension build as her muscles clamped down around his cock, squeezing him with exquisite pressure.

Her eyes had narrowed down to tiny slits and her lips were parted. Gavin watched her, mesmerized by the sight of her passion, by her wanton willingness to both give and receive pleasure, her clear enjoyment of the act of love. Her easy acceptance of him as a lover, as a man; her faith in his ability to drive her to states of ecstasy—the knowledge that she wanted him to do so, that she welcomed his attempts to please her—ignited something that had long been dormant within him. Something that had been nearly extinguished during his marriage. Pride. Self confidence. Self respect. Call it what you will, it was something he'd never thought to feel again and he reveled in its return. And, as for the woman responsible, the woman who'd given him back to himself, he'd do anything for her. Anything but let her go.

As she dug her nails into his arms and arched against him Gavin groaned in pleasure. The growing tightness in his balls signaled that his climax was not far off. *Aye, now. I need this.*

But his anticipation was cut short by a mournful protest from the woman beneath him, "Oh, nay, do not stop!"

He glanced at her, startled by her request, surprised to be able to recognize the signs that she was once again approaching climax, herself. But not as quickly as he was. With her recent criticism of him still fresh in his mind, *"There's much you do not know about pleasing a woman, and you seem little inclined to change,"* he forced himself to stop. The action drew another groan from him, and an answering one from Aislinn, as well. But he gritted his teeth and remained still. This was his chance to prove her wrong, after all, and he *would* see to her pleasure before his own—if it killed him. But how? "What can I do to hurry things along for ye?" he begged, chest heaving. "Tell me! For I canna last much longer."

She stared at him for an instant, as though gauging his sincerity or his intent. Then, "The angle. If ye lift my hips it might change it."

It took a moment for her meaning to register. When it did, he rose to his knees between her legs and slid his hands beneath her bottom, tilting her pelvis upwards and then thrusting into her again. The breath hissed between his teeth as he felt they way her body gripped him; tight as a fist yet softer than a velvet glove. "Saints," he muttered in wonderment for as good as he'd always thought it before, it felt even better now.

"Aye, like that," Aislinn groaned as he hooked her legs over his shoulders. Her eyes closed in bliss. "Doona stop."

Unable to form even a single word of assurance, Gavin nodded. He kept his own eyes open as he rocked slowly in and out of her, needing the external focus to distract himself from the heat that pulsed in his veins as he pushed her steadily closer and closer and closer to the brink. Moisture sheened her skin. His own body dripped with sweat. The slow pace was torture, but any faster and he wouldn't last another second.

As it was, it was close. Her body arched suddenly, she cried out and, as fast as that, he was following her over the edge. Wave after wave of his seed poured from him as his body shuddered and his mind reeled and, for an instant, he forgot how to breathe.

When the storm finally passed, he gazed at her wearily. She smiled back at him, seemingly delighted. And when she opened her arms to him, he collapsed gratefully into them, sighing in contentment as she held him close, stroking his hair and murmuring endearments. "Ah, Gavin. *A thaisce. A chuisle mo chroí.*"

Her words registered slowly through his exhausted haze. *A thaisce?* He raised his head to look at her. "A treasure, is it? And is that what I am to ye now?"

Her hands played lightly over his back as she returned his gaze and a small smile glimmered on her lips. "Aye. 'Tis what I said. What of it?"

"You surprise me, Fae," he replied hiding both his pleasure and his embarrassment behind a joke. "For I'd not thought *treasure* would be a word that one such as yourself would use lightly. Are not the fae all supposed to be greedy, grasping, mercenary creatures always jealously hoarding their gold?"

"Ah, what nonsense is this?" Aislinn scoffed, pouting a little as she stretched sensuously beneath him. Gavin drew in a quick breath. The feel of her body, arching against his, was almost enough to start him shuddering again. "For shame, O'Malley, to be spreading such lies. And me having just shared myself most generously with ye too."

"Aye. I think, perhaps, you were a little too generous, my girl." Gavin grimaced. "For I'm feeling quite worn out from all the generosity you've shown me tonight." But, in the very moment he said it, Gavin was surprised to realize that it was no longer true. His energy, which had been flagging no more than an instant earlier, seemed fully restored, as was the lust he'd so recently sated.

"Are you, indeed?" Aislinn's eyes gleamed with mischief as she ground her pelvis against his rapidly stiffening cock. "For sure, 'tis not how it feels to me. But, I use no words lightly, mortal, and if I call you my treasure, you may be certain 'tis how I regard you." Her face turned serious as she laid her fingers against his cheek. "The truth is you've surprised me tonight, Gavin. It seems I may have once again done you a disservice—this time by thinking you inattentive rather than inexperienced. My apologies, sir."

Gavin bent his head and nipped at her shoulder, and then proceeded to lay a trail of kisses up her neck to her ear. "Nay, lass, do not apologize. At least not with words." In truth, he had no problems with her continuing to feel as though she was in his debt, for such a thing could well work to his advantage. But there was only one way he wanted her to make it up to him tonight.

"Again," she murmured, so softly Gavin could not determine whether she was expressing her own desires, or inquiring after his.

Not that it mattered. For the answer to each would still be the same: "Aye. Always. Again and again."

Chapter Eight

And so it continued, again and again and again, until Gavin had quite lost count of the number of times he'd had her. The night seemed endless, the darkness within his room, unvarying. Occasionally, he'd doze, falling exhausted into brief, fitful bursts of sleep, only to wake again, instantly, eagerly, whenever Aislinn summoned him.

Towards morning, or close to what he thought must surely be morning, though time seemed hardly to have passed at all, Gavin became aware of a strange, hammering sound. Distant and faint, it clamored at the very edge of his consciousness.

"Is that the wind I'm hearing?" he asked as he paused to listen. But rather than answering, Aislinn took his face between her hands and covered his mouth with her own, kissing him 'til lust flamed again in his heart and he was lost, once more, in the wonder of her. He kissed her back, ravishing her mouth, tangling his hands in her hair, pressing her back into the bedding...

Until the noise intruded again.

He lifted his head. "Whist. What *is* that sound?"

"'Tis nothing for you to be worrying yourself over, *mo chroí*. Pay it no mind."

But, this time, when she tried to pull him in, he held her off, straining his ears to hear; frowning at the effort it took, for it seemed his mind was oddly befogged. His eyes widened when the fog cleared a little and the noise, at last, resolved itself into something recognizable—into the sound of a fist being diligently applied to his own front door.

Sitting up, he pushed aside the covers. "Who the devil could it be coming 'round at this time of night?"

"Please," Aislinn begged with fear in her eyes. "Don't go."

One look at her had Gavin's temper rising. "Is it that bastard Tiernan, then? Is that why you're wanting me to stay here, cowering beneath the covers? Well, be easy, lass. For if either of you are thinking he can just come to my front door and I'll hand you over to him, you've got a lot to learn. That may be the way the fae go about dealing with such threats, but the O'Malleys are quite a different breed and we handle such matters very differently, as well."

Aislinn clutched at his arm. "'Tis nothing of the kind. It doesn't matter to me who it is, Gavin. Only, please, come back to bed now, do. No one can harm us here."

Gavin shook her off and reached for his clothes. "'Twill be no one harming ye here in any event, lass. Have I not given you my word on that? So long as you're under my roof, you've naught to fear. But, all the same, I'll not stand for either of us being harassed."

As he got to his feet the room seemed to spin. He had to grab hold of the bedpost to keep from falling over.

"Gavin, no. You doona know what it is you're doing. No good will come of it. Stay here with me, I pray you."

"'Tis all right, lass," he muttered, taking deep breaths until the dizziness receded. "I only just got up too fast, that's all. You stay right where you are now, and keep the bed warm for me. I'll be back directly—as soon as I've gotten rid of the beggar."

Gavin swerved and stumbled his way across the room, slowly, because the air seemed as dense as water. As he opened his bedroom door he knew another moment of disorientation; when it passed he was surprised to realize that the darkness was nowhere near as complete as it had seemed only an instant earlier. Was it morning already, he wondered. For, if so, perhaps it wasn't Tiernan at his door after all. Just to be on the safe side, however, he made a small detour to his hearth to pick up the iron poker he kept there.

By the time he reached his front door, the room had filled with daylight. He flung open the door to find Auld John standing on his doorsill. "Well, 'tis about time." The old man looked him up and down. "Glad I am to see you're not dead, but whatever were you doing, that it took you so long to answer the door?"

"John?" Gavin squinted at him, nearly blinded by sunlight. "Is that you?" And then, remembering the fae's shape-shifting abilities, he jabbed the old man in the side with the poker. "If it is, then what are you doing here, eh?"

"Here now, what's all this?" Auld John scowled as he took a step back, out of range of the poker. "Yerra, 'tis a fine, neighborly way for you to be acting. Of course it's me, you bloody imbecile! What's gotten into ye, man? Is it the drink then?"

Gavin shook his head. "'Tis nothing. I'm just not altogether myself at the moment. You caught me sleeping and I'm not quite awake yet."

"Well, I can see that for myself," John replied, frowning suspiciously. "For sure and you look like hell itself, you do. And why you should be lying abed this late in the day—and on such a fine one as it is, too—is a right mystery, I'd say."

"Oh, is that so? Well, thank ye, John. And what is it brings you out here, old man—other than to be commenting unfavorably on my health and appearance, and giving me a weather report into the bargain?" And, then, still not convinced as to his identity, Gavin poked him again.

"Jesus, man," John protested, finally grabbing hold of the metal with his bare hand and pushing it aside. "Put the fekkin' tool down now, would ya? Or have you lost your senses entirely? Do we need to fetch the priest out here for to perform an exorcism on you? For here you are trying to ventilate an old man and me just doing my duty as a Christian coming out to see how you are."

"And why would I not be all right then?" Gavin countered. "What cause have you to be worrying over me, all of a sudden, like you were my ma?"

John looked at him in surprise. "Sudden, is it? When there's not a soul as laid eyes on ye in nigh on six weeks and you failing to show up for Mass yesterday? Naturally, after that, I got to thinking something was amiss. And, despite your protests to the contrary, I can see now I was right. For sure as I'm standing here there's something that's ailing ye."

"Weeks!" Gavin rolled his eyes. "Well, you're daft, that's all. Who is it told you it had been that long? For sure and they must all be touched as well. Why, 'tis not even six *days* since I was last in town and there was plenty as seen me. And, as for my not being at Mass yesterday, why the devil would I have—" A bird flew across the yard, calling Gavin's attention to the inexplicable, bright beauty of the day. "What the bloody hell is going on?" he demanded as he blinked and scrubbed his hand across his eyes. His blood running cold, he scanned the world outside his front door, expecting snow and meeting only sunlight. "Holy Mother of God. What mischief is this then?" Gone was the cold gray landscape of Winter. The apple tree that grew against his garden wall had put forth an avalanche of blossoms, seemingly overnight; the surrounding hills were robed in green once more and the sweet scent of Spring was everywhere in the soft, warm air. "What day is it, John?"

"Why 'tis Monday, of course," the old man replied and then quickly added. "April the third, if that's what you're asking. 'Tis the day *after* Easter, don't you know."

"Oh, bloody hell. *Tá sé Earrach.* 'Tis Spring then," he said, in the same tones as anyone else might have said, *'Tis death.*

"Aye. 'Tis indeed. And about time, too, after such a turrible Winter as we've had. But, why the surprise, boy? Have ye been ill, then?"

"Nay." Shaking his head, Gavin gently pushed the old man off his doorstep. "'Tis nothing of the sort. But ask me no more questions now, for I'll say no more about it. I'd invite ye in, John, if I could, but I can't. So I'll say good day to you here and wish you good health." And so saying, he closed the door in the old man's face and bolted it shut with hands that shook.

When he turned around he found Aislinn, still in Mairead's form and dressed in one of her old gowns, staring warily at him from across the room.

"What have ye done to me, witch?" he demanded hoarsely as fury at having been deceived warred with the fear that he might have already lost his chance to stop her leaving. "You've stolen weeks from my life. How dare ye do such a thing?"

"Stolen, is it?" Her eyebrows rose. "I've done nothing of the sort. Nor have I done anything at all to *you*. 'Least, nothing you seemed to find objectionable. 'Twas but a small enchantment I placed over your cottage, taking us out of time for a bit. The old man must have fae blood in him to have broken though my spell as he did."

"Aye, so he claims. And a good thing for me an he does. How much longer were you planning to keep me ensorcelled, then? Weeks more? Months? Years?"

Aislinn sighed. "Nay, nothing like that. Only a few weeks longer perhaps, no more. Just 'til Winter was truly past. For you know I doona have years to spend in such a pleasant fashion. But, speaking of pleasure, what cause have ye to complain? Sure and you're not going to say you didn't enjoy our time together as much as I did, are you? For, if you do, I'll know ye for a liar, Gavin O'Malley. And one with a very poor memory, besides. Did I not tell ye it would take more than a single night to accomplish all you'd asked for?"

Frustrated, Gavin glared at her. "'Tisn't the point. 'Tis the trickery I object to. For you knew damn well I had no idea what you were up to and I'll have your word on it, right now, Fae, that you'll not do any such thing again while you're living under my roof."

She gazed at him sadly. "Nay, *mo chroí*, though it pains me greatly to have to disappoint ye. You'll not have my word for I'll make no such promise to you."

"You will, I tell you," Gavin insisted. "By what right do you refuse me? Are you not still indebted to me for the bargain we made last Winter?"

Aislinn's gaze turned crafty. "Aye, indeed I am. But is that all you're wanting then, in exchange? Sure and I thought you'd hold out for a bigger prize than that!"

Gavin nodded. "I never said 'twas *all* I wanted. But 'twill do for a start." He crossed his arms over his chest and steeled himself before continuing. "Just so you're knowing, I'll also be wanting you to continue on here as you have been; taking the place of my wife and giving me everything I might otherwise have had with her had she not died aforetime."

*****

Aislinn cocked her head to the side and studied at him thoughtfully. "And why would you be after making such a request of me now? Am I not already doing that very thing? Why would you be looking to waste your boon on something you have already?"

"The why of it is not your concern," Gavin replied after a slight pause. "'Tis my own business that. Now, do we have a bargain or not?"

"Nay, we do not. For only a fool would make such a bargain as that and whatever else you are, you're not a fool. Sure and there's something you're not telling me."

"What do you mean, 'nay'?" he demanded, with more bluster than the situation seemed to call for, further arousing Aislinn's suspicions. "Anything that's in your power to give me—was that not what you promised me last December? And I think we can both agree that I'm asking for nothing you canna give!"

"Which is my point exactly. You're asking for *nothing* more than what I've *already* given. Freely."

"So? If all I'm wanting is more of the same, what of it? You owe me, Fae. And, whether you think it sensible or not, you canna deny me that for which I'm asking ye without going back on your word and proving *yourself* a liar."

Aislinn shook her head. "You know I am as incapable of lying to you as I am of rescinding a promise, once it's given. Nor would I seek to deny thee anything to which you're rightfully entitled, *mo chroí*. But, you forget one thing. Did I not also agree to give you a year and a day in which to decide what ye wanted? And did ye not thereafter tell me you wished to take your full measure of time and would not be rushed? As a result of that, I am now not obliged to grant you any wish at all until next midwinter. In fact, it might even be argued that I'd be doing you a disservice if I concluded our bargain aforetime."

Gavin's eyes flashed. "More trickery!" he growled as he stalked over to where she stood. "Do you not still plan on leaving here come Summer? For, if you do, by next midwinter you, my fine lady, might very well be dead. Is that not what you told me?"

Aislinn nodded mutely, too surprised to speak; and, for an instant, she had to fight down the sudden impulse to launch herself into his arms. He was speaking the truth, and, indeed, she thought she'd come to terms with her probable demise. But to hear it put so bluntly made her realize she'd been fooling herself. The reality of her situation terrified her.

"So then, how is it you plan on fulfilling your end of our bargain if you're no longer living?" Gavin pressed.

"I do not know." Nor could she bear to even think about it. Once again, the monumental unfairness of it all crashed over her and left her brain reeling. She wanted to cast herself upon the ground, keen long and loud and give voice to her grief and her rage. But, she kept her composure.

She was both daughter and sister to queens and not one to bend, even in the face of defeat. If it was her fate to die so that Summer might be saved, then so it must be. She would *not* weaken, turn craven and seek to forestall the inevitable. She would meet her doom with pride and an unbowed head and never let *anyone*, least of all this mortal, see her despair.

Straightening her spine, she smiled serenely. "Perhaps, after all, it *would* be best if you did not wait until then to decide. Can you not think of anything worth asking for now?"

Gavin's eyes, as they met hers, looked troubled. "I've already told you what I want from you, Fae. And I'm thinking you've no reasonable grounds on which to refuse it to me."

"Reasonable? Nay, perhaps not. But 'tis a point of pride with me, mortal. After all, 'tis my very existence I'm owing ye for. And, I have to ask myself, is it because ye value my life at so little that you're so reluctant to ask more of me? For, if so, 'tis very ungallant of you."

He shook his head. "If it seems I'm asking for too little then perhaps 'tis *my* life which *you* hold in too little regard. For I'm asking you to stay on here and take the place of she who was my wife. That's no small thing to me."

The sincerity in his tone touched her. Stepping closer she placed her hand upon his cheek and gazed deeply into his eyes. "My apologies, *a thaisce.* For, truly, I did not mean to belittle either of us. But, as I've told ye, no one is truly dead as long as there is yet someone alive to remember them. So, rather than give ye something so fleeting, my Gavin, I would much prefer to leave thee with a gift that will outlast me. So that, when I'm gone, you might remember me with fondness; rather than as the Fae who cheated ye out of all that ye deserved to have."

To Aislinn's surprise, rather than softening, Gavin's expression turned even more grim. "And I would prefer that neither of us were cheated out of what we deserve, Fae. Which is why my answer must remain the same: I would have ye stay."

Aislinn stared at him, puzzled by his continued resistance, until his final word caught her ear. "Stay? For how long are we speaking then?"

Gavin's mouth tightened. His eyes searched hers as though looking for something he could not find. "'Tis not how I'd planned to do this," he said at last, regretfully.

Do what? she wondered. "Answer my question, Gavin. Ye know I canna remain here beyond June, do ye not? For how long would ye have me stay with ye?"

When he finally answered her, it was with a voice as implacable as it was firm: "I would have ye stay for the rest of my life, Fae. I would marry with you, and have children with you—aye, now, the children, they would be gifts that might outlast us both, would they not?"

She stared at him, shocked into silence. For one, breathless instant, a wild wave of hope rose within her. Did he mean it? And, if so, was it not a way out of her sad predicament? Should she take this chance? Could she risk it?

Mind racing, she considered the matter and all it would mean, not just for herself but for everyone involved. And, against that hard rock of reason, her hopes were dashed.

It would be a disaster.

She shook her head. "Nay, *mo chroí*, you know better than to ask for that. 'Tis not possible for me to stay past midsummer. My kinsfolk will surely come for me if I do not return to the realm before then, and I must go with them when they do."

"Let them come then. I'll turn them all away, same as I did Tiernan last winter."

"Aye? And for how long do ye think ye can defy us? There's no doubting you've a strong will, and you're more resourceful than many would believe. But, ye canna pit yourself against the whole realm and hope to come out the winner. Sooner or later, they will find a way to defeat ye, Gavin. Even if ye were to live to a ripe old age, by your standards, it will still be but a blink of the eye to the fae. Nor will Tiernan e'er abandon his quest to make me his. Every winter he will return, until I'm either dead or captured. Is that the life you're wanting for us?"

"Did you not say that, as your husband, Tiernan would have greater claim on ye than even those of your own folk? Why would ye not have the same protection as *my* wife?"

"Because you are not fae. You're not bound by the rules of either court, nor are you under their protection. And this house, located in the outer world, as it is, is on neutral ground, accessible to all. I'm fair game if I remain here, O'Malley, as are you, if you choose this fight, and that can ne'er be changed. Nor would a mortal marriage deter Tiernan for even an instant. And may your God help ye an he e'er takes it into his mind to entrance ye and put you out of time as I have so recently done. Given your objections to my own sweet spell, think ye you would enjoy falling prey to Tiernan's brand of sorcery? I promise you would find it most unpleasant."

Gavin merely shrugged, clearly unwilling to be moved by either fear or reason. "You argue your point well, but it matters little to me. I'm thinking you'd not find death so pleasant either, Fae, for all your brave words. Just as I'd not find it pleasant to go back to the life I'd been living, now that you've opened my eyes to what I might have had instead—nay, to what I *will* have, for I'll not release you from your promise. You said you'd give me anything I asked for, and I've asked for this. Now, come and kiss me, lass, and seal the bargain. And doona look so glum, for I dare say we can contrive to make a good life for ourselves. After all, I'll not be the first man to take a wife over her family's objections."

Aislinn gazed at him in sorrow. "Why will ye not listen to reason? Have ye not heard me say I'm under no compulsion to grant you anything 'til next midwinter? Would you really have me leave you with nothing at all? For that's all you'll get from me, you stubborn man, if I canna return here at that time: Nothing."

"Aye, Fae, I've listened and I've heard. But, let's say a miracle occurred and you *were* to be here at midwinter, you'd have to give in to my demands then, wouldn't ye?" He smiled grimly when she nodded. "Very well, then. If that's how it's to be, I'll have to make sure you don't leave here aforetime."

"Insolent, ignorant, arrogant man that ye are!" Aislinn stamped her foot in fury. "Have you *any* idea who it is you're dealing with?"

"I do, aye." Gavin grinned at her cockily. "I'm dealing with my future wife and the mother of my children,

God willing, in three quarters of a year's time. Well, the children'll take longer, of course, but you take my meaning."

"Wrong, you insufferable fool! I am Aislinn Deirbhile, daughter of Ireland; I'm no one to be trifled with—least of all by the likes of you. In the last year alone I have defied the will of two Fae Courts, outsmarted my enemies at every turn, rescued myself from the clutches of doom time and again and yet *you* think to get the better of me? Why, I bested you at midwinter—when my powers were at their absolute nadir. You've yet to see me rise. I am still nowhere near my full strength. Do you honestly think you can imprison me here through summer, through my own period of ascendancy? Pray, tell me what magic will you use to create this, this...miracle I think you rightly termed it?"

"The very same magic that's kept you here 'til now. Or did ye think I'd not figure out that you can no more move through my doorway unassisted than your friend Tiernan can?"

Aislinn grimaced. "Aye, I'd hoped it might have escaped your notice. But do not make the mistake of thinking me defenseless. I can take other forms besides this, you know. And, mayhap someday, an it suits me, I'll take the shape of a wee mouse and ride out of here in your coat pocket or the cuff of your trousers, with you none the wiser."

"Thank ye for the warning," Gavin replied nodding earnestly. Then his smile peeked out again. "I'll bear it in mind—and you best hope that I don't decide to get myself a cat, in the meantime."

"Ah, I suppose 'tis my own fault for being too easy on you up 'til now." She smiled maliciously. "Perhaps, instead, I'll simply sing ye into another trance. You'd asked me to show you Annwn, did you not? I could make you think you're there now, if I so choose, and you'll be begging me to let you leave this place and glad you'll be to carry me out with ye if I ask you to."

"That's enough." Gavin's face blanched, but his gaze remained as determined as ever. Reaching out suddenly, he grabbed hold of her wrist and began to pull her towards the door. "I hadn't wanted to do this, lass, but you leave me no choice."

"What are you doing?" she asked as he unbolted the door. She shivered at the chill that raced through her as he yanked her through the iron-warded doorway. "Gavin, stop this foolishness at once!"

"Answer me something, Fae," he said, ignoring her request as he stormed across the yard, seemingly headed for the forge, dragging her along behind him. "You told me once that iron has power to bind your magic, is that still true for one at the height of her ascendancy?"

"I suppose it must be so," she answered, gazing wildly around at the landscape, half fearing Tiernan would choose this moment to make another appearance. "For what else could possibly account for the ease with which you defied Tiernan last winter? I'm sure it gave him quite a shock when you did so for you shouldn't even have been able to see him, an he didn't want you to."

Gavin gave a satisfied sounding grunt as he shoved open the forge's heavy door, then he pulled her inside. The bitter cold scent of iron assailed Aislinn's nostrils, chilling her from inside out and setting her heart to racing. Whenever else she'd been here there'd at least been the heat, pouring from the fire pit, to warm her and she'd at least been wearing shoes. Now, there was nothing to ease her discomfort or protect her from the touch of the foul metal. And even the cold soot dusting the ground held enough iron residue to sting her bare feet. "Take me back to the house now," she begged. "I hate it here. Whatever you're thinking of doing, surely it can wait for later."

"Aye, I'm sure it can," he agreed, throwing open the lid of the old oak chest in which he kept his tools. "I'm sure it can wait for at least another month or so. But, I canna trust you not to try and trick me again, even before that time, and I'll not take any such chances where my future is concerned." He turned his head and flashed her an apologetic look. "I'm sorry for what I'm about to do to ye, lass, but I'm only thinking about what's best for both of us. I hope someday you'll see the truth of that."

"Why? What is it you're doing?" Aislinn asked, gasping in surprise when he pulled the chain from the chest. "Gavin, nay, put that thing away now." She didn't know what, exactly, he planned to do with such a thing, but she knew it could be used for nothing good. Heart hammering in her chest, she tried to pull away from him, but his fist tightened, his grip on her wrist intensifying almost to the point of pain.

Murmuring soft sounds, intended to soothe, he backed her across the room until the backs of her knees connected with the edge of the bench. She sat down hard, then immediately leaped to her feet again, when she felt the icy sting of the nail heads with which the bench was studded.

"Sit back down," Gavin ordered, pushing her down once more.

This time she shrieked with the pain that lanced up her back and legs. She tried once again to stand but Gavin had already knelt and took hold of one of her legs, lifting her foot from the floor, putting her off balance. Moving quicker than she would have thought possible, he slid a loop of chain over her foot and a cold agony, more excruciating than anything she'd ever yet known, followed along with it, stunning her into immobility. In the instant it took her before she could respond, he'd wrapped the metal around her ankle once again.

*****

"Take it off! Take it off!" Aislinn screamed as she changed, without warning, back to her true form. Blonde curls tumbled about her suddenly haggard face as she rose from the bench and clawed at him.

Gavin shoved her back on the bench once again. "Easy, now. I'm not going to hurt you. 'Tis just to keep your magic under control."

"Not hurt me?" An odd sound—something between

hysterical laughter and a sob—broke from her lips. "Nay, nothing so kind. 'Tis killing me you are!"

Gavin snorted. "Sure and I'm doing no such thing." But doubt assailed him and he found himself studying her suspiciously. The color seemed to drain from her face, even as he watched, until her lips began to turn blue. Even the gold of her hair seemed to fade. "Stop this glamour now, for I know 'tis just one of your tricks."

Gasping for breath, she shook her head. "I have no strength for glamour and can barely think with the pain. Take it off me, please," she begged, her voice faint, thready, worrisome. "Please, Gavin, I beg thee."

He hesitated. "Will you swear you'll not try and escape, if I let you go? That you won't run away or trick me or use your magic against me in any fashion?"

She nodded weakly, slumped against the bench with her eyes shut.

"Answer me!" Gavin demanded. "Say the words, Fae, or you'll get no relief."

Aislinn's eyes opened. The pain in their depths took Gavin's breath away. "I pray thee...what is it you wish me to say?"

"What I just now told you. That you'll not escape, or use magic or trick me or—"

"Aye. Aye, anything, I swear. Only please..."

Muttering angrily, and certain he would regret giving in to her request, Gavin reached for her foot, only to stop when he spied the faint wisps of smoke pouring from beneath the hem of her gown. Hastily, he swept her skirt aside and felt his heart seize at the sight that met his eyes.

"O, Holy Mother," he breathed, staring in horror for Aislinn's foot was withered and blackened, hardly recognizable, looking more like a bit of charred wood left over from a fire, or a piece of coal. It was cold when he touched it, too, like something long dead. "Why didn't you tell me it would do this to you, Fae? Why?"

But she seemed too far gone to do more than to shake

her head from side to side and weakly murmur, "Please..."

It took him almost a minute to remove the chain for it seemed to be melting into her ankle, eating away at the flesh. He cursed himself as he worked, hampered by the sweating of his hands and the powdery, gray ash that continually furred the wound. Railing against his own stupidity, he raced against time for the blackness was spreading, traveling steadily up her leg, and with each breath she took she seemed to be slipping further and further away.

She was barely conscious by the time he finished, still breathing, but unnaturally cold. Picking her up, he rushed for the house and laid her down on his bed.

"What must I do?" he begged as he knelt by her side, stroking her hair back from her face. "Please, *a stóirín*, tell me. What will make it better?"

She said nothing, merely shook her head, raised one hand as though to touch his face, then let it drop again.

"I'll go and get Doctor Butler for you then," he said, rising once more. For an instant, he stood there, looking down at her, reluctant to leave her side, but what else could he do? "You're not to die while I'm away," he told her sternly. "I couldn't bear it. Do ye hear me, Aislinn? You're not to die on me. I forbid it."

For the space of another heartbeat, he waited, but she didn't answer and he knew he couldn't delay any longer. His only hope of saving her lay in leaving now and getting back as quickly as possible with whatever help he could muster.

He rushed from the house and clambered up the boreen towards town, and it seemed some luck was with him that day, after all, because he'd gone no more than a few hundred meters before he heard the sound of hoof beats. And a minute later the very doctor he'd been on his way to fetch appeared from around the bend.

"Here now, what's all this?" Doctor Butler protested, after Gavin, having flagged him down, arms waving, in the middle of the road, took hold of his horse's bridle and all but dragged the animal back with him down the road leading to the forge. "What are you doing, O'Malley? Let me go, now, for I'm on my way to see a patient!"

"Well, whoever it is will have to wait. For I've something you need to see first," Gavin replied, as he pulled on the rein. "Now, come along."

"I tell you, I've no time for this. There's a new babe being born over t'the O'Faolain's and I'm wanted there even as we speak. So whatever is ailing you, unless you're about to drop dead of it, you'll just have to be patient."

Gavin shook his head. "Nay, that I canna do. 'Tis a matter of urgency, I tell ya. And, babes are born every day, are they not? If this one canna wait, it will have to greet the world without you. It wouldna be the first time. Besides, 'tis unlikely O'Faolain's wife could be in *that* great a hurry to expand her brood. I should think she'd be glad for the delay of a few more hours."

"Babies die every day, too," the doctor reminded him. "Being born is a perilous business, at times. As you, of all people, should well know."

"Aye," Gavin growled, fighting to hold his temper in check. "You know, Doctor, I'd gladly bloody your nose for you right now, an I didn't fear it might swell and obscure your eyesight. But, if you e'er speak thus to me again of my loss, I might decide to risk it just the same."

Frantic though he was to get help for Aislinn, Gavin did retain just enough sense to insist that the doctor himself unlatch the cottage door and precede him into the house. For the thought had occurred to him that it might not be luck, at all, but more fae trickery that had put them both on the same road that morning. As soon as the doctor proved himself human, however, Gavin hustled him into the bedroom as quickly as he could.

Doctor Butler's face grew grave as he examined Aislinn's foot and ankle. After no more than a minute, he pulled Gavin aside.

"Poor lass," he said, sighing heavily. "I suppose it was frostbite and left too long untended, but that foot's quite done for now. I fear the gangrene's reached almost to her knee."

"There must be something you can do for her?" Gavin insisted. "Isn't there?"

The doctor nodded. "Aye, there is, though I haven't the tools with me to deal with it now and I must see to this baby first anyway. Now, don't be looking at me like that, son," he said hurriedly, for Gavin had begun to scowl. "I know it looks like the girl's in a bad way, and indeed she is, but I tell you there's no rush about it now. The damage is already done. However, the wound's not infected, and that's a blessing, nor is she running a fever, so you just keep her quiet 'til I get back and if you've any whiskey about, give her a good shot or two of it to keep her comfortable. In fact, give her as much as she'll have from you; for sure and it'll be easier on all of us an she's unconscious when I take her leg."

Gavin stared at him, aghast. "When you *what?*"

"Aye." he nodded again. "You heard me correctly. There's no hope for it, I'm afraid. It'll have to come off."

After the doctor had gone, Gavin stood in the bedroom doorway, shoulders sagging, feeling once again all the guilt and grief and self-loathing that had lain heavy on him for most of the past ten years and which had only recently begun to abate—all thanks to her. She'd come to him for help last winter, but it seemed that he was the one who'd benefited the most from their association. He didn't know if she'd ever come to realize how much she'd given him over these past weeks and, if he were honest with himself, he hoped she never would. For, after all she'd done for him, this was how he repaid her!

Tears tracked slowly down his face as he gazed at Aislinn's still form and perhaps she felt the weight of his stare for she opened her eyes and met his gaze. "Gavin," she whispered, holding out a hand to him.

"Aye, *a muirnín*," he murmured when he'd crossed the room and was kneeling by her side, holding her hand in his. "What is it you're needing? Tell me. How can I help?"

A faint, wry, ghost of a smile curved her lips. "There's naught for you to do now. I'm dying."

"You're not! Do not be saying such things. The doctor will be coming back shortly and he, he—" But he stopped there, unable to tell her the rest of it, unwilling to admit how badly he'd served her.

She shook her head. "Nay, 'tis over for me and perhaps...perhaps 'tis better thus. What's a few months more or less, after all? Why, 'tis hardly worth the shedding of a single tear over so small a thing. And...I think now, 'twould have been harder than I first thought 'twould be to give my life up willingly in my own home. I might have fought it, at the end, and so disgraced myself before my kin. I would not have wanted that. This way, too, I can be sure that Tiernan won't have me. So I thank you for that."

And with that, Gavin broke. For her to be thanking him now, after what he'd done, was more than he could bear. "Ah, Aislinn. *A ghrá geal. A ghrá geal mo chroí.* What have I done to thee, lass? Never would I have put the cursed thing on ye had I known. And your poor little foot..." Overcome with remorse, he pressed his lips against the blackened, brittle remnant and kissed it tenderly, murmuring, "Ah, God, I'm sorry, Aislinn, so very sorry."

Tears leaked from beneath his closed eyelids as he continued to kiss her foot. His shoulders were shaking so hard he almost missed the shudder that passed through her frame and the sharp, shattered intake of her breath. It was the startled urgency in her tone when she softly cried his name that finally broke through his grief to capture his attention.

Alarmed, he glanced first at her face, and then, following her gaze, he turned his eyes to her foot. A change had occurred, but it took him a moment for his mind to register the reason for her foot's mottled appearance. "Saints be praised," he whispered, staring in wonder and disbelief. For wherever his tears had fallen, wherever his lips had been pressed, her skin had been restored to the pink, unblemished hue of healthy flesh.

He wasted no time after that, applying his lips again and again to her foot, her ankle, her leg, until no sign of injury remained other than a faint brown mark, in the shape of joined links that circled her ankle.

"How?" he asked at last, when he'd finally finished and was lying beside her on the bed, holding her close, sending up silent prayers of thanks. "How is it possible?"

Aislinn shrugged. "Who can say? Very little is known about the magic contained within the human heart and soul and 'tis not a subject to which I've ever given much thought before. To be honest, *mo chroí*, I've never had much use for your kind until recently."

Gavin smiled down at her, mockingly. "Oh, is that so? Well, I might say the very same thing about your kind, too, you know. What say ye to that?"

"I'd say that, perhaps, in the future, it would behoove us both to give a little more thought to such matters." She returned his smile, then, with a sleepy one of her own. "Now, let me rest for a bit. For I'm quite worn out from the ordeal and just thankful you did not try it any sooner. For had I suffered such an injury last winter, I'm sure I'd never have survived it." And, so saying, she laid her head upon Gavin's chest and fell instantly to sleep, leaving him to ponder her words.

He supposed, having nearly killed her, he owed it to her to set her free with his blessings. But he couldn't. If anything, coming so close to losing her made him even more determined not to let her go back to her homeland where she'd face an even more certain death. His only hope lay in the promise he'd wrung from her at the forge. But would she feel herself honor-bound to keep such a promise—one so vague, made under such duress? Or would she even remember having promised him anything at all?

And so he lay there awhile, fingers toying with the bright curls that cascaded down her back, enjoying the guilty pleasure of holding her for once in this, her true form and wondering what the future would bring. Until, eventually, he, too, fell asleep.

*****

For the second time that day, Gavin was roused from sleep by the pounding of a fist on his front door.

"Devil take the man. What is it he's wanting this time?" he growled as he sat up in bed and rubbed his eyes.

"'Tis probably the doctor come back for to treat me," Aislinn replied, looking worried.

Gavin nodded agreement. "Aye. I was forgetting about him. I'm sure you're right, lass. All right, then, I'll just go and get rid of him. I'll tell him his services are no longer required."

"You can't," she said as she clutched his arm. "He'll be wanting to see me then and, once he does, word of my miraculous recovery will be all over the county by nightfall."

"Well, what are you suggesting I tell him, then? For it's sure I am that I'll not be letting him cut off your foot merely to preserve the illusion you're still hurt!"

"If I could put a glamour on him it would make him forget what he'd originally come here for," she suggested. "I could then have him believing that his horse had thrown a shoe and he'd come to you for to have it fixed."

"Aye. That would do the trick, I suppose. Go ahead then."

A faint frown crossed her features. "I cannot."

"What do you mean, you cannot?" He glared at her. "Did you not just tell me you could?"

"I said 'if I could'. But I promised you I'd not use any magic. So, therefore, I cannot."

"No magic used against me is what I said. 'Tis not against me if I'm telling you to do it, now is it?"

"It could be."

The knocking came again at his door; louder this time. Gavin sighed in exasperation. "Well, could you not then make an exception, just this once?"

Aislinn's lips pursed. "Aye, I suppose. But I must be very sure, first, that it's what you want. Having just survived death, I'm not about to run the risk of cursing myself now by unintentionally breaking my word to you."

"You'd not be breaking your word over something like this," Gavin told her. "For I'm the one you gave your promise to and I'm telling you this is not what I asked you to swear to."

Aislinn sighed unhappily. "Very well, then. Now, go and answer your door and keep the man occupied. It might take me a few seconds to gather my strength for I'm still not yet quite myself."

Chapter Nine

"What took you so long?" the doctor grumbled when Gavin finally opened his front door. He tried to enter, but Gavin placed a hand against his shoulder and pushed him back a step. "Here now, what are you doing?"

Gavin stepped out onto the stoop as well and pulled the door closed again behind him. "Just taking a minute or so to enjoy this beautiful Spring weather," he replied quite truthfully, for he couldn't help but notice that the day was more than fine with late afternoon sunlight gilding the green hills and the scent of apple blossoms perfuming the air. "You said earlier there was no sense in rushing things, now didn't ya?"

Doctor Butler sighed. "Let me go in to her, O'Malley. I know it's a hard thing, and not what you were wanting to hear, but it'd be best to get it over with whilst we still have daylight on our side. 'Tis nothing going to be gained by putting it off, you know. She's not going to get any better that way."

Gavin couldn't suppress a grin. "Well, now, I don't know as I'd be so sure about that, if I were you. She's looking marvelously improved already, in my opinion."

"Oh, is she indeed?" The doctor shook his head. "Yah, not bloody likely. I'm telling it to you plain, man, her own dead flesh will be poisoning her soon, if it's not already. She'll only improve when it's cut away and the surrounding tissue cauterized. And the sooner I get to it, the more of her leg I'll be able to save."

"Aye, we'll go in directly," Gavin promised. "But, first, tell me about O'Faolain's newest addition. Boy or girl?"

"They've another fine, stout girl with a full head of hair and a grand set of lungs on her. She'll be keeping them all from their beds at night for a long time to come, is my prediction."

"In good health then?"

"She is. Although, the poor wee thing does seem to favor her da in looks."

"Ah, you don't say? Sure and that's a shame now; his is not a face I'd be wishing on anyone. And Mrs. O'Faolain? Is she doing well?"

But the doctor made no answer. A strange, wistful, enraptured expression had crept over his face as he glanced around, as though searching the very air for something he could not see. "What is that sound I'm hearing?" he asked, at last. "Is it a nightingale then?"

"A nightingale!" Gavin all but gaped. "What nonsense is this? Surely, an educated man like yourself should know there's not a single nightingale to be found in all of Ireland!"

"Aye. I do know that. And, indeed, it's been so many years since last I heard one, not since I was a young man away at school—and, sure and that seems a lifetime ago, now, but—Oh, surely that must be what it is I'm hearing. I could ne'er be mistaken about such a thing..."

Curious, Gavin strained his ears to hear what the other man was hearing. But all he could hear was the *ceol sidhe*. A thrill of delighted recognition ran through him but, for once, the exquisite beauty of Aislinn's song seemed to have no effect on him as it wafted, soft and warm, on the still Spring air. He was surprised to find himself almost disappointed by that, and even felt vaguely envious of the doctor.

"How much am I owing ye then?" Doctor Butler asked, startling Gavin from his contemplation.

"What's that?" he asked, forgetting, for a moment, the subterfuge that he and Aislinn had agreed upon.

"For the shoe. For my horse? Is it the Spring Fever that's got to you, or are you bewitched, that you're forgetting why I'm here?"

Gavin smiled. "Nothing of the sort. Of course, I'm remembering. But, there'll be no charge for that today. Think of it as a gift to celebrate your part in bringing O'Faolain's daughter safely into the world. Besides, on so fine a day as this, I'm sure 'twould be a sin to be thinking of commerce."

The doctor looked surprised—and a trifle confused—by the smith's unexpected generosity. But he thanked him profusely, just the same, and went on his way.

Gavin, for his part, was happy to hurry back to Aislinn's side.

*****

"Well, now, my little songbird," Gavin said, grinning as he re-entered the bedroom, after having seen the doctor off. "It would seem you played your part very well. 'Tis a great loss for the good doctor, to be sure, but I do believe he's quite forgotten your existence."

"'Twas my intention he should do so," Aislinn replied, aware of a faint feeling of trepidation as she gazed on him now. The events of the day had changed many things—not least of all, the balance of power between them.

"He thought 'twas a nightingale he was hearing. Did you intend that, too?"

Aislinn shook her head. "'Tis the sound of that which is most dearly loved and longed for that you're hearing, when I sing in that way. Which is why, even if you're knowing what it is, you still find yourself bound to listen to it."

An odd expression passed across Gavin's features, wiping the smile from his face. His eyes narrowed. "Is that a fact, now?" he asked in a voice that seemed strange as well.

"It is," Aislinn answered and then they both fell still and, for a long moment, neither of them had a word to say. For her part, Aislinn was longing to open her arms to Gavin. She longed to press him close, ached for him to make her feel alive once again.

She'd been ready to die today. She would have welcomed it—or anything that would have offered an end to her pain. But, she wasn't ready now. Her narrow escape had served only to draw her attention to how sweet, how fleeting life could be and, if truth be told, she was not entirely certain she could bear to face losing hers again. There had to be some way for her to survive, other than by throwing herself on Tiernan's mercy.

And, perhaps there was.

Having felt the energy with which Gavin had healed her—power such as she'd never suspected any mortal could possess and which she could only assume must be an attribute of his soul—had given her cause to once again consider the druid's words. Up until now, she'd taken it for granted that Gavin would have to imperil his soul, or lose it entirely, in order to foil Tiernan's plans. But what if she were wrong?

What if all that was needed was for Gavin to gift her with just a small portion of his own soul? It was not unheard of. In fact, one of the few things she remembered having been told about human souls was that they were often shared. Between lovers. Between parent and child. Between the best of friends.

Anamchara. That was the name she'd heard mentioned. Soul friend. A person who had grown so close to another human's heart that their souls merged, married, flowed together; until the two became one.

Could a man ever join himself in such a fashion with a fae? she wondered. And, if he did, what would that mean for them both? Would they each only have half a soul? Could that ever be enough for either of them?

Surely, with even half a soul would come extraordinary benefits. Like self-determination and the right to decide for herself which court her power would serve, Winter or Summer; or the strength to survive the breaking of a *geis*.

While still retaining all the magic that made her what she was, she might also be rendered impervious to iron; independent of the seasons; subject to nothing but her own free will; able to go back on her word, if she so chose it; even to lie with impunity.

She could be—in a word—invulnerable.

Or, almost invulnerable. She could still be killed, of

course, under the right circumstances, and Tiernan could still imprison her, but to what purpose? He could no longer hope to control her—even in Annwn—and, court politics being what they were, he would hardly want her there to serve as a constant reminder of a plan that had failed. No, it would be in his best interest to try and forget he'd ever even thought of it.

"A penny for your thoughts, Fae," Gavin murmured, startling Aislinn out of her reverie.

She looked at him in surprise. "What's that you say?"

"Out with it, my girl. For you must have been thinking of something pleasant, just now, judging from the smile on your face and I'm thinking it would cheer me to learn of it."

But Aislinn was reluctant to share her thoughts just yet. "Pleasant enough, aye, they were. But, all the same, I'll keep my thoughts to myself, at the moment, if you don't mind."

"'Tis your right, I suppose," Gavin answered, though his eyes betrayed his disappointment. "Would you care for some supper, then? Or tea, at least? It feels like an age since last we ate."

"I would," she replied, smiling in an effort to assuage any hurt feelings she may have caused. "Thank you most kindly."

With a nod, Gavin turned toward the door, and then stopped and turned back to her, frowning doubtfully. "But, I'm forgetting about how much time has passed—weeks, in fact. I doubt there'll be anything fit to eat, at this point."

Aislinn shook her head again. "Nay, you've naught to worry about. Time has barely passed at all within these four walls. Your food's still as fresh as though it were only last night since last you ate."

"Well, that's a blessing," he sighed. "Will you not join me beside the hearth while I fix our meal?"

"Aye." Aislinn nodded and, sitting up, swung her legs off the bed. She sucked in a quick breath as her feet made contact with the floor; the faint stinging sensation served as a graphic reminder that the iron-rich dust she'd been forced to walk through, earlier in the day, still clung to her soles

Gavin was beside her in an instant, scooping her into his arms. "Ah, 'tis a fool I am for forgetting you're only just recovered. You're probably still too weak to walk, aren't you, lass?"

"Nay," Aislinn protested weakly. "'Tis not that."

But Gavin cut her off with a shake of his head and, in a voice that brooked no argument, said, "Aye. I'm thinking, indeed, it is that."

He carried her from the room and set her down gently in a chair by the fire, then went about getting their supper started. Aislinn watched him surreptitiously as he cooked. She was right about things having changed between them. Why else would her heart still be racing from nothing more than being held in his arms? Sure, it could well be fear, remembering the pain he'd caused her, but would that explain the way her gaze kept traveling to his mouth, or the way her mind insisted on replaying the moment when he'd pressed his lips to her ruined foot and brought it back to life?

Her breath caught as she recalled the tingling tide that had raced up her leg to flood her sex with warmth before expanding, upward and outward, until her entire body was infused with heat, with want, with desire, with...something more; with a feeling for which she had no name.

It was like nothing she'd ever known, like being re-born, perhaps. It was an entirely new experience—which was noteworthy all on its own, it having been ages since anything had been entirely new to her.

All of which surely went a great ways toward explaining why she felt herself somewhat in awe of him tonight. Or why she longed to feel his mouth on her again, longed to feel her body consumed by the nameless flames he'd conjured forth in her today.

It was towards the end of their meal that Gavin got up from the table and took two cut glass tumblers down from the top shelf of the hutch where he kept his dishes. He poured a couple of fingers of whiskey into both glasses and handed one to Aislinn. Then he seated himself across from her and gazed at her earnestly.

"I was never intending to hurt you, lass," he said quietly while his eyes pleaded with her to believe him.

Aislinn nodded. "I know that."

"I was only trying to keep you safe." He glanced away from her as he added, "I cannot allow you to go to your death. But to bind you with chains was my only plan and now I'm quite without knowing how to stop you from leaving."

"I've no wish to die," Aislinn answered, suppressing the shudder of fear she felt upon hearing the steely determination in his voice. "But neither am I willing to become Tiernan's captive, for that would be even worse than death, I think. To what lengths are you prepared to go to ensure my safety?"

A self-contemptuous smirk twisted Gavin's mouth as he lifted his glass to his lips. "I shouldn't think you'd have to ask such a question, Fae. Sure and it's obvious from my actions today, I'm willing to give up all claim to decency and reason in my efforts to keep you here. A better question, perhaps, is what wouldn't I do and, in truth, I can think of very little."

"Would you give up your soul, then, or a fragment thereof?"

Gavin choked on his whiskey. "M-my soul?"

"Aye." She nodded. "Do you not recall? 'Twas the only thing the druid mentioned as being capable of foiling Tiernan's plot. But only an it were offered willingly. 'Tis not that unheard of you know. Sure and it must be how your own young come by them, for where else would they get them, if not from their parents? Are you not knowing that's the main reason why the Brownies and other Imps are always looking to leave their offspring as changelings? Sure and it's in hopes that their human foster parents will overlook the exchange and gift their new charges with all that should have gone to their natural children."

"My soul," Gavin repeated, shaking his head in thought. "By all that's holy, could you not have asked for something else? For sure and it was in the very hope of keeping my soul intact that I first conceived of making you my wife."

"'Tis only a piece I'd be taking, you know," she told him, smiling encouragingly. "And it'll grow back in time. I'm almost certain such is the case. For, otherwise, those parents with large broods would be walking around completely soulless, and surely your Church would have something to say about that, would it not?"

"Aye, so you'd think," Gavin agreed, sighing heavily. "But, all the same, I cannot give you an answer tonight, Fae. 'Tis a weighty matter. I'll have to think upon it, you know."

Aislinn inclined her head. "Indeed, I understand. And I can wait 'til midsummer for your answer, but no longer. I've promised I'd not try and escape, or trick you into letting me go, nor will I use magic to accomplish the same. But, if you tarry beyond that point my kinsmen will surely come for me and I have not promised I would resist their efforts to take me. Nor will I. For even now I am certain death would be more palatable than a life of servitude in Annwn."

Gavin nodded. He tossed back his whiskey and then got to his feet. "Would you be wanting me to carry you back to bed now?" he asked.

Aislinn held out her arms. "Aye. If you please."

Once she was safely snuggled within the circle of his arms she tried again to explain. "'Tis not that I canna walk," she said, but faintly, because her heart was racing again. "'Tis merely that I can still feel the dust from the forge upon my feet and even the small particles of iron it contains cause my feet to sting when I try and stand upon them."

For an instant, Gavin's stride seemed to falter. "Lass, if you're that sensitive to the substance, this canna be the first time you're feeling the effects of it. You've been out to the forge many times before and...and certainly today is not the first you've been in contact with the stuff?"

Aislinn looked at him in surprise. "Aye, I'm sure you're right. For, now that I think on it, there have been many occasions I've felt a similar sting—though much milder, of course—even, at times, when you've touched me; as though you'd absorbed the essence of it through your skin's pores."

"If such was the case," he replied with a scowl, "you should have mentioned it sooner."

"And so I would have done," Aislinn answered, "had I recognized it for what it was, but it was not until today that I made the connection."

Still scowling, Gavin deposited her in his bed then left the room again without a word. Aislinn bit back her disappointment and busied herself by removing her gown— not so easy a task as it would have been had he stayed to help her, or if she could have stood. She'd no sooner settled herself into bed then Gavin returned.

She glanced curiously at the towels and pitcher he was carrying. "What are those for?"

"For washing the dirt from your feet," he said as he poured the steaming water into the washbasin and dipped one of the towels into it. After wringing the towel out, he moved back to the bed, tossed the covers aside and picked up one of her feet.

At his very first touch, Aislinn felt a shudder run through her. She practically purred in contentment as he carefully laved first one foot then the other; making sure every inch of skin was attended to; pausing periodically to re-immerse the towel in the warm water.

"Is that better then?" he asked after he'd dried them, just as meticulously.

"Aye. Much better, thank you kindly," Aislinn replied, her eyes widening when Gavin picked up the pot of butter he'd brought in with him. "And what is it you think you're doing with that?"

He shrugged, his gaze locked on the foot he held so

tenderly. "I know naught of the kind of injury you suffered today, lass. Burns are the only things I'm knowing how to treat and for those we've always used butter. I can think of nothing better to use in this case. It might do you no good but, at the very least, I'm fairly certain it will do you no harm." He raised his eyes to her face and asked, "So, may I?"

Aislinn nodded once again, then sucked in a quick breath as he slathered the butter over her foot and began to rub it into her skin. The butter seemed to melt almost on contact, adding its comforting, homey scent to the air. It felt good. No, it felt better than good. Much better.

She sighed in contentment as his strong hands soothed and caressed and kneaded her flesh, closing her eyes to better enjoy the sensations. Warm waves of pleasure seemed to lap at her senses causing her sex to spasm and swell, her juices running like honey in July.

Then he raised her foot to his mouth, nibbling and sucking on each toe in turn and Aislinn cried out in surprise as she was overtaken by a sharp, sudden climax that ran through her like wildfire leaving her dazed and trembling, her nether lips drenched.

"Liked that, did ya?" Gavin's chuckle rumbled sensuously in her ear, low and amused, and heat blazed in her cheeks. "Why, Fae, is that a blush I'm seeing? I didn't think the fae were given to such displays."

"No more are we," she replied with as much dignity as she could manage, honestly forcing her to add, "For the most part. 'Tis very rare, but not impossible." She opened her eyes, not at all surprised to find him smiling rather smugly, his own eyes twinkling as they raked her body, pausing at her nipples, which were tenting the thin material of her shift, then dipping lower.

"Raise your skirt then," he murmured, his voice thick and husky. "And let me see the rest of you."

Though the fae had never been overly concerned with nudity, and she had never been an exception in this regard, his request caused Aislinn's heart to race and her cheeks to

grow even hotter. Still, she did as he asked. Allowing her
legs to fall open, she slid the thin material slowly upward in
hopes that the sight of her pink folds, coated, as she knew
they must be, with cream, would help to re-establish her
dominance over him.

For a moment, it seemed to work. Gavin's eyes
darkened and his breathing hitched. "Ah, that's lovely, it is,"
he sighed, as he released the foot he'd been fondling. Then
he took hold of her other ankle, lifting her foot and spreading
her legs even wider in the process. "Now, stay just like that
and let's see if we can't do the same with this one." And the
smile he flashed was ripe with confidence and as meltingly
sensuous as the butter for which he was once again reaching.

Aislinn moaned blissfully. She thought it a long shot
she could climax again so soon, but as the erotic sensations
began to course through her again, her certainty diminished
and a whimper escaped her lips when he brought her foot to
his mouth once more.

This time, it was the action of his tongue that did the
trick; edging between her toes, lashing at the underside of her
arch, although the weight of his stare, focused as it was on
her dampening sex, added to the effect and helped to push
her over the edge.

As her body arched helplessly, she found herself
longing to feel him inside her; an unspoken desire he
partially answered, sliding his palm up along the inside of her
leg until he could push one finger between her pulsating lips.
"More," she begged as her muscles tightened around the
digit. "I want to feel all of you there."

Groaning, Gavin pulled his finger from her weeping
sex. She opened her eyes to find him rapidly shucking out of
his clothes. She opened her arms in welcome as he came
down on top of her, nuzzling at her neck, nipping at her ear
lobe, firing her blood once again.

He felt wonderful on top of her; right and familiar
and...different, all the same. It took an instant for the reason
for the change to register and when it did, it caused a

stabbing sense of disappointment within her heart.

"Wait," she rasped, pushing him away and holding him off, waiting until he raised his head to meet her gaze, before she continued. "If you're wanting me to change, you'll have to make it very clear you're wishing for me to use my magic in this fashion. Otherwise, I can no longer oblige you."

"Use your magic for what?" he asked, his expression guarded.

"To transform myself," she replied, refusing to elaborate further, unwilling for the name of the woman whose likeness she'd been assuming all these months to pass her lips; wanting him now for herself alone.

Gavin's brow furrowed. "Nay," he answered harshly. "No magic."

But why? she wondered. Was it because he didn't trust her not to turn his acquiescence to her own advantage, in some fashion? Or could he be wanting to make love to her—in her own form, face to face—in the very same way, and for the very same reason she wanted him to?

Before she could decide whether or not to risk asking, he was lowering his head to capture her mouth, his lips fitting hers so perfectly she gave up wondering anything at all; choosing, instead, to believe it was just as she wanted it to be. "Here, now." She wrenched her mouth away to beg. "Help me take this off." For even the sheer fabric of her undergarment seemed suddenly too cumbersome. She wanted to feel him skin to skin, with nothing separating them and nothing in between, no clothes, no lies, no subterfuge, no disguise.

With Gavin's help, she had soon divested herself of the shift. But, when she attempted to pull him back down on top of her, he eluded her grasp. Kneeling between her thighs he studied her, his eyes hot and dark as they slowly perused her nakedness. Aislinn propped herself up on her elbows, returned his gaze and waited.

"Lie back, now," he murmured and she willingly

obliged, sighing happily in anticipation as he followed her down. This time, he avoided her mouth, kissing her everywhere else, however, as though attempting to map her face with his lips.

"Gavin," she whispered, feathering her hand through his hair until he caught her hand in his and then proceeded to kiss each finger, her palm, her wrist; and then slowly moved up her arm. "What is it you're doing?" she asked teasingly. "Is it your intention to pleasure my hands now, sir, as earlier you did my feet?"

"Nay," Gavin replied raising his head to grin at her. "Although, it is something to keep in mind for the future." Then his smile faded. "I was thinking of what you'd said a little while ago. About my touch having caused you pain at times."

"Ah, no," Aislinn murmured, framing his face with her free hand. "Pray, do not think about that now. 'Twas a very small pain, to be sure, and nothing for you to be worrying yourself over."

"All the same, I thought if my kisses could soothe your foot, as they did today, perhaps the same would serve to make amends for all those earlier injuries."

"So you plan on kissing me...everywhere, then?" she mocked gently.

But Gavin nodded, his face serious. "Aye. In all the places I've touched you or wished to touch you. As well as all those places I've yet to even think of touching you but will probably want to, just the same, at some point."

Aislinn laughed. "A worthy endeavor, to be sure. And far be it from me to discourage you from making such a valiant effort, sir. But, surely, we have time enough to undertake such a task on another night? Right now, there's only one part of me that's aching. And that part will only be satisfied by the length of your cock. I wish to feel you inside me, *mo chroí*. Will you not oblige me?"

Gavin groaned. "Ah, Aislinn, no one else has ever spoken to me thus. To hear you speak of such things— 'Tis like putting a spark to dry tinder. For, in truth, you set me aflame with your words."

Aislinn pulled him tight against her and whispered in his ear. "Then do as I ask, *mo chroí,* and take me now. Put your rod inside me and I'll speak such words as will make your hair ignite."

But, apparently, he must have thought she'd said enough, for he sealed her mouth with his and thrust into her in just the way she'd grown to crave; with a fierceness that took her breath away. Again and again he rocked into her until they were both groaning unchecked, until his skin was slick beneath her hands and she was once again mindless with pleasure. When he erupted inside her it triggered yet another climax; this one composed of slow, rolling tremors that swept through her like a warm wave of bliss. Her nails scored his back as she lifted herself against him and her muscles milked his cock. He dropped his head to her shoulder and whispered her name, softly, reverently, like a prayer. Finally they both collapsed, sated and spent, in each others arms.

As Aislinn's heart returned slowly to a normal rhythm and her satisfied body slipped gratefully toward sleep, a single thought, shiny and bright as a new coin, dropped into her exhausted brain and put a sleepy smile on her face. It had been *her* name he'd whispered tonight in the midst of his passion. *Her* name. For the very first time.

*****

Sleep did not find Gavin as easily. He lay awake for a long while, studying her face in the moonlight and brooding. She'd looked beautiful at dinner tonight, idly rolling her glass between her hands as they talked; the whiskey casting amber colored shadows against the table linens as she explained all the ways in which having a soul might aid her. She'd leaned forward earnestly as she made her case, speaking with all the persuasive passion she possessed.

And, all the while, her long, elegant fingers had cradled the glass as lightly as they might have held a frozen soap bubble, or a crystal ball—something rare and magical. As magical as she herself could be. He'd found himself staring at the glass, unable to look away; thinking of all the ways in which she and it were similar. Both were things of beauty, shiny and bright, fit for a palace; divinely inspired creations of earth and fire and breath commingled.

Both were delicate yet strong; durable unless they were handled carelessly or callously. Or cruelly. Fragile enough that, if they were treated without the respect their beauty and refined natures deserved, they would not just chip or crack, they'd shatter. Irreparably. As had nearly happened to her today in the forge. As could happen again—at any time—if the threat against her could not be finally and definitively eliminated.

She'd caught him off guard when she'd asked for his soul and even though it was clear from all she'd said that she thought it the perfect solution, at the time, he could think of nothing to say. He still could not. What answer could he give her that he would not end up regretting?

However much he might wish to oblige her, to atone for the hurt he'd caused or repay her for all she'd given him, how could he honor such an impossible request? He had nothing to gain from such an exchange, and everything to lose.

With a soul, Aislinn need no longer answer to anyone. Endowed with free will, she could choose to disregard the *geis* by which her sister had all but given her to Tiernan. She could refuse Tiernan, and by extension her sister, without repercussion. She could refuse anyone. Even him—though she'd been far too careful to mention that last fact.

And, even if she were to marry Gavin—in gratitude for the gift of his soul, perhaps—what of it? She'd need be no more faithful to her vows than any human spouse. She might choose to leave him at any time and for any reason. Or for no reason at all.

Without a soul, on the other hand, she'd be forced to

remain as she was: At his mercy. His to command. Bound by the iron that kept her imprisoned here. Bound by the promises he'd wrung from her today, at the point of death, and by her own words last winter. Bound by the *geasa* that still threatened her existence. And, perhaps most of all, bound by her abiding fear of being imprisoned in Annwn.

The fact that fear was his greatest ally in this war to keep her was a source of great shame to Gavin. He knew that a good man, one who was generous, chivalrous, disinterested, would be willing to aid her—without hope of recompense— not just in evading her enemies, but in defeating them, once and for all. Such a man would be willing to let her go, if need be, and if it was what she truly wanted; or even give up his life for her. But Gavin doubted he had ever been that good in his life, and he had no wish at all to be that man.

Chapter Ten

So then it was Spring. For the life of him, Gavin could not recall a more beautiful season—nor a more poignant one, nor one which seemed to pass more swiftly. Not a single day went by that he failed to notice how blue the sky was, or how soft the breeze. Or without his taking note of a new flower just coming into bloom or some other sign of new life—from the spring lambs grazing on the nearby hills to the birds nesting in his eaves.

But, although he was an altogether happier man than he'd been in years, there was still one thing spoiling his enjoyment of the season, one trouble weighing ever more heavily on his spirit, one issue he must all too soon resolve: what should he do about Aislinn's request?

As had quickly become apparent, there was no room for compromise in either of their positions, and it seemed no amount of discussion was ever going to change that.

"So, is it your plan to simply keep me here then?" she'd griped, as they lay in bed just the night before.

Gavin groaned inwardly, exasperated as much by her decision to resume the argument at all as he was by her timing. *Damn it, why now?* He'd been feeling pleasantly relaxed. In fact, he'd just been contemplating the various ways in which he might pleasure her, in an attempt at improving her mood and making up for the sullen silence he'd maintained throughout dinner—in an obviously futile effort to forestall any more discussion of the topic.

"'Tis clear what *your* plan must be—'tis to talk to me to death! Or why else would ye be covering the same ground over and over again?" Surely they'd both said all there was to say about the subject. The decision was his to make. His alone.

Not that Aislinn seemed to have realized that fact.

"Imprisoned unfairly," she continued, in mournful tones, just as if he hadn't spoken. "Without recourse, without hope, without even the possibility of fruitful discourse—and, until when pray tell? Until such time as Tiernan finally succeeds in tricking you into releasing me to him? Can you really not see the absolute foolishness of such a course?"

"You owe me a wish, Fae," he countered stubbornly, his affectionate mood effectively spoiled. "And you know what it is I'm wanting. Likening your stay here to a term of imprisonment does naught to persuade me to give ye the means by which ye might end your torment and leave. As for Tiernan, and your own folk as well, I'm thinking 'tis in your own best interest to make *sure* I am not tricked by either of them. Nor do I consider my treatment of you to be in any way unfair, if you must know. After all, is it not the same kind of dealings your people and mine have always had with one another?"

"Aye." She glared at him disdainfully. "It is indeed. 'Tis *exactly* the sort of short-sighted, heavy-handed selfishness I'd expect of most mortals. 'Tis the very reason my people have almost no dealings with your kind, as a rule, and even less use for them."

"Oh? No use, do you say? And yet, 'twas not I who came to you last Winter begging for shelter, now was it?"

"A regrettable necessity." Aislinn eyed him for a moment, her grim expression gradually softening as she finally entreated, "But, come, why must we fight one another on this? You claim you want to marry me, do you not? Well, what of that, then? Is it not common, among your kind, for a man to wish to join his soul with the woman he weds?"

"Perhaps, in most cases," Gavin replied grudgingly, angry with her for putting him on the spot. For, certainly, this was *not* like most cases—and he was sure he'd never said *anything* to her to suggest it was. If he wanted her merely as a convenient substitute for Mairead; someone he might wed and bed without completely breaking his promise to his late wife, then, no, what need had he for to be giving away any part of his soul?

And, if that wasn't the case? If he wanted Aislinn for herself alone? *Then, may God have mercy on my foolish soul.*

No, he wouldn't even contemplate the idea that such could be the case. For a man to have those sorts of feelings for one of the Gentry could only lead to disaster and he refused to believe he could be that stupid.

"If I were to give you my soul, what assurance do I have that you'll not go back on your word?" he asked. "What guarantee are you willing to give me that you'll abide by your promise to live as my wife and ne'er return to your own home, or resume your own true form, until after I've been laid to rest?"

"You know I cannot, in truth, offer any such assurances," she answered, reluctantly. "As I have told you already. Since I've never before been faced with either the choice or the ability to renege on a vow, how can I know how I'll react when I do? But, surely, the same could be said for any human with whom you'd wed. Such was the case with your first wife, was it not? And yet that did not stop you from marrying her."

"Only because I was in love," he replied without thinking—silently cursing himself, and her as well, when her eyes widened in hurt surprise just before her expression iced over.

"Ah. Of course," Aislinn murmured, in dangerously silky tones. "A thousand pardons, sir. I pray thee will forgive me my foolishness. I should ne'er have presumed you might have similar reasons for wishing to marry me."

Gavin rolled his eyes toward the ceiling, mentally counting to ten while Aislinn, with a sulky sigh, turned onto her side and gave him her back. What he should have said, he supposed, was that he'd been young and foolish and it had never occurred to him that his wife might not reciprocate his feelings.

He knew better now. And, if ever he were to be giving his heart away again—not to mention his soul—he'd be damned certain it would not be torn to pieces and trod upon, but received with gladness. Viewed by its recipient as something of value, something worthwhile; a gift to be cherished, or even treasured.

"I use no words lightly, mortal, and if I call you my treasure, you may be certain 'tis how I regard you."

Aislinn's words, spoken weeks earlier, returned to haunt him and guilt struck at his conscience. Fae or not, perhaps he should be more trusting of her, and not hold her accountable for another woman's failings. "'Twas not what I meant, exactly," he muttered, awkwardly patting her shoulder by way of apology. Aislinn jerked away from his hand, her breathing hard and irregular—as though she were about to burst into tears. "Now, don't be crying, lass, for sure and you know I never meant to hurt your feelings."

"Crying?" Aislinn repeated, her voice low and vehement, throbbing with so much spirit, pride and anger that Gavin couldn't help but grin. "Pray, do not speak any more foolishness, mortal, if you can at all help it. Wondrous rare would it be for a Fae to be crying, especially over something as staggeringly insignificant as the childish prattling of one such as yourself."

"Oh, is that a fact?" He slid a hand around her waist and pulled her close; until his shaft was pressed snug against the seam of her butt, exactly where he wanted to be. "And how rare is it, then?" he asked, as his hand dipped lower. "Is it as rare as a blush, perchance?"

Still frowning, Aislinn craned her neck around and gazed up at him curiously. "What nonsense is this? Are you suggesting I'm blushing now, too?"

"Nay, not at the moment. I was just reminding you of the fact that I've made you blush more than once already, and I can do so again, if I choose to. Perhaps you'd like for me to show you what I'm meaning?"

For another instant she stared at him, her expression one of almost pained surprise. Finally, "How very like a man," she muttered, shaking her head in disgust. "Hard it may be for's not every problem between a man and a woman that can be resolved by fornication."

"Not resolved perhaps, no," he agreed. "But, all the

same, it's certain I am that we'd both of us be feeling much better if we were to indulge in a bit of it."

"Is that really all you can think about?" she asked in the instant before her gaze turned crafty and a carnal smile curled her lips. "But, aye, I can see that it is. And, so, if such is the case, and that's truly all you're wanting from me, then why can we not come to an agreement now and put an end to all the arguing? With or without free will, I know myself well enough I can easily swear to share your bed on a regular basis for as long as you wish it. Surely I've given you no reason to doubt my sincerity in this regard, at least. And, if you're willing, I would gladly enter into such an agreement with you in exchange for your soul. Do we have a bargain then?"

Gavin stared at her horrified, cold dread running through his veins. Her argument made sense and, surely, a promise such as she was offering should be sufficient for him. Why, then, did it leave him feeling empty, disappointed, bereft?

'Twas a trick of some sort. Sure and it had to be, for the alternative—that he wanted her for more reasons than he was willing to admit to—was unacceptable. "Is it a fool you think me?" he growled in response, hiding his dismay behind an angry scowl. "Is the loss of half my soul not enough for ye then? Must you tempt me into losing all of it by sleeping with ye out of wedlock? I don't even know why it is we're having this discussion at all. Sure and I must be daft for ever entertaining the subject! I saved your life last winter, you bloody ingrate, and this is how you think to repay me? By stealing my soul? How very like a fae!"

Aislinn's eyes narrowed. For another instant she stared at him, her expression inscrutable. Then she shook her head and turned her back upon him once again. "Oh, go to sleep now, you benighted fool of a man, and bother me no more. Sure and there's no use reasoning with you. Why couldn't you have let me die when I was injured? For I'd have been content to go then and I'm sure it would have been

161

kinder than whatever else the future has in store for me."

"Doona say such things," he protested weakly. "Of course I wouldn't have let you die. How could you think it? And, as for the rest...it doesn't have to be that way, you know."

She snorted angrily. "Oh, indeed, I'm thinking it does. And, from this moment on, I'm washing my hands of it. Whatever will be, will be and if it's endless winter for all the world you're wishing to create, then so be it. I've done what I could to stop it but 'tis on your head now, Gavin O'Malley. Sure and I should have listened to Eoghan in the first place. The bloody druid must have been fekkin' mad to have sent me to you."

"Well, I've been telling you that from the start," Gavin couldn't help but point out. "Have I not?"

"Aye. So you have. And the shame of it is 'tis the only thing you've ever said to me that made sense, or I might otherwise have heeded it sooner."

Gavin gazed at her helplessly, unable to think of a single thing to say in response. He was angry, frustrated, unhappy, twice as miserable as before. After a moment, he reached for her, once again, and pulled her back against him. She resisted, at first, jabbing her elbow into his ribs and kicking at his shins but he bore it uncomplaining and refused to let her go. Eventually she gave up and lay still and he held her, not knowing what else to do, until finally they both fell asleep.

*****

The weeks continued to pass and it seemed to Gavin that if only time were not rushing away from him, as it was, he might find the time to think rationally about the matter. But time did not stop and rationality was nowhere to be found, and all too soon it was summer.

All at once, the roses were in bloom and the constant chirping of baby birds begging for their next meal had been replaced by the lazy drone of bees foraging among the flowers. The branches of the apple tree, which had long since

Iron

lost their blossoms, were bent now under the weight of green
fruit and the warm, sweet scent of clover greeted Gavin
whenever he stepped foot out of doors.

But the changes to the landscape were insignificant
next to the alteration the season had wrought in Aislinn's
appearance. She was even lovelier now than she'd been when
first he saw her. Though how that was possible he didn't
rightly know, for she'd seemed then to be the most beautiful
woman he'd ever laid eyes on. Now, however, her cheeks
were rosy and flushed—even though she'd not set foot
outside since that day he'd dragged her to the forge—and
there was a new lushness to her body that held him utterly
transfixed. It was as though she embodied summer; as though
the season itself radiated from her, charging the atmosphere
around her until Gavin would have sworn he was living
within a sun-drenched glen, or a palace of sorts; anything
other than an ordinary cottage.

But, that was just by day. At night, her presence
infused his rooms with all the warm, wild glory of a sultry,
star-studded night—and she the brightest star of all—until
the mere sight of her, lying beside him in bed, left Gavin
awe-struck and dazzled, too hesitant to even touch her.

"You've a peculiar look about you," she observed, on
one such night, her brow puckering slightly as she studied his
face. "Is aught wrong with ye?"

He started to shake his head no, and then changed his
mind. "Aye," he answered, struggling for words. "Perhaps.
Or, nay, now I think on it. 'Tis you. 'Tis everything about
you...do you know how beautiful you are?"

An amused smile curled one corner of her mouth. "I
do, aye, for 'tis summer, is it not? Do you not recall my
saying you knew naught of my true nature, having never seen
me at this time of year?" She cast back the covers so there
was nothing hiding her from his sight and stretched
languidly. "So, Gavin O'Malley, do you like what you see?
Does it please you? What is it you feel when you look at me?
Tell me. For 'tis been a long time since I've been admired by

163

a man who was seeing me thus for the first time."

Gavin's eyes roved greedily, taking it all in. But his thoughts were a muddle and, "How do I feel?" Ah, if only he knew the answer to that. He felt...distracted, conflicted, confused, humbled and, "Fearful," he replied at last.

"Fearful, are ye?" A silvery laugh broke free from Aislinn's lips and swept through Gavin, brightening his spirit like a sudden shower after a dusty day. "And what is it you're afraid of then, my darling one? Surely not of me?"

He nodded, still reeling from the effects of her laugh. "Aye, of you, indeed. Mortally afraid, I be."

"You silly man," she murmured, circling her arms around his neck and grinning up at him. "And why, pray tell? Dost thou think I would ever hurt you?"

Gavin sighed. Reaching a hand to her head, he fingered a strand of her hair, which still gleamed gold, even in the starlight. "Lass, I think you could very well destroy me. And I think you know it, too." He shook his head. "I'm a simple man, Aislinn, whereas you..."

"Are not so simple?" she supplied helpfully, as her smile dimmed and turned mocking.

"Not even a little bit."

"Perhaps not. But, I didn't ask for it to be thus, you know. Besides, *mo chroí,*" she murmured wickedly, her smile returning as she rubbed her mound against him. "I've always been one who's enjoyed the simple things life has to offer."

"Have you now?" He took hold of her hips and pulled her against him, letting her feel the growing length of his shaft, enjoying the smoky look it brought to her eyes, the slight hitch in her breathing. Fearful or not, he planned to take full advantage of all that she offered; for he was a man, after all, and she was a risk well worth the taking. "And would I be one of those simple things to which you're referring, then?"

"Oh, you are indeed, *mo chroí,*" she breathed delightedly. "Without a doubt."

*****

But stunning though her beauty was, it was marred occasionally by a certain look that appeared in her eyes, at times—such as when she gazed through the window, or out the open door, at the world beyond. It was a look that was at once haunted and hungry, frightened and forlorn. It tore at Gavin's heart to see her thus but, whenever he tried to ask her about it, she shrugged it off.

"'Tis nothing of consequence," she told him. "Pray do not concern yourself about it."

And, indeed, with so much else on his mind, he found it easy enough to ignore. For he was also, and more pressingly, aware of a growing sense of urgency, a feeling that time was running out on him. With every day that passed, the thought of losing her became progressively more painful to contemplate. And, yet, the alternative—the idea of keeping her here against her wishes, of staying the course, holding to his plan and risking her life in the process— seemed even worse.

If his soul was not already damned due to all the wrongs he'd committed, all the promises he'd broken, he knew it surely would be lost, utterly and forever, if he failed in his efforts to protect her. He'd die a thousand times over if her kinsfolk were to somehow spirit her away to her death. Or, Heaven forbid, if her worst fears were realized and she was taken, instead, by Tiernan.

For weeks, he tried to close his eyes to the grim reality. But, finally, the day arrived when he could no longer deny what had probably been true from the start. He loved her, God help him, and he wanted to marry her for no other reason than that. Not as a stand-in for Mairead or a convenient means to get what he wanted. Not in the now forlorn hope of possibly finessing a place for himself in Heaven. Not even for the sake of satisfying his lustful cravings.

The knowledge left him feeling both elated and—just as he'd predicted—destroyed. For though he'd never loved this way before, nor likely ever would again, he knew she'd never return his feelings; not in the way he wished she might, for she'd assured him only humans ever loved in such a fashion. But even that no longer seemed to matter. Her safety and well-being were of paramount importance to him now, his own needs came in a poor, distant second. And, that being the case, there was really only one thing for him to do...

"I must be off to town today," he told her at breakfast one morning just a couple of days before the solstice. "Will you be all right on your own then? I'll be back before it's time for supper."

Aislinn transferred her gaze to his face and left off fingering the petals of the roses that stood in a bowl in the center of the table. He'd picked them for her the day before, in the hope they might brighten her spirits, for she'd seemed, in the past few days, even more withdrawn than usual. "Where is it you're going?"

"To town," he repeated patiently, as he finished his tea. "There's people I must see and...and stops I must make along the way."

"And you'll be back when? In time for supper, is it?"

"Aye. 'Tis what I said. Why, were you going to cook for me then?"

Though he smiled as he said it, the idea was not as unimaginable as it once had been. In an effort to make the idea of living for years as the wife of a blacksmith more palatable to her, he'd been helping her find her way around the kitchen. Aided by the purchase of various, odd utensils such as covered earthenware dishes and wooden spoons and a tin rack for toasting bread, she could now fix a decent meal for herself without fear of injury.

Aislinn returned his smile with a wan one of her own. "Aye, perhaps. Would that please you?"

"It would indeed," he replied. "Very much, in fact." And, rising to his feet, he went 'round the table and kissed her. Her lips were sweet, soft, succulent, tasting faintly of the berries she'd been eating. And when she wrapped her arms around his neck and kissed him back it was all he could do to keep from sweeping the dishes from the table and laying her right there upon the worn wooden surface, amid the scattered petals. She'd look glorious with her hair fanned out across the boards, and even better when he'd removed her clothes...but he'd never get to town today if he started in with that; so, reluctantly, he pulled away from her.

"Ah, Aislinn," he sighed. "What a distraction you are. I'm like to forget all my business when you kiss me and spend the day here with you, instead, making love 'til we're both too weak to move."

Her eyes were dark with heat. Her chest rose and fell rapidly, the swells of her breasts threatening to spill over the top of her gown with each breath she took. "Then perhaps you should do so," she purred huskily. "Whatever this business is, it cannot be so important as all that. Sure and it can wait 'til tomorrow, can it not?"

Gavin sighed. "Nay, I've put it off long enough. But, important as it is, my darling girl, 'tis not near as important as coming home to you. So, kiss me once more, quickly, and then let me go. For, the sooner I'm gone, the sooner I'll be back again."

She lifted her face willingly and kissed him far too briefly, just as he'd asked her to, and yet it was still a struggle to leave her. He forced himself to do so, however, turning away and striding across the room, not daring to look back at her even once for fear he'd confess to everything he had planned.

*****

Aislinn remained where she was, after Gavin left; seated at the table, listening to the sound of his footsteps fading into the distance. And trying her best to ignore the other sounds—the summer sounds—the ones that called to her so insistently

"Come out. Come join us!" they seemed to say, as much an assault on her senses as Winter had been, albeit in a very different way.

Propping her elbow on the table, she rested her cheek

on one hand and resumed her contemplation of the roses, finding comfort in their warm, sun-steeped presence. Just stroking their petals was enough to ease the craving, the pressure, the endless longing for home. *Home.* She shivered, now, at the thought that, in the past few weeks, had become both a temptation and a torment.

She'd known the exact moment the gates to the Summerland had opened for her; she'd felt the singing in her mind—nay, in her very veins. *"Come out. Come join us. Come home, darling Aislinn. Come back to us, now!"*

It was a familiar voice and a beloved one; a voice she could not disobey. It was the voice of her sister bending all her will toward finding her. But, though it continued night and day, not even the dulcet tones of the Summer Queen could compel her wayward subject to pass through iron wards.

Even though it pained her to be stuck inside *any* four walls when the summer sun was shining, Aislinn was grateful for the protection of her iron cage; for the druid's forethought in sending her here; even for Gavin's stubborn intractability. For they were all that stood between her and certain death.

No matter how sweet the words, Aislinn was in no danger of mistaking her sister's meaning. She was being summoned home, ordered to return without delay, and it was clear no joyful reunion awaited her. All she'd meet with there was doom, a lonely prison cell, a final fading from existence.

Bile rose up her throat at the thought of it and her stomach churned with sudden panic. She was almost overwhelmed by her feelings of loss, betrayal, fear. Unexpectedly, it was thoughts of Gavin that steadied her. No matter how selfish his reasons were for wanting her—and no matter how foolhardy she thought him, how blind to the danger in which he was placing them both, how unlikely he was to succeed—it was still nice to know her life held some value for someone.

And, perhaps...perhaps it *was* worth chancing the odds to stay here awhile longer. Another year, perhaps. Or five. Or ten. Or—

"Milady Aislinn! Are you within?" another familiar voice hailed her from outside the cottage.

"Eoghan?" Startled, Aislinn rose from the table, ran to the window and peered outside. A delighted smile spread across her face at the sight of the spriggan's homely visage. It is you! 'Tis good to see you, my friend. But, whatever are you doing here?"

Eoghan frowned, his gaze taking a wary measure of the cottage's walls as he answered, "The Summer Queen did bid me seek you out and escort you home, milady. Will you not come out?"

Aislinn sighed. Eoghan's refusal to make eye contact had shattered her happiness at seeing him, even as it laid to rest any last, lingering hopes she might have had about her sister's intentions. "Pray convey my regrets to Her Majesty," she murmured dryly. "As well as my thanks for the kind offer of your services. But, in truth, I find myself unavoidably delayed, at present, and am therefore unable to comply with her request."

"So," Eoghan growled, his face darkening as he met her eyes for the first time. "'Tis as I warned you last December, then? 'Tis imprisoned you are?"

Aislinn's heart rebelled at the assumption—and at the thought of assigning Gavin the label of jailer. The reality was, and despite having made similar suggestions to Gavin herself, in truth, she did not feel herself imprisoned—not when she was where she wanted to be. Still, honestly bade her answer. "Aye. In a manner of speaking, that I am."

Eoghan nodded grimly. "Hmph. I thought as much. But, be easy, milady. 'Twill not be for much longer. When does the smith return?"

"Before nightfall." Doubt assailed her as she studied the spriggan's expression. "Why? What is it you intend on doing?"

"I'm to dispatch him, of course." Eoghan answered calmly, throwing back his cloak to reveal the sword belted at his waist. "What else would you expect?"

"Eoghan—Nay!" Aislinn struggled for breath as bile threatened to choke her once again. "You, you cannot. I forbid it!"

Eoghan's eyebrows rose. "*You* forbid it? Is it, then, as the Queen has feared? Has your mind been changed since last we spoke? Would you seek to challenge her supremacy then? Or is it that you've chosen to ally yourself with Annwn, after all?"

"In a desperate attempt to preserve my imperiled?" She shook her head. "Nay, of course I would not—even then. Surely, you know me better than to think such things. 'Tis merely that my confinement here has naught to do with that. 'Tis the result of a private matter that has arisen between the smith and I—nothing more sinister than that—and he does not deserve to die because of it. If my sister thinks otherwise, she is mistaken," she added bitterly. "'Twould not be the first time. But though I shall not shirk my responsibility to my people, no matter what the cost to myself, I *will* bear that cost alone. Gavin O'Malley has done naught to threaten the Queen or the realm. He has offered me shelter and friendship—aye, and protection from Tiernan, too, when none of my own people could do so. Are we become like the *Sluagh Sidhe* now, who repay those who assist them with betrayal? He will *not* suffer harm on my account."

"'Tis the Queen's command that I see you safely home without delay," Eoghan answered stubbornly. "If the blacksmith would interfere with her wishes, what am I to do?"

Aislinn snorted angrily. "Oh, aye, my sister's concern for my safety is quite touching, indeed. But, who is she to command *you*? The Spriggans are a sovereign people, are they not? Or so they were, ere last I heard, and not under the sway of either court. Have things changed that much since I've been gone?"

"Naught has changed," he replied. "'Tis always been our honor to serve as bodyguards to both the *Seelie* and

Unseelie, as you will well remember. Yet, ne'er before have you thought to question my loyalty to those I choose to serve."

"And I am not doing so now, my friend. But, tell me, have ye not asked yourself who it is I could possibly need to be guarded from at this time of year? For, other than the Summer Queen herself, who among the fae is stronger than I am right now?"

Eoghan sighed. "I know only what I am told, milady. But, as you yourself have observed, we know each other well, you and I. Your sister has been requesting your presence most urgently these past weeks and yet you have not responded to her summons. So, what am I to think? Were it not for this mortal delaying ye, would you not have returned to the realm by now?"

"Aye," Aislinn answered grudgingly. "Indeed I would, as I would have had no other choice."

"Then, despite what you claim, I judge him to be a threat, possibly even an agent for Annwn. Perhaps he's intending to ransom you off to the highest bidder. But, whatever the case, if even your own *glamoury* is not sufficient for the task then I know of no better way of convincing him to let you go than with the point of my sword."

"Eoghan, nay, 'tis not at all what you think. Indeed, he knows naught of the Queen's request, for I have hidden the matter from him. Give me the chance to talk to him, I pray thee. An I convince him to release me, you will have no need to kill him. Please, Eoghan," she begged when the spriggan hesitated. "For the sake of our long friendship, will you not grant me this one request?"

Eoghan gazed at her sadly, his expression pained. "Milady..."

Aislinn set her teeth. "Enough. I have no wish to harm you, spriggan," she said, as she drew herself erect. "And I know you cannot wish to fight me now. Do as I ask and I promise that, as soon as I am released, I will return with you to the realm—and offer no resistance along the way."

Even through the window, she knew he felt the force of her vow. He nodded slowly. "Very well, then. I can give you one day. But no more than that. If you are not set free by tomorrow morning, I'll have no choice but to remove the impeding factor. And, if that means a fight between us...then so be it."

Eoghan's grim expression left Aislinn with no doubt as to how little he liked the prospect. She was not surprised. They both knew what the outcome of such a fight, waged now, must be. It was unlikely he would survive it. Still, "Promise me he'll not be harmed," she insisted, unwilling to take any chances.

He nodded again, his look reproachful; for theirs was, indeed, a long friendship and had never before required such solemn assurances. "Aye, Lady, I do so swear. But, 'tis as I've said. I can promise only to stay my hand for a day—no longer."

Relieved, Aislinn sagged against the window frame, almost too weak to stand. "I understand and I trust it will be long enough. Thank you, Eoghan. *Go raibh míle maith agat.*"

"*Tá fáilte romhat,*" he responded with a shrug then added, softly, "*Tá brón orm, mo chara.*"

She nodded sadly. "Aye, my friend. I, too, am sorry." Then, raising a hand in farewell, she turned from the window to gaze at the room around her. It was a bitter irony to realize, now, how happy she could have been here—for the year, or five, or ten she'd been imagining—if only things had been different. Although, of course, if things had been totally different, she supposed, she never would have come here in the first place.

It was almost laughable, that her greatest sorrow could have held the seeds for what might have been her greatest joy. The shame of it was there was no one with whom she might share the joke.

She just hoped Gavin would be reasonable. For, surely, when he said he wished her to stay for the rest of his life, he hadn't intended on his life ending quite so soon!

There was still one gift she could give him. One final night in his bed and the supper she'd promised to cook for him. And, while it wasn't nearly as much as either of them would have liked, it was all they'd have and so, it would have to do.

*****

"I'll be needing to get myself back to the forge soon, Father," Gavin observed with a weary sigh, rolling his eyes at the faint sounds that emanated from the other side of the confessional's wooden screen. It wasn't hard to decipher what they were. The old priest's muttered prayers. The rattle of his rosary beads as he crossed himself again and again. The slight pause, each time, as he pressed the crucifix to his lips. "Can you not leave off kissing the blessed cross 'til later, and absolve me now?"

He'd just finished confessing his sins—all the masses he'd missed, the impure thoughts and deeds, the breaking of his solemn promise to his dead wife, his wish to marry Aislinn.

It was hard to say which had shocked the good father more. "Absolve you?" he gasped. "You're consorting with the devil—or with a demon, at least. For, so she must be an she's looking for to steal your soul. Is it forgiveness you're wanting? Then, first, you'll have to foreswear your sinful ways. Do you do so?"

Gavin squirmed uncomfortably for there was no way he could answer in the affirmative. "She's not a demon, Father; you can be very sure of that. And 'tis just a small piece of my soul she's wanting. Is it not the very same as happens when a child is born—for how else do we come by them, then?" he asked, repeating Aislinn's suggestion, for it made as much sense as anything he could think of.

"I do not have the answer to such a question," Father Cullen replied. "Such a mystery 'tis best left to God, Himself."

"Well, then, you can't rightly call it a sin, now can

173

ye? But, I am most heartily sorry for having broken my promise to Mairead—and twice as sorry that I ever gave it to her in the first place. And I never was meaning to miss Mass, you know. But, as for the others...if ye cannot absolve me, will you not marry us? For then, 'twill be my own wife with whom I'd have been sinning and I have your word for it since last December that 'twould not even be a sin, if that were the case."

"Aye, if your wife were a good Catholic woman, it wouldn't be. But you're talking about wedding some soulless, demonic, heathen...*creature*. 'Tis unnatural, my son, surely you can see that? Why, I'd as soon marry you to my horse."

"Careful, Father," Gavin growled. "Or I'll be forgetting you're a priest. 'Tis my future wife of whom you're speaking and I'll not have her referred to in that manner—not even by the likes of you. And, nay, it does not seem unnatural to me at all. Nor would it to you, an you'd met her, I'll wager. For she's a Fae, Father, and a more beautiful creature you never did see. And though she may not be a human—not as you or I may be—it's certain she's no sort of animal, either."

"Oh, she's a fae, is she?" Father Cullen sighed. "Ah, sure and you've gone mad, my boy. 'Tis children's faery tales you're speaking of now. I did hear you'd been taken ill and a high fever can easily addle a brain. Why don't you go round and see the doctor?"

"I've seen Doctor Butler," Gavin said, smiling broadly as he thought about it. "And, if anyone's gone mad, it's him. Or haven't you heard? The man thinks he's hearing nightingales, right here in Kilbanning. Perhaps, I should bring my lass 'round to meet you? Methinks, once you hear her sing, you'll be thinking she's an angel."

"Aye, bring her around then, if she'll even consent to step foot inside a church. I'll sprinkle holy water on her and we'll see, then, whether or not she's a demon. An she survives those tests and agrees to be baptized, I'll withdraw

my objections and marry you on the spot."
*****

So, he had the priest's blessing. Gavin considered the matter while sipping a pint at his usual, dark, quiet table, at the back of The Starry Plough. He was now one step closer to making Aislinn his wife—assuming she'd even agree to marry him. Though they'd discussed the matter, she'd never really said she would. She'd only ever mentioned it as a possible means of getting her hands on his soul. Which, if Father Cullen was correct, was not even necessary. In the priest's learned opinion, all that was required was for Gavin to agree to give up his soul for the deed to be done. And, if that was true? Then, he supposed, it was a damn good thing Aislinn didn't know it. Otherwise, she might already have left, since he was quite certain he'd given up both his heart and soul to her already. Small wonder, then, he was so ready to surrender his freedom to her, as well. Except...he really wasn't ready, was he?

Finishing his pint, he called for a second and passed the time until the drink arrived considering the sorry state of his nerves. He was as jumpy as an unshod horse this afternoon. Far more nervous than he'd been in the days before he'd asked for Mairead's hand, which struck him as exceedingly strange. After all, this time there were no dour parents to convince of his worthiness, no future in-laws whispering speculations as they sized him up, no womanly mysteries to descry, no dark imaginings to trouble his sleep or all consuming worries about the marriage bed. There were no worries at all about that part, now that he thought on it, only joyful anticipation of the bliss to come. And yet...

Perhaps the difference lay in the fact that he'd never doubted that Mairead wanted to marry him. Whereas with Aislinn...would she even have him? Or would she take his soul and leave him, damned and desperate, to a lonely life of longing and regret?

He swallowed half his second pint in the time it took him to contemplate the bleak future he might be looking forward to. But, ah, well, he thought at last, the past was pretty bleak too. What worse could the future hold? At least he'd have the solace of knowing she was still alive. At least he could console himself with the thought he'd done the right thing by her. Though not nearly as satisfying as 'twould be to have and to hold her for the rest of his life.

The rest of the pint disappeared while he fantasized about a repentant Aislinn returning to him, years from now, in trouble once again and needing his assistance. Perhaps he'd help her. Perhaps he'd turn her away. Or, maybe he'd be dead already when she returned and, too late, she'd realize her loss and then spend the rest of *her* long life regretting him. Gavin wasn't sure which version he liked best— probably the version where she never left in the first place.

Over the third pint, he mulled the question of soul loss. Would his soul ever grow back, as Aislinn had suggested, or would it be forever stunted? Would he be left with so little that, in the end, both Heaven and Hell would refuse him when he died? Not that he was still holding much hope he'd ever see Heaven now, himself. But...could Aislinn's part of his soul ever be damned to Hell? Was he giving her something that would save her life now, only to cause her eternal suffering? And, what would occur when they'd both, at long last died? Would the two halves of his soul ever re-unite, somewhere on the other side of the grave? Could he and Aislinn ever be together—whether in Heaven or Hell—for eternity? Or was this life all they could ever hope to share?

By the time he'd drained his glass again, he was no closer to answering any of his questions and only marginally less nervous. No, on second thought, he was maybe more nervous than he'd been before, he thought; for he'd somehow managed to put the entire day behind him and now...now he had no choice but to head home and take his chances.

Chapter Eleven

The day was passing. Long shadows stretched across the empty road. Frustrated, Aislinn turned away from the window, her glance falling on the fireplace where the supper she'd so painstakingly fixed awaited Gavin's return. It would be a miracle if it wasn't ruined by the time he got back. Where was he? She'd expected him hours ago. What business could he have had that would take this long to complete?

Bending over the hearth, she rearranged the dishes in an attempt to salvage what she could—moving those that looked in danger of burning up or drying out away from the heat, and pushing those that were growing cold closer to the coals. Straightening, her eyes went back to the window.

The road was still empty. Where was he?

Not knowing what else to do, she began to pace; anxiously crossing and re-crossing the room, feeling, for the very first time, as though she really were caged. What if he'd been delayed in town and didn't come back 'til morning? She'd have no time to talk to him, no time to reason with him. No chance to save him. What if he'd been hurt, somehow? Or what if something else had gone wrong?

The thought stopped her. Like what, pray tell? What else could have possibly gone wrong? But, she had no answer for that. She knew precious little about his life outside of the forge and, until today, she'd felt no need to know anything more—what did it have to do with her, after all? Now, however, she wanted to know everything. Like, did he have friends he could have gone to see? Or family, perhaps? Might one of them have needed his help?

Passing the looking glass, she paused to assess her reflection and practically groaned in dismay at what she saw there; her cheeks flushed from the unaccustomed labor, her hair escaping the clasp in which she'd secured it, her gown liberally splattered with flour despite the care she'd tried to

177

take. She'd wanted to look especially nice for him, instead, she barely recognized herself.

Impatiently, she shook out her skirts and patted her hair back into place, in hopes of repairing some of the damage. Not that it would matter what she looked like, if he failed to appear! Damn it, what could be keeping the man? Perhaps he was dead. It seemed as plausible as anything else. In fact, she could hardly imagine his missing his evening meal for any lesser cause. But, no, of course he wasn't dead. For, who would be looking to end his life other than Eoghan; and he had sworn the smith would remain unharmed...

Or had he? Heart clenching, Aislinn recalled Eoghan's exact words to her, examining them with the care she should have given them earlier. He'd promised to stay his hand for a day. His hand, yes, but, what if there were others? What if her sister had sent an army to escort her home?

"'Twould make sense," Aislinn muttered in grudging respect. It would make a great deal more sense, now that she thought of it, than to have sent a single spriggan to do the job. "For, sure and it would take an army to subdue me, had I truly intended to stand and fight. But, oh, Eoghan, my friend, would ye really deceive me in such a manner? Would you be that cruel?"

Only, she knew he wouldn't have thought of it as cruelty. He would have counted it as a kindness, not telling her truths she hadn't asked to hear and, likely, didn't want to know. And, considering how soon her own life might be over, he could have hoped she would never have to learn of his betrayal; that she'd go to her death happy in the belief that Gavin was alive and well, having merely tarried too long at the pub, perhaps.

Hands shaking, she pulled out a chair and sank into it. She felt as though her legs would buckle under the weight of all these unaccustomed emotions—for what had she ever known of grief, and fear and loss before this past year?

It made her heart ache in a manner she'd never before experienced to think that Gavin might be dead—even now, as she sat here, trapped, awaiting his return. Or, even worse, perhaps, that he was lying mortally wounded somewhere along the road—alone, unattended—and she unable to go to him. She wanted to cry out in her rage and frustration; give voice to her grief like one of the *bean sidhe* loudly mourning the loss of her lover.

"And if you've truly come to grief because of me, *a chuisle*, then I wish I'd never come here. For sure and I'd rather Tiernan had taken me last winter than for me to be the cause of any harm to ye now."

Again, she raised her eyes to the window, expecting nothing, breath stuttering at the sight of a lone figure, his hands shoved deep into his pockets, making his slow way up the road. *Gavin?* Her grief forgotten, she jumped from her seat and ran to look out. *It is! Ah, by the Sun and the pale Moon, yes!* Relief sluiced through her and she couldn't suppress a smile at the sight of him, meandering along, without a care in the world. And—*hark at the man*—whistling!

She met him at the door, flinging her arms around his neck as soon as he'd stepped foot inside, and pressing her face against his chest; happy to have him back, happy for the way his presence made the summer sounds recede and the unexpected comfort of his embrace. But, in the very next instant, relief gave way to anger; for how dare he so carefree, how dare he be living and breathing and *well*, after causing her hours of grief?

"Wherever have you been?" she demanded as she pulled away from him, barely controlling the urge to slap him.

Gavin's brows rose. "I've been just where I said I was going. Up to town on business."

"Oh? And what business is it that took you so much longer than you planned on? You did say, did you not, that you'd be home before supper? Well, you weren't and now, 'tis quite ruined it is."

"Did you really cook for me then?" An odd, crooked

179

smile curved his lips as he glanced at the hearth. "Ah, well, I'm sure it's not ruined at all. And, even if it is, since it's you that's made it, I'll eat it no matter what. And gladly tell you it's the best I ever had."

Hands fisted on her hips, she glared at him. "Oh, aye, tell me lies, by all means, for 'tis just what I'm wishing to hear spilling from your mouth after I've spent the bulk of the day working to please you."

"Well, you're fae, are you not?" he asked, blue eyes twinkling. "If it was so important, why'd ye not simply twist time, as your kind is wont to do, and let the meal wait on my return?"

Aislinn stamped her foot in impotent fury. "What game is this now? You know very well why I could not have done so." Eyes narrowing, she sniffed suspiciously. "This business of yours, were you conducting it in a pub, perchance?"

Gavin stared at her, for an instant, his expression unreadable. Then, with a shout of laughter, he grabbed her up and swung her around in a circle. "Good lord, Aislinn, you're already sounding like a wife! 'Tis music to my ears to hear you scold me so. Tell me now, do you mean to be always nagging at me like this?"

Aislinn's fury evaporated with his words and fear almost choked her. For there would be no always for her—and even less for him, if she could not convince him to let her go. "Gavin, put me down."

He did so at once. Setting her on her feet with a flourish and a bow. "Aye, my lady, your wish is my command."

"Don't." Aislinn winced at the title. She hated being reminded they inhabited such different worlds and she felt almost sick at the loss of his touch. She wanted nothing more than to hurl herself back into his arms, confess all her fears and the danger she had placed them both in, and beg him to keep her safe. But to do so would be craven and cowardly and...useless.

At best, she would be setting him up to fail, and to die in her defense. At worst, he would see the impossibility of their plight and deny her. So, instead, she pulled herself together and forced herself to speak calmly. "We must talk."

"Aye, that we must," he answered with a sigh. "But let me get all the way in the door first, if you don't mind."

She stepped back and watched as he strode across the room with quick, impatient steps, his hands clenched into fists. She followed more slowly, wondering at the restless energy he exuded. And, wondering, too, whether it would be better to wait to broach the subject until after he'd eaten. Or perhaps they should skip dinner and go straight to bed. Would he likely be more amenable to suggestion after she'd pleasured him, or would that work against her by making him more loath to let her go?

Before she could reach a decision Gavin swung around, took hold of her arms and pulled her toward the chair in which she'd been seated earlier. "What are you doing?" she asked as he wordlessly urged her to sit.

"Something I probably should have done weeks ago," he admitted, looking nervous and ill at ease as he lowered himself to his knees before her. "I've been selfish, *a muirnín*," he said as he clasped her hands in his. "I've been thinking only of my own wants and needs, and 'tis for all the wrong reasons I've tried to keep you here."

"And what would the right reasons be then?" She gazed at him, perplexed. And, recalling Eoghan's suggestion she added, "What is it you could possibly hope to gain by keeping me here, O'Malley, if it's not to satisfy your own wants and needs?"

"Lass, please." Gavin looked at her pleadingly, his expression pained. "'Tis hard enough as it is, without your asking such foolish questions. Let me get through this first then you can talk."

"Oh, by all means, do go on, then," she replied, trying hard not to be affronted by his suggestion she was being foolish, trying even harder not to be annoyed at having to waste so much of the short, precious time they had left together in cryptic conversation.

"'Tis like this," he said after hesitating briefly. "'Twas wrong of me to ask for so much from you and yet give naught or little in return. I feared losing you, 'tis true, but all the same, 'twas not fitting. 'Tis an important decision and not a prize to be bargained over. Nor would I want to be winning you in such a fashion." He took a deep breath, his grip on her hands tightening, almost to the point of pain. "And so...'tis yours I am, Aislinn, body and soul and whatever else it is you're wanting from me. Will you not marry me, then, and make me a happy man?"

Gavin's last few words didn't even register for a wild, radiant flood of energy had infused Aislinn's being. Up her arms from their clasped hands and straight to her heart it flowed; then outward, until every last cell was saturated. It was joyous and sweet, but there was a darkness to it, as well; a shadow side she'd not expected. It carried the best and worst of life itself, along with every emotion she'd ever heard of: greed and compassion, hatred and hope, passion and pain and fear. And love. Love, most of all.

"Aislinn." Gavin's voice, unexpectedly harsh and unsteady, broke the silence. "Do you think you might be giving me an answer sometime today, lass? I'm dying here."

"An answer?" she repeated, confused, her mind still reeling with the shock. "Was there a question, then?" Had he given her his soul? Was it that made her want to tremble at the mere sound of his voice, or which caused the unbearable swelling of her heart when she did no more than gaze into his eyes? *'Tis no wonder they live such short lives, these mortals*, she thought in astonishment; *sure and they must burn themselves up from the inside out if they feel like this all the time.*

"There was, aye. I asked you to marry me, to live with me here, as God intended, as husband and wife."

"Oh." Aislinn felt her gaze falter. How was it possible to want something so much, she wondered, and yet dread it at the same time? If only it was for herself he wanted her, she'd have said yes at once. But how many times had he told her exactly where her primary value for him lay: in her ability to take the place of his precious Mairead. Suddenly, the idea of being no more than a surrogate bride, of living with him in the guise of another, seemed too hard. How long did he think she could stand such an arrangement? Certainly not the years he expected. Yet, even if she wished to make the attempt, she could not. She'd given her word to Eoghan and she must keep it—if for no other reasons than, if she did not, then he surely would. Gavin's life would be forfeit; and that she could never accept.

*****

The silence stretched out for several seconds and Gavin's hopes died. "You do not seem very taken with the idea," he said at last with a sigh.

Aislinn gazed at him appealingly. "Ah, *mo chroí*, 'tis not that. 'Tis just...I cannot stay here now. For I've given my word and I must return home by morning."

"I might have known," Gavin grumbled as he got to his feet. "And what about your word that was given to me last winter, then?" he asked, moving swiftly away from her, in an attempt to put as much distance between them as he could. "What about your promise that I might have anything I desired? Is that all to be forgotten now?"

She shook her head. "I have forgotten nothing that has passed between us, I assure you. But you've set me free, have you not? Shall I not avail myself of the gift, then? Or would you have it back from me already?"

"Nay," he answered grimly. "Even if that were possible, I'd not go back on my word; for I've yet some honor left to me, thank God. I've given my soul to you, Aislinn, and your freedom along with it. I've given you every blessed thing you've asked of me, in fact. And, while you can do what you will with them now—take them and go, if it's what you're wanting—is it too much to be hoping that you might give *some* thought to the idea of staying here, instead?

Has this all meant nothing to ye, then? Can ye not even give my suit the consideration it deserves?"

"Ah, Gavin, what am I to do?" she asked in helpless tones. "So much has changed. The Queen is demanding my presence in the Summerland even now. And, in truth, I should have been expecting it, for did not the druid warn me that we'd both face danger an I stayed here past midsummer? Tomorrow night is the Solstice and 'tis your life I'll be putting in jeopardy an I do not go before then. 'Tis not a risk I'm willing to take."

He gazed at her resentfully. "I'm a grown man, Aislinn, not a child, that I need you to be making decisions for me. Your own life has been at hazard for as long as I've known you. If I choose to take the same chance with mine, 'tis my own business and no one else's. Not even yours."

"I must go, *mo chroí*," she said, as she stood and moved toward him, stopping only when he stiffened and drew back a step. "'Tis the only way. Nothing else will convince my sister that you are not a threat to her, that you are not holding me against my will, nor seeking to profit from my confinement here. 'Tis through no fault of your own you have been placed in this position, Gavin, but 'tis foolish of you to talk of taking risks that need not be taken. Allow me to rectify the situation, I pray thee. For the sake of my honor, if nothing else. For, to see you come to harm for my sake would be too grievous for me to bear."

At her words, a bitter smile curved Gavin's lips. "I see now how it is. 'Tis *another* favor you're asking for. Shall I then give up what's left of my honor, in exchange for yours and cower here behind my own walls while you brave forth to defend me? 'Tis a lovely thought that. You've quite unmanned me, Fae, I thank thee."

"Ridiculous man," Aislinn groaned. "You know 'twas not my intention to offer ye insult. Nor call your manhood into question. But since you're so insistent on being treated like one, will you not then act like a man, rather than a sulky child, and attempt to see the sense in what I'm telling ye?

'Tis not asking for a favor, I am, but attempting to repay one. You've given me my life back, *mo chroí*. 'Tis a precious gift and one I'm grateful for, beyond measure. And, whether you wish it or not, I *will* do the same for thee, and not suffer you to be killed for the sake of proving to you your importance to me. Now, come, must we have enmity between us on this, our last night together?"

"And why would it be our last night then?" Gavin asked, more stung by her criticism than he wished her to know, trying hard to keep both the desperation and any trace of sulkiness out of his voice. "Other than because you want it to be. For I thought you were free to do as you will now. After you've proven your allegiance to your Queen, and removed the threat against us, why could you not come back again? Unless you do not wish to do so."

"Oh." A cautious smile broke over Aislinn's face; its loveliness tore his heart in two. "Indeed, you're right, and I beg your pardon, for I hadn't thought that far ahead. For too long the threat of imminent death has been looming over me. But, surely, an there's nothing impeding my return I could, indeed, come back to ye, Gavin, *mo chroí*, and gladly would I do so. How could you doubt it? Have I not already said as much?"

"Aye, that you have. But for how long?" he demanded, steeling himself for one more try; and assuring himself he could handle the outcome—whatever it was. "And to what purpose? I want a wife again, Aislinn, and I'm not willing to settle for anything less. You've still not given me an answer to my question. So, I ask ye again, will you have me?"

Pain filled her eyes for an instant, or so it seemed, but it was gone too soon for him to be certain. At last she shrugged and, dropping her gaze, she answered softly, "Perhaps, I might."

Gavin eyed her reproachfully. "'Tis not an answer, that. And if you're thinking to spare my pride or my feelings by letting me down gently, you can save your breath. I'm not needing to be coddled or cosseted. I've put it to you simply, without guile or pretense, and I'd appreciate your answering me in kind."

Aislinn's mouth tightened and, once again, something shone briefly in her eyes as they met his own—pain or surprise, or possibly spite, he couldn't be sure. "Then so be it. And, if it's the truth you're looking for, here it is: 'Tis a wife you're wanting, to be sure. So you've said and, indeed, I believe you. But 'tis not me, Gavin O'Malley. And, as to whether I could act the part of your wife, under these conditions and for as long as you'd want me to...'twould be terrible hard, I'm thinking, and I don't know that I could stand it."

Gavin nodded, buying himself a bit of time while he labored to catch his breath. He'd been lying to himself thinking he was prepared for the worst. He wasn't. "I'm answered then," he murmured at last and, turning away, his glance fell on the hearth. "Shall we have supper now? For, in truth, despite your complaints about the lateness of the hour, it does not look so bad, what you've made here. And, quite famished I am, in any case."

"Gavin, please." The pleading tone in Aislinn's voice was almost enough to make him lose all resolve. "Don't turn from me like that."

He hadn't wanted to turn away, either. He'd wanted to band his arms around her and demand she stay. Instead, he forced himself to smile. It was a small smile, to be sure, but enough of one to conceal his pain, or so he hoped, so he was content with it. "Why not then? 'Tis nothing else to say about it, is there, lass? I'm sorry to have troubled you with my foolishness. Now, come, let's eat before we both perish from hunger."

"I have only 'til the morning to be with you," she said mournfully, her voice barely above a whisper. "And, much more than food, what I'm longing for is to feel you holding me close. Will ye not lie with me, Gavin, one final time?"

Gavin's breath shuddered out on a long, slow sigh. It

was truly the worst thing she could have thought to ask for. He knew he did not have the strength to say no to her and once he had her in his arms again, how could he ever let her go? There was only one thing he could think of doing to make the situation more bearable. And so, just as he'd done when she'd asked him a similar question the night she'd shown him her home, he asked, "Will ye not transform yourself into Mairead for me, Fae?"

Aislinn inhaled sharply and two bright spots of color appeared on her cheeks. She didn't answer, at first then she took a step back from him and nodded. "Very well, then."

Gavin groaned inwardly and cursed himself for being a fool. He did not want to lie with Mairead tonight. Even knowing it was not really her, it would still feel wrong. For, it was Aislinn he wanted, and no one else. He waited, dreading the transformation to come, but nothing happened. "Well?" he snapped impatiently when almost a minute had passed. "Where is she then?"

A faint frown appeared on Aislinn's brow. "I-I cannot do it."

Gavin could have sighed with relief, instead he scowled at her. "And why is that? 'Tis never been a problem for you before."

"Your memories of her," she said, eyes widening in surprise. "They're gone. I can no longer reach them."

Gavin's eyes widened. He knew his memories of Mairead were safe; they'd merely been displaced and were no longer front and center in his mind. But, too late, it occurred to him that, in order to comply with his request, Aislinn would have had to invade his mind. He knew very well what she would have found there: the dashed hopes, the shattered dreams, the ruined remnants of his foolish heart. The thought of putting his still-bloody wounds on display, exposed to her view, like trophies for her to gloat over, was more than his temper could tolerate.

"Get out," he ordered, pointing toward the door. "You devil's hag, are you saying you've cost me my memories now too? What next will you take? Will you leave me with nothing at all? Out, then, be gone!"

Aislinn just stood there, as though frozen. The stricken expression on her lovely face struck his nerves like scalding water.

Snatching up a poker from the hearth he brandished it at her. "Out with ye now," he repeated. "*Amach libh.* Be gone, or I'll take this iron to you." But, even as he said it, he knew he'd never make good on his threat. And one look at her face, at the compassion gleaming in her eyes, the pity and remorse, the total lack of fear, told him she knew it too.

"Gavin, please," she murmured taking a step toward him, her hand outstretched, the faintest smile glimmering on her soft lips. "Just give me a chance to—"

"Never," he growled as he took hold of her arm and dragged her across the room toward the door. "I'll give ye nothing more, I tell ye. You've had all you'll get of me, my girl, for I've done with ye. Now, go." Throwing open the door, he pushed her through it. "And you can count yourself lucky for having gotten away with as much as you have—just as I will for having finally seen the last of ye."

*****

Aislinn stumbled blindly across the yard, her thoughts tumbling over one another in confusion. What she'd just read in Gavin's heart and mind cast all her previous thoughts about his motives and emotions into disarray. Could it possibly be true? Did he really love her as much as he seemed to? If so, she'd done him a huge disservice. She'd hurt him—worse, far worse—than she'd realized. He'd suffered so much already. How could she leave him now, to bear more pain alone?

She couldn't, she realized. So, as she reached the gate, she paused and turned back toward the cottage. Gavin was still there, standing in the doorway, frowning as furiously as ever, but she wasn't fooled. "I'm sorry, *mo chroí*, but I can think of naught else to do for thee."

Even though he'd accused her already—and falsely,

at that, as she very well knew—of taking his memories, she was sure there were some he'd be happier without. Those of her, for instance. Hadn't he just said as much? It took but an instant to gather her power. It was summer now, after all, and she was at the peak of her strength. Heart breaking at the necessity, at the loss she was already feeling, she sent the *ceol sidhe* wafting over him; knowing he could not help but respond to it. "Forget me," she ordered, sad but firm, her voice but a whisper within the song, "Forget, forget, forget..."

For a moment, just as she'd expected, Gavin's face went slack; but then his frown returned. "What mischief are you up to now, Fae?" he demanded, his voice clearly audible to her sensitive ears as it carried across the yard. "I'll have no more of your trickery. Stop with your bloody singing and go back to where you belong now. Leave me alone."

Aislinn stared at him in surprise. Clearly, he'd felt the compulsion in her song and yet he'd refused the relief it offered. Why? "I'm sorry, *mo chroí*," she said again. "I was just trying to ease your pain."

"Go now," he repeated. "'Tis no concern of yours, but my memories are mine to keep, if I choose to. And, I do." For another moment they stared at each other, both wordlessly pleading. Until Gavin added more softly this time, his voice breaking. "Please..."

Understanding, when it came to her, was swift, stinging sharp and bittersweet; it left Aislinn breathless. Lips trembling, she nodded and turned blindly away. If he'd wanted to forget her, he would have done so. The *ceol sidhe* would have ensured it. But, painful as his memories of her had to be, he apparently cherished them enough that he did not want to lose them.

She could not comprehend the why and wherefore of such reasoning—yet—but she suspected her newfound soul would shortly make its meaning clear to her. Despite her curiosity, it was not something she was looking forward to, for she did not doubt the lesson would be a costly and extremely painful one.

"Is all well, Milady?" Eoghan inquired, appearing suddenly at her side.

Aislinn turned to him. "It is," she said as she studied his expression, searching for some sign of guile and finding none. "But, tell me, my friend, had you realized, when you came here, that you were being sent to escort me to my death?"

"T-to your death, milady?"

The shocked horror in his voice, the stricken look within his eyes, told Aislinn all she needed to know—about both his loyalty and her sister's cunning. For, how better to keep from arousing Aislinn's suspicions than to send only one guard, ignorant of the plot against her, to coax her into coming home?

"'Tis all right, my friend," she replied soothingly, refusing to hold the mischief he might have committed in his innocence against him. In the difficult days to come, she was sure she'd have need of all the friends she had. "The damage has all been done. 'Tis over now. Come then, let us go home."

Chapter Twelve

The rest of the summer passed without incident, although, to be sure, the beauty of the season was quite wasted on Gavin. His heart ached in a way that was worse than he'd ever known and the emptiness he felt within his cottage each night, when he returned to it from work, was surpassed only by the emptiness inside himself. He was missing his soul, he told himself, in an attempt to stir up some righteous anger. How could he not feel empty, after suffering such a great loss? His soul. His heart. His peace of mind. His honor. His self-respect. His last chance for Heaven. He was missing things he should have never given up; things he'd been tricked and deceived and seduced into surrendering.

But, the plain fact of it was, no matter what he tried to tell himself, he knew it to be a lie. He was a much less bitter man than he had been before and, when all was said and done, he had to admit that all he was really missing was *her*.

He had changed. And the way he viewed the world around him had changed as well. But, since he continued to keep to himself, as had been his custom for almost ten years, weeks passed before anyone else seemed to notice that fact.

He'd gone to see Father Cullen right away, of course, to keep him from talking. The good father was much relieved to be told that he'd been right; that Gavin had indeed been temporarily suffering from an addled brain as a result of his earlier illness. The old priest heard Gavin's confession and absolved him of his sins—the impure thoughts, the breaking of a solemn promise, the lies—and then happily wrote the whole episode off. He was content to believe that there was no Fae, no impending, unholy marriage, and no need at all to worry over the potential loss of Gavin's soul. And, for his part, Gavin, once what was left of his soul had been washed clean of his transgressions—the lies in particular—was content to let him.

191

As the weeks progressed Gavin found himself better able to deal with his loss. There were entire huge blocks of time now when he didn't think of her at all. Why, toward the end of August, there even came a day when he was pleased to realize he'd gone for a good, solid hour before some stray memory crept in to torture him.

Some days however, were not as good. The memories were often agonizing, it was true, but even so he had no regrets about keeping them. There were other things, though, that he did regret. Like the anger he'd shown at their final parting. Like his foolishness at turning down the chance to bed her one last time. Like the stubborn, blind stupidity that had kept him from realizing sooner what a treasure he'd found. Or the fact he'd wasted every, last, blessed opportunity he'd been given—and was now ever likely to get—to tell her he loved her.

Would it have made a difference? As summer came to an end and the days and nights turned cooler, that was a question he asked himself over and over again as he sat brooding before the fire.

...'twould be terrible hard, I'm thinking, and I don't know that I could stand it, she'd said when she refused him. Her words gnawed at his mind during those evenings until, finally, he found a measure of solace in them. For it seemed, indeed, that nothing would have made a difference. That it was just never meant to be.

He was lucky to have had her at all, he decided at last, for she was an adventure such as few men could claim. And, that being the case, he should be happy. Even though she'd left him destroyed, as he knew she would, she'd also left him—in other ways—a far richer man for the experience. And, so, even as summer breathed her last, and the nights grew long and even longer, Gavin resolved to himself that he *would* be happy and he *would* be grateful and he *would* put the past behind him and find a way to move on.

*****

Autumn brought odd rumors swirling like leaves

through the streets of Kilbanning. For, it seemed that Gavin O'Malley had been heard singing as he worked.

The villagers wondered greatly at this for it seemed the smith had at last begun to put his long grief behind him. His manner improved to the point where he actually smiled, now and again, and his mien became so much more genial that the village children no longer feared to go to him with their requests that he fix their broken toys.

Several of the boys, in fact, became so bold they took to hanging 'round the forge, fascinated by the noise and the sparks and the heat and the smells. Gavin took great pleasure in their company—and in their interest, as well—and he asked often which of them it was, again, as wanted to grow up to be a smith? And then laughed out loud to hear them all claim it was just the thing, and that nothing could be better.

Many was the night he'd send them off with souvenirs tearing holes in their pockets—nails and links and horseshoes and little, useless scraps; things he'd made for them, or helped them make for themselves, or that they'd picked up off the floor. Things which, so he whispered to them, conspiratorially, were good to have close to hand especially if they were out and about at twilight; for they were useful in warding away the *Sluagh Sidhe*.

They didn't believe him, of course, for they knew such things didn't really exist, but they thanked him just the same. And, if his smile, at times, turned wistful as he watched them go, none of them ever noticed.

*****

The leaves fell from the trees and the wind blew cold as October fled away. And, on the second of November, after attending mass for The Feast of All Souls, Gavin stopped in the graveyard behind Saint Ita's to pay a visit to his wife and their child.

"Well, my dear, and here we are again," he said as he stood there, at the foot of the grave. As was his usual habit, he didn't bother with any sort of preamble. Why should he, after all? Though his ideas of what the souls of the departed did in Heaven was somewhat vague, he had no doubt they spent the bulk of their time idly waiting for their loved ones to stop by for a chat.

"I hope you're doing well, Mairead. And the babe, too, of course, though I imagine he's not a babe any longer, but a big, fine boy. Ah, I wish that I could see him," he sighed, trying to picture the child—almost ten years old, happily running and jumping through fields of clouds. "I hope he has his mother's eyes, for I do remember them, you know, quite well. Blue, they were; a beautiful, bonnie blue."

He paused then, and kicked for a bit at the weeds that grew among the stones, for the next part was harder to get out. "I think I must be saying good-bye to you, Mairead. I'm sorry to be breaking it to you like that, my dear, but the truth is I don't believe I'll be joining you in Heaven after all. God knows, I tried to keep to the promise I made you, but it was too hard for me to do so. I'm not yet an old man, you know—though no doubt I seem so to you, now, if you're watching me—and I can't be giving up all my hopes for this lifetime. Not yet.

"I want a family, Mairead. I never sought to deceive ye about that, and you can't say I did. And so...it was wrong of me to make you that promise when you lay dying. And, I have to tell you, lass, I think it was wrong of you to ask for it too. I know you were going through a terrible hard time of it just then, and I don't hold it against you, really I don't. But, all the same..."

His voice trailed off and he dug his hands deeper into his pockets before continuing. "All the same, if you'd truly loved me, I don't think you'd have asked that of me. Or, at the least, you wouldn't be angry with me now for failing to keep to something like that. I hope you've forgiven me for all the hurt I caused you. But, whether or not you have, I thought you should know that I forgive you. We were both of us young and didn't know any better and I suppose that's the crux of it." Again, he paused, remembering his marriage, the grief, the pain, the hope, the love, but with a new detachment; even a sense of peace.

"The thing is, Mairead, I'll probably be getting married again after all. Though, the truth of it is, I don't know to whom, at this point, or when. I've fallen in love again, you see, and while that didn't work out as well as I'd hoped, it got me to thinking. I don't want to be alone any longer, Mairead. Maybe that's hard for you to understand, up there in paradise with all the angels and such. But...I'm lonely down here on my own. I've no one to talk to, you see. No one to laugh with, no one to share my bed or wake up to. I don't think 'tis good for a man to live like I've had to do; at least, it's not been good for me. Had ye lived, I swear, I'd have been the faithfulest husband ye ever did see—even despite your not wanting me most of the time, which, I have to tell ye, I think was more your fault than mine. But, you didn't live, my dear, and...and I did. And I can't go on any longer as I have these past years.

"Anyway, I thought you should know that, in case ye were wondering. And, like I said at the start, I don't think I'll be joining you. But, I hope eternity's turning out to be everything you deserve, Mairead. Kiss our boy for me, and tell him how sorry I am that I never got to know him before and will now not be meeting him again. Take care, my dear."

And, so saying, Gavin blew a kiss off the tips of his fingers toward the simple stone tablet that bore his wife's name. Then he turned and headed for home.

The sky overhead was leaden gray, barren but for the occasional raven. The air was still and smelled of snow. It was winter now, and perhaps it was inevitable, because of that, that his mind should turn to thoughts of last winter; to thoughts of Aislinn with her smiling face, her bright hair, her hot, dark eyes...

He hoped she was well, that she was warm and happy, that he'd given her everything she needed to live a long, satisfying life. He doubted he'd ever know for sure, for he had no expectations of seeing her again. Still, it gave him solace to think of her, safe in her home now, with a piece of his soul growing inside her.

It made him smile to think of that. To think of Mairead and his child in Heaven. And Aislinn in her Summerland. And a piece of his soul living on in each place—truly the best of both worlds. And, even if he never did make it to any kind of paradise when he died, still he was content. For, brief and fleeting though it had been, he'd had his paradise, right here on Earth.

And how many other men, he wondered, could boast of that?

Chapter Thirteen

It was on yet another bleak, midwinter day that Aislinn returned to Kilbanning. She stopped, once again, on the snowy rise above the forge with her heart beating swiftly within her chest. The day was cold, and the wind that blew across the frozen landscape was a bitter one; but it wasn't that which caused her to tremble as she surveyed the prospect before her.

Perhaps she was a fool for coming back, she thought, as she made her way through the gate, stepping lightly, quickly, soundlessly across the stones. She knew the chance that she was expected here today was small, indeed. But, even if there'd been no chance at all, she couldn't have stayed away. Her heart would not allow it.

Because it was Christmas Eve, and a Sunday at that, she had not expected anyone to be working in the forge itself, but the steady beat of the hammer told her that's where he was. She paused at the open door and drank in the sight of him. A tremor of a far different nature rocked through her then. His back was to her as he stood at the anvil, muscles shifting smoothly under gleaming skin as he worked the black metal, and she felt herself go molten to the core, desire rising like a hot, thick wave to sweep over her.

She took a moment to compose herself; and then another to steel herself to enter the place. For, although her wounds were long healed, she could still recall the agony of iron links melting into her flesh, her life-force wilting helplessly away beneath the violent assault.

Panic threatened to overwhelm her then, but she took a long, slow, deep breath and reminded herself why she had come. *Gavin...*

Finally, when the hammering had ceased and he'd paused to return the iron to the fire, when she was certain she had herself well under control, she stepped inside the forge, gliding past the heavy doors on their iron hinges, just as though she had not a care in the world. "Good day to ye, Gavin O'Malley," she said in a cool, distant voice. A small smile played over her lips when a thrill of surprise ran through the smith and he stilled, his entire body stiffening at the sound of her voice.

Slowly, he released the hammer he'd been holding and turned to face her. "Fae," he replied in a voice that was almost as cool as her own. "'Tis good to see you well. What are you doing here?" Gavin's eyes, blue as ever they'd been but colder than she'd remembered, drifted disinterestedly over her. His face, likewise, was stern and harsh. Remote.

Aislinn smiled back at him, just the same. "Why, were you not expecting me then? For, sure and you must know why I'm here? I've come to settle my account with thee. I'm still after owing you for your kindness to me last winter, as I'm sure you remember, and 'tis now a year and a day since we made our bargain."

"Is it?" he asked, in a voice that was only slightly unsteady. "I'd quite forgotten."

"Did you, indeed?" Laughing softly in disbelief, Aislinn crossed to where he stood. "Ah, *mo chroí,* sure and it is a shocking liar you've become since last I saw thee. Why is that?"

The smith shrugged, his gaze faltering as she approached. "Does it really matter?" And, though he could not stop the subtle darkening of his eyes, the tell-tale flush in his cheeks, he continued to keep his voice in check. "In any case, you're wasting your time. For my answer now will be the same as it was then: You've naught that I want."

Aislinn sighed, biting back the disappointment she felt. So. He was going to be difficult, was he? "Well, then, sir smith, my response to you, now as then, is also the same. There must be something you're wanting."

"Many things," Gavin agreed. "Just not from you."

She gazed at him reproachfully. "Ah, Gavin, come now, how long must we play this game? I know what it's in your heart, *a chuisle,* will you not admit to it and give in?"

Blue fire blazed in Gavin's eyes when he met her gaze; and in their depths Aislinn read fury, hurt and bitter resentment. She drew in a startled breath, but before she had time to do more, he grabbed hold of her shoulders and pulled her flush against him. He kissed her once, one fierce branding of his lips on hers then just as quickly he thrust her away.

"There, now," he spat, wiping a shaky hand across his mouth. "I'm repaid. And I'm done with ye. Now, leave me, Fae."

Aislinn stared in dismay. Had she read him wrong last summer? Or could his feelings for her have changed that much in only six months? But, no. She would not believe it. Had she not just felt the hunger in his grasp, tasted desire on his lips?

Without a word, she launched herself into his arms, again, and kissed him back. Time stopped. Through no art or intention of her own, the stars simply ceased their spinning. And for one, breathless, solitary moment that seemed determined to stretch itself into eternity, the two of them melted together, body and soul.

As Gavin slanted his mouth over hers with a feral sounding growl and banded his arms tightly around her, Aislinn speared her fingers into his hair and gave into her own feelings of hunger and desire. And love. Love, most of all.

"Ah, Aislinn," Gavin murmured at last, pushing her away again, but gently and more slowly this time; his arms shaking as though the motion cost him everything he had. "You shouldn't have come back."

"Oh," Aislinn gasped, startled and dismayed once again. "That-that's not very gallant of you, sir. Why, I feel myself quite rebuffed."

Gavin sighed. "Then perhaps we're both repaid." He took a few steps back then, and eyed her unhappily. "Did you think it was not hard enough on me, being refused by you last summer? Why the bloody hell are you here now? Is it for any

199

other reason than to have me on my knees again, that you might have the pleasure of denying me once more? You say you've looked into my heart and know what I'm feeling, so then why? Is it for sport, you do it? I'd always heard the fae were cold at heart, but I hadn't thought ye this cruel."

"Gavin, nay." She pressed a hand against her chest, to ease the pain caused by his words. But, the pain, like a dull blade hacking away at her heart, continued. "*A thaisce*, of course it is not—never think it!"

"Then why?" he repeated, stubbornly.

Aislinn hesitated. "When you asked me to marry you, I didn't think. Was it I, myself, you wanted? For, if so, I-I thought it wasn't, you see. I thought your only reason was to have me to step into another woman's shoes. To be *her* for you, never myself. And, to live in such a fashion...indeed, it seemed more, at the time, than my heart could bear."

"Nay," Gavin answered, shoulders sagging. "'Twas you I wanted, *a muirnín,* and no one else. 'Tis you I want still and always will, or so my heart is telling me. And sure and I must be cursed, marked at birth for a life of constant sorrow, for I know that I can ne'er have you—not as I want to. Not as a wife."

Relieved, Aislinn breathed a heavy sigh. "And why can you not, then, *mo chroí*? For did I not promise ye aught that was in my power to give? And am I not standing here now, ready to fulfill that very promise? Ask me again, why don't you and see if my answer now is not more to your liking?"

But Gavin shook his head. "Nay. That I'll not. Since you've been gone, I've had time to think on it. I'm not so blind or foolish as I was last summer. You were right to leave me, lass, for things could ne'er have worked out for us. Only look around you," he said as he flung his arms wide. "Do you not see where you are? I'm a blacksmith, Aislinn. 'Tis the only life I know. And you— What kind of wife would you make for such a one as myself?" Scowling, he nodded at her foot. "Have we not both seen what the iron can do to you, lass? I nearly killed ye once already with it—and me after swearing on my life I'd ne'er cause ye any harm! Are you thinking I'd ever want to risk putting either of us through something like that again? Never, I tell ye. Never again."

Aislinn could not repress a shudder—though whether it was at the memory of that day, or fear for Gavin's safety, for the price he might yet have to pay for his broken promise—she couldn't be certain. "But, things are different now," she insisted. "Did I not walk in here today under my own power; unaided by you, unaffected by the very thing which once held such sway o'er me? I do not know what the cause of it is, whether it is an attribute of your soul within me, or a result of the very injury that nearly ended my life, but your iron no longer has the power it once did to affect me. You've set me free, Gavin."

Gavin's eyes widened. "T-truly?"

"My love," Aislinn murmured in gentle reproach. "Have I ever yet lied to thee?"

He made no answer, but the look on his face was so heartbreakingly hopeful it very nearly brought tears to Aislinn's eyes.

"Ask me again," she urged quietly.

*****

Heart pounding, Gavin closed the gap between them. Aislinn lifted her face, clearly expecting to be kissed. Instead, he cupped her face in his hands and stared searchingly into her eyes. "'Tis not just for the settling of old scores between us that you're doing this, is it? If so, tell me now," he implored, heart sinking when she frowned at the question, her displeasure apparent. He shook his head. "'Tis as I told you last summer, lass, that's not how or why I want to win a wife. There must be more between us than that, for otherwise—"

"I know," she replied solemnly, stopping the flow of words from his mouth with a finger pressed lightly against his lips.

Disappointment knifed through him again, stronger

than before, when she reached up and took hold of his hands, gently prying them from her face. Sighing reluctantly, he tried to prepare himself for what he knew was to come. But instead of dropping his hands and stepping away from him, instead of admitting she'd been wrong to come back; instead of doing or saying anything he was expecting—even in his wildest dreams—she held tight to his hands and slipped gracefully to her knees.

"Aislinn, get up," he said, his face growing uncomfortably warm as the awareness he'd been trying his best to ignore raced down his spine and tightened his balls. It felt far too good to be with her again. The sight of her, gazing up at him as she was, with the faintest trace of a smile, ignited memories of other times she'd knelt between his legs—under far different circumstances—and his randy cock, never fully at ease in her presence, came more fully to attention. "Stop this foolishness. Get up now."

"Nay." She shook her head. "For there's a question to be answered first." And though there was a promise of tenderness in her eyes, there was also a touch of steel in her voice. "Grateful I may be to you, Gavin O'Malley, for all that ye've done for me, but, even so, I can assure you I would not be here today offering myself in marriage for the sake of that alone. Nor to honor a promise or repay a debt, or any other such reason you might be thinking of. And had ye managed, last year, to force me into such an arrangement for any of those same reasons, you may be very certain I would have made you pay dearly for the insolence. Are you answered now?"

"Aye." Gavin tugged on her hands impatiently. "I am. Now, get up off your knees."

"Not yet. And, since you've thought to mention the matter, did you not also question whether I might not be taking pleasure in the prospect of having you once again on your knees?" Letting go of his hands at last, she spread her arms wide. "And, yet, as you see, 'tis I on my knees, instead, asking you to believe me when I tell you that *never* could I be so cruel and...for the sake of sport, did I hear ye say?" She shook her head, her gaze turning reproachful. "My love, when have I ever treated you so shamefully?"

"Never," he sighed, feeling helplessly exasperated as he fisted his hands on his hips and gazed down at her. "Will ye not stand up then, that I might apologize properly? For 'tis sure I cannot make amends to you while you're kneeling at my feet."

"I am still not quite done," Aislinn replied with more than a hint of malicious glee in both her voice and her eyes. "For there's still yet another question I recall your having asked me, several months back, and which I have yet to answer."

Rolling his eyes toward Heaven, Gavin groaned. "Aye, no doubt and may God strike me dead an I am ever so foolish as to ask another question. For, whatever it was I said, I'm sure you will tell me I was wrong then too. Can we not just leave it at that?"

Aislinn chuckled softly, shooting so heated a glance at the front of his trousers that his shaft jerked in sudden anticipation. "The question to which I'm referring was whether or not you could ever become so accomplished a lover as even I would be unable to resist." She raised her eyes to his then and the carnal gleam in her smoke colored gaze left him speechless. "Would you not be wanting to hear the answer to that now?"

There was only one thing Gavin was wanting from her mouth, in that instant, and it wasn't words. Memories of her lips closing over the head of his cock had shudders of remembered pleasure coursing through him.

"I shall take your silence for consent," Aislinn murmured in mischievous tones as she slipped her hand into his trousers and fondled his cock. "From the very beginning, O'Malley, I found you most intriguing, and so had no great *wish* to resist you, even then. My *will* to resist—ah, now that was another story, or so I told myself. But, in all honesty, I do believe it was well nigh gone even before you'd posed the question. And, now, 'tis completely lost I am; utterly at your mercy. Will you not be taking pity on me, then, and allow me but a small taste of what I am so craving?"

As she'd pulled his cock free of his pants while she spoke, and was now squeezing and stroking along the shaft, her meaning was perfectly clear. And the eager droplets already pearling from the tip of his achingly stiff rod were making something else clear to Gavin as well; he'd be disgracing himself, in another minute or two, if he didn't let her have her way with him.

A rush of exultant heat shot through him with the realization that his cock would soon be exactly where it most wanted to be: sliding between the sweet, soft lips that smiled up at him so encouragingly. And he couldn't keep from laughing. "Well, lass, when you put it to me so nicely, I hardly see how I can refuse your request."

Aislinn grinned slyly back at him. "Indeed, *mo chroí*," she said as she tightened her grip on the shaft of his dick, leaned in and swirled her tongue over the shiny red crown. "I do not believe you can."

Gavin groaned in appreciation as she opened her mouth wider and, inch by tantalizing inch, his cock disappeared into the warm, moist cavern...only to reappear, a moment later, just as slowly. Aislinn flicked her tongue once more across the crest while she readjusted her hold on his cock. When her other hand slid inside his pants and cupped his balls he groaned again. Then he was spearing his hands into her hair, pressing his hips forward, offering his cock, helping to feed it into her hungry mouth.

While continuing to squeeze and pull his sac with exquisite gentleness, Aislinn slid her other hand around to take hold of his buttocks. Her grip was firmer there, her fingers digging into his taut muscles, urging his hips into motion; while her mouth moved up and back, swallowing the length of him, over and over again.

Six months, he thought, as his legs began to tremble from the tension. *Six months. Six months. Six lonely months.*

Six months too long. That's how long he'd been without her—without this. But, never again. For, just as he'd predicted last summer, now that he had her again, he could not let go. She was his. And if, in another minute, she disappeared and was gone from his life forever, she'd be his still. His one and only. His own, true love. He knew his heart would belong to her until it beat its last.

His heart was beating now, though—*like a bloody drum, it's sounding*—hot and fierce, fast enough to rival the most skillful *bodhran* player ever to have wielded a tipper. Aislinn's pace quickened now too, as she sucked him harder, faster, deeper, taking him with such greedy abandon that he could feel the tip of his cock hitting against the back of her throat with every stroke. He felt his balls draw snug, heard—and felt—her anticipatory growl of pleasure as it vibrated over his shaft, and went over the edge. As his cock pulsed, pumping his seed down her throat, he shouted aloud with his climax. "Ah, Aislinn, for the love of God!"

His heart was still hammering against his chest when she pulled back and smiled up at him. Sitting on her heels, she licked the last few drops from his softening shaft and it was all Gavin could do to keep from moaning at the loss of her engulfing warmth. He needed to be inside her, joined with her still, his cock buried deep, his seed filling her. He needed to feel her body, pliant and giving beneath him. He needed to cage her in his arms and prove to himself that she was here, that she was his, that never again would she leave, never again would he find himself without her.

Reaching down, he pulled her to her feet, pulled her to him, and kissed her soundly, loving the taste of musk and desire on her lips. Still kissing her, he hoisted her into his arms, glancing around, from the corners of his eyes, for a suitable place to lay her down, finding only the bench.

Gingerly, half fearing to find she'd lied about the iron, he set her atop the worn oak. He sighed in relief when she reclined willingly, showing no reaction to the very same nails that had so tormented her in the past.

He followed her down, covering her body with his own, pinning her beneath him. She kissed him hungrily, making love to his mouth as voraciously as she'd just done his cock, while he pushed at her clothing, seeking the sweet flesh he knew awaited him. He could scent her arousal in the air and it drove him wild.

"My, you're a greedy one today," Aislinn teased when he found what he was searching for, when he'd paused, with the tip of his cock just nudging against her opening. "Are you ready for more so soon then?"

"'Tis been six months," he said in explanation, kissing lightly along her throat, trying his best to go slow. He knew he should be giving more thought to her pleasure, at this point. But, he couldn't. He was driven by a need that seemed only partially physical; by a feeling that he must make every moment count; by a fear that this moment—this very one—might be all the time they would ever have.

"Six months, is it?" Her eyebrows rose. "And has there been on one else in *all that time*? You astonish me."

"Of course there's been no one." Lifting his head, he scowled at her. "And what about you, then? Have you had others in that time?"

"Why, what is this look now?" she asked, merriment dancing in her eyes. "Is it upset you'd be, an I said I had? Ah, nay, do not answer, for I can see that you would." She shook her head. "Nay, *mo chroí*, though you must surely realize by now that we fae do not share your same human scruples or sense of shame, nor find such activities to be at all unseemly, there has been no one for me as well."

"Good," he answered, feeling more relieved by her admission than he would have thought possible. He regarded her sternly. "And glad I am to hear that you realize such behavior is unseemly to us. You'd best not forget that, my girl. For sure and I'll be expecting you to behave like a proper wife to me from now on."

Her smile held a hint of challenge. "Oh, will you now?"

Gavin had been leaning in to kiss her when her words stopped him. She hadn't said she would yet, had she? He pulled back to look at her. "Aislinn, you will be marrying me, won't you?"

Still smiling, she tilted her hips up just enough so that the tip of his cock just breached the soft flesh of her sex. "Is this how you would propose to me then?" she asked, in a voice both husky and amused. "While I'm flat on my back beneath you? And will you say *that* is not unseemly?"

He nipped punishingly at her lip. "Aye. 'Tis most unseemly, wench. But there's no help for it. I need your answer without delay and were I to go down on my knees before you now, with the intention of proposing to you in a more appropriate manner, sure and it's distracted I'd become—as ever I am by you it seems—and forget what I was about. And then neither of us would be capable of talking for a good long while."

She laughed at that, canting her hips back and then up again, forcing him a little deeper inside her. "Well, now, seeing as you're asking so nicely, how could I ever refuse?"

Cock pulsing eagerly, he grinned at her, recognizing his own words as she repeated them back to him, ready to respond in kind: *Indeed, you cannot.* The words were trembling on his tongue in the instant before he realized he could not give voice to them. For, as he himself had told her, this was no fit subject for jokes. So, shrugging a little he replied instead, "Very easily, if 'tis what your heart is telling you to say. Is it, Aislinn?"

Smiling sadly, she shook her head. "Sure and you should know exactly what my heart is saying, *a chuisle.* 'Tis telling me I was a fool to refuse you last summer and would be a fool, ten times over, an I did so again. So, aye, Gavin O'Malley, I will marry you. And will do my best to keep in mind all that your kind expects of in a wife, so as not to disappoint you."

"Never," he murmured, bending his head and kissing her fiercely, again and again in an attempt to give vent to all the joyful emotion overflowing his heart. "Never *a chuisle, a thaisce, a chailín mo chroí. A bhean chéile.* Never, could you disappoint me. *Gráim thú.*"

*****

Gráim thú. I love you. Gavin's declaration struck a chord of recognition somewhere deep inside Aislinn. The same truth his words carried, the same emotion that prompted their utterance filled her heart, as well. "*Is tú mo ghrá,*" she murmured in reply as she wrapped her legs around his hips and pulled him into her. "*Tá mo chroí istigh ionat.*" *You are my love. My heart is within you.*

Given the fierce passion she was feeling—and which she knew he was feeling too—she'd expected him to fuck her quickly, with reckless, wild abandon. She was hoping for it, in fact, for he was not the only one for whom the past six months had seemed an eternity. But, once again, he surprised her.

Tangling his hands in her hair, he took control of the rhythm, rocking into her slowly, his eyes never leaving her face, steadily stoking the flames within her until her entire body was on fire for him. Until she cried his name with every stroke. Until the need for more, for everything, had her wanting to tear the clothes from both their bodies, to meet each other skin to skin.

She whimpered as he slid one hand between them, dragging it slowly down the length of her body, skimming over her breast, longing for his touch, finally gliding between her legs to cup her mound. Then he used the pad of his thumb to pet her clitoris; and that, in tandem with the steady stroking of his cock inside her, sent her over the edge.

Slow, shimmering waves rippled through her and she forgot to breathe. As her muscles tightened around his shaft, she felt him stiffen. She smiled when she felt the flood of his release as it filled her.

And, then, just moments later, as Gavin rested his head upon her breast, in an attitude of total exhaustion, she felt something else, as well: A contentment greater than anything she'd ever known.

They were lying there still, too indolent to move, when a sudden clatter of hooves in the yard outside startled them. A horse neighed frantically and a man's voice could be heard crying out, "Hey, there. Blacksmith. Some assistance, if you please."

"Bah, what the bloody hell is this now?" Gavin growled, hurriedly pulling away from Aislinn and adjusting his clothes.

A dreadful foreboding swept through Aislinn's heart then and she clutched at Gavin's arm, begging. "Don't go out there, Gavin. Send him away, I pray thee. 'Tis dangerous."

"Calm yourself, lass," he said, patting her hand and pressing a last kiss on her cheek before he stood. "For, after all, 'tis unlikely anyone would be out on the road this late on Christmas Eve unless they had to be. 'Twouldn't be right to send such a one away unaided, now would it? I'll just see what the fellow is after and then I'll be closing for the holiday. We'll have the rest of tonight and all day tomorrow to spend together—in any unseemly way that you wish. You'll have me on my knees yet, my girl, I can promise ye that."

Chapter Fourteen

There was a spring in Gavin's step as he headed for the door. Aislinn watched him go, aware of an inexplicable feeling of grief that weighed on her spirit.

"Now, now, my beauty," she heard him say as he stepped outside. "Take it easy, there. Whoa, whoa. What's all this now, eh?"

"My mount is a touch skittish, as you see," a man's voice replied. And although Aislinn didn't recognize the speaker something about the timbre of the voice seemed oddly, and unpleasantly familiar. The hairs rose on the back of her neck as she crept closer to the door, hoping to hear more clearly. "If you'll but take hold of the bridle and lead us inside, I'd be much obliged," the voice continued.

"Oh, very well, then," Gavin said. "But, in future, you might want to learn how to control your horse somewhat better, before you're setting out with him again. He's a fine, feisty creature, indeed, but I'll warrant he'll be the death of you yet if you're not careful."

"I shall strive to keep your words in mind," the stranger answered

Aislinn held her breath and waited, listening to the sound of Gavin's voice speaking quietly, in soothing tones; then watching as he reappeared, using one hand to gently stroke the horse while, with the other, he led the creature—a magnificent, pewter-colored steed with eyes of coal—forward.

For an instant, it seemed that all was well. But, before the horse was more than head and shoulders through the doorway, its eyes went wide with fright and it reared, screaming, its hooves beating the air above Gavin's head.

Unable to move, Aislinn watched in horror as Gavin fought to regain control of the creature, without being struck; while the rider, making no attempt to help in the effort, leapt to safety, landing lightly on his feet within the forge. With a final kick that seemed to connect with Gavin's ribs and sent him sprawling, the horse broke free, pivoted wildly and bolted out the door.

Aislinn was halfway to Gavin's side when the stranger gave a low laugh that froze her in her tracks. The blood thudded loudly in her ears as she turned to face him. "Tiernan."

The other fae smiled mockingly as he swept his leg out in a courtly bow. "Well met, Lady Aislinn. 'Tis been too long since we've seen each other."

"Do you think so, then?" she answered, drawing herself up straight and glaring haughtily. "And here was I, thinking it had not been nearly long enough."

"Ah, bloody, fekkin' hell," Gavin groaned from the floor behind her. "Of course *you* would show up now, you bloody bastard. I shoulda known. 'Tis all the day was missing."

Aislinn cast a quick, uncertain glance in Gavin's direction. Relieved to see him climbing to his feet, even if it was with difficulty; but worried, too, half wishing he would have stayed down and let Tiernan think him more badly wounded than he was. For she knew her enemy would never have let himself get trapped, here within the forge, unless he had a plan for escape. In all likelihood, that plan must involve using Gavin, in some fashion.

And the plans of the dark fae were unfailingly cruel and hard.

"What is it you're after, Tiernan?" she demanded, as she faced him again, hoping to draw his fire and distract him from Gavin for as long as she could. "There's naught for you here. You cannot touch me now. Your gambit has failed. Why are you not still skulking in Annwn, licking your wounds?"

But Tiernan refused to be drawn. A mocking smile curled his lips. "And what conceit is this, then? Why should you think 'tis only you I'm after?" His gaze flickered coldly over Gavin. "I have a score to settle with this fellow here as well. Is this your champion then, Aislinn? In truth, he does not seem to be a very prepossessing specimen, though I'll admit he did catch me off-guard last winter. But, whatever were you thinking, choosing to ally yourself with him, rather than me? I'd credited ye with better taste, although, why I do not know. In truth, the ways of the *Tylwyth Teg* have always been a mystery to me. How is it that creatures so soft and malleable could yet be strong? 'Tis a wrong I shall ne'er cease trying to correct."

"You're what's wrong." Gavin took a step forward, wincing a little at the pain. "And, if she's chosen anyone over you, then perhaps there's a clue for you in that fact. She doesn't want you, Tiernan, or whatever your name is. And, I'm thinkin' the most obvious reason for it is that she probably couldn't bear the thought of having to look at your ugly face every day."

Tiernan's eyes turned a shade colder. "Lo, it speaks," he drawled, fixing Gavin with a disdainful look. "Though I find I don't care for its tone. However, that is easily fixed."

"Stop it," Aislinn demanded, as she felt him begin to gather his power. "Tiernan, don't. Your quarrel is with me, not him." But, even as she said it, she knew it was already too late.

*****

"Silence, mortal," the dark fae commanded, raising his hand and gesturing in Gavin's direction; and, just as happened last year, Gavin gasped in shock. Bitterly cold, like ice invading his veins, the spell hit him. It was even worse this time, though, for he had no iron in his pockets to ward against the fae's power. He felt his tongue cleave to the roof of his mouth. His heart labored to beat. His lungs, already aching from the kick he'd taken to the ribs, simply gave up, it seemed, and refused to work at all.

Struggling for air, he reeled backwards until he hit the bricks at the edge of the fire pit and his retreat was brought to a swift, stumbling halt. *Help me*, he thought wildly as his legs gave way and he slid to the floor; *I'm dying. I'm strangling.*

I'm...falling. And through it all—and worst of all, it seemed—was the sight of Aislinn's eyes as they locked with his; wide and horrified, burning with all the wild grief he'd once fantasized about her feeling for him. But, not now. Not like this. *Turn your face away, love,* he begged silently. *Don't watch.*

"Let him go," Aislinn ordered sharply, turning once again toward Tiernan. "'Tis unseemly to involve mere mortals in our fight. Let us resolve our differences like the civilized people we are. Let him go, Tiernan, and we'll talk."

"Pretty words, when you know you're beaten," Tiernan scoffed. "But, truly, what can you possibly have to say, that I'd care to listen to at this point? Had you thrown yourself on my mercy when first your sister turned you out, perhaps *then* might I have been willing to hear you. If you'd surrendered gracefully, admitting defeat at the very start, *then* might I, perhaps, have considered whatever request you cared to beg me for. *Now*, though? After mocking my suit, eluding me all last winter, collaborating with such as this..." Once again, his eyes raked over Gavin and the cold intensified. "This *thing* here...and rendering yourself useless to me in the bargain, *now* you think to plead for parley? Nay, Aislinn, you will not have your way in this. Beg all you like for the mortal's life, but I shall kill him anyway—slowly, while you watch—and then it will be your turn."

"Kill him?" Aislinn tossed her head, a hint of barely concealed amusement lacing her voice. "Is that what you plan to do? And, is it a fool you've become since last I saw you? Go on, then, an it pleases ye to do so, but 'tis yourself you'll be spiting. For how do ye think you'll be getting yourself out of here, if you kill him?"

Tiernan smiled coldly. "Oh, I shall get out all right, ne'er fear that. For I'll have you to assist me."

"I? Never. I'd sooner die here, myself."

"Hark at you—speaking as though you had a choice," he replied with a shrug. "Which, of course, you do not. I need only put a compulsion on you to have you doing whatever I say."

"You may try, my Lord," she answered coolly. "For all the good 'twill do you, for I'm fae too, am I not? What makes you think I shall not be trapped here, as well? 'Tis only because I carry a piece of the smith's soul that I might bypass the iron's warding. Who can say what will happen when he expires? Mayhap the pieces of his soul will be rejoined, at that time, and so seek the afterlife as one. You and I may very well both find ourselves defenseless, dependent on the mercy of whatever human happens by. Let us hope we are both not so weak, by then, that we are seen for what we are and trapped into bargains not of our choosing." She shook her head. "I've had some experience with such, thanks to you. A greedy, grasping lot, these mortals be, and always after something."

Tiernan frowned suspiciously. "'Tis a trick."

"No trick," Aislinn promised. "Only let the smith go now, that he might free us and, once we are quit of this place, I will go with you wherever you wish. I will ally myself with Winter, if you so command it, renounce Summer, do anything you ask of me. I swear it."

Gavin stirred. *Aislinn, nay!* From the very first, she had feared being forced into just this place. It maddened him to think that it had all been in vain, that it had all gone for naught. And, furious at the prospect before him—of losing her to Tiernan, at being an unwilling participant in the bastard's victory—he forced his frozen, aching lungs to expand, forced himself to think. There must be something he could do. He'd outwitted the bastard once. Surely he could do so again?

So long as I live you'll come to no harm here. On pain of death I swear it...

Over and over again, his words to her last year rang in his mind, galvanizing him into action. He'd sworn to keep her safe, sworn to protect her, sworn he'd love her unto death. And, unto death, he would.

"Do you think I'm unmindful of all that's transpired

in these last six months?" Tiernan demanded. "You've already as good as renounced Summer, from what I've heard. Or do you deny that you are no longer bound to obey your sister the queen, nor subject to her *geasa*? 'Tis not just in your own country that the story has been spread, you know. 'Tis said you could have taken her place this past summer, an you wanted to, and be ruling now in her stead. Do you deny it?"

Aislinn shrugged. "It makes a pretty story, I suppose, but I'll leave it to your lordship to decide the truth of it. As you are well aware, I am not queen. And what reason could I have for turning down Summer's throne? For what more could anyone wish?"

Tiernan shook his head. "I would not know. For the truth is no longer in you, Aislinn Deirbhile, as I'd been warned was the case. And what need have I now for your useless promises? When well I know how apt your sweet assurances are to being recanted at your merest whim. Were I to take you back to Annwn now, I do not doubt but that I'd find myself dead, come summer, when your power waxes."

"Indeed, you'd do well to worry about that, Tiernan ap Annwn," Aislinn answered grimly. "And, if you believe nothing else I have told you, believe you this. I swear to you now that if you kill the smith you still will not win me and woe to you an I get away from you, as in all likelihood I shall. For, come summer, no matter what else befalls us, and no matter what lengths to which you go to avoid it, I *will* hunt you down. I *will* find you. And, when I do, then you will find out just how s*oft* the *Tylwyth Teg* are *not*. You will count yourself lucky, then, if I let you die. For 'tis more likely I shall not. More likely I shall rend you into pieces and scatter the parts throughout the realm so that you might live on and suffer untold agony 'til the end of time."

Tiernan nodded. "I do believe you, Lady Deirbhile. And so, since I can no longer hope to use you for my original purpose, and have no wish to taste death at your hands, I think I will change my mind, after all. I will kill you first.

Here—in the outer world, where your body will turn to dust and your spirit be lost forever. And now—before summer returns and you become a threat to me again."

Once more, the dark fae waved his hand. Gavin watched in horror as the color drained from Aislinn's face, leaving it white, bloodless, frozen; as pain filled her eyes and the bright orbs clouded over. Still she stood where she was tall and adamant, immovable, proud. For an instant it seemed she tried to fight the spell. Shimmers of bright, sparkling light, like dying stars flared to life around her and then went out. The air in the forge was filled, suddenly, with all the sultry, soft, fecund scents of Summer.

On pain of death I swear it...on pain of death...on pain of death...

Gavin struggled to his feet. Fingers numb with cold he scrabbled for the one substance he knew better than any other, having devoted so much of his life to it; the only thing capable of taking the dark fae down; the one chance he had to save Aislinn.

The iron rod he'd been working on earlier had lain forgotten in the fire since Aislinn's arrival. Gavin knew when his nerveless hands had found it by the sizzle and smell of burning flesh, by one brief, excruciating burst of pain that all but blinded him with its intensity as he took hold of it. Mindless of the pain, mindless of the damage he was likely inflicting upon himself, he lifted it from the bricks. Its power flowed through his veins, shattering the paralysis affecting his heart. His cracked ribs still protested violently as he swung around but he ignored them and, staggering drunkenly forward the couple of feet necessary to bring him into position, he raised the iron high and then brought it crashing down hard across the fae's shoulder.

The crack of breaking bone was almost lost beneath Tiernan's agonized shriek. The fae stumbled, half turned, and fell forward. As his hand clutched at Gavin's neck another wave of black, bitter cold swept through the smith, piercing his heart, freezing him to the core. With the last bit of strength left in him, Gavin struck again, thrusting upwards this time. The hot metal passed easily through the fae's clothing, through skin and muscle and bone, to lodge in his heart.

Blackness swept outward from the wound like a fell wave, like a killing frost. Smoke poured from Tiernan's mouth, stretched open in a last, silent scream. Then his clothes burst into flame. His body fell to dust. The iron rod Gavin had been wielding fell from his useless fingers and he, himself, would have fallen too, if Aislinn wasn't suddenly there beside him, supporting him, murmuring softly in his ear, "Come away now, my love, I have you."

"Is he dead?" Gavin demanded, stubbornly refusing to be moved until he knew for sure his enemy had been vanquished. Even though the fact that he could breathe again, albeit with difficulty, coupled with the returning sensations— of heat and pain, mostly—in all but his one, damaged arm, seemed to indicate that such was the case.

"That he is," Aislinn said as she led him toward the bench. "Well and truly. Come...just a few steps farther then you can rest."

"And you? Are you injured, lass? He didn't hurt ye, did he?"

"I am well." She lowered him slowly onto the bench. "Here, seat yourself."

"Good," he sighed, feeling greatly relieved. "By the saints, I feel strange, though."

"Aye. I've no doubt you do," Aislinn replied tightly, sounding far more cross than Gavin thought reasonable, under the circumstances.

Surprised, he glanced at her face; at the pain etched there, at the tears sparkling in her bright eyes. "Tears is it, Fae? And here I thought your kind had no use for such."

"Nor do we," she retorted, with mock haughtiness, though her voice seemed close to breaking. As she sat down beside him and cradled his head in her lap he noticed, once again, that she no longer shrank away from the touch of the iron nail heads. "We've no use for them at all, in fact. Nor any for the likes of thee, either, if you must know."

Gavin snorted weakly and smiled—a faint, satisfied smile. He closed his own eyes. "Aye, so you've said."

"That was a foolish thing you did just now," Aislinn murmured. Gavin could feel her fingers trembling as she brushed the hair back from his face. "Brave, to be sure, but...very foolish, indeed. And, oh, *mo chroí*, how I *wish* you had not!"

His smile grew broader to hear her scold him. "Ah, stop with your complaining, woman. Is this how 'tis always going to be with you, then? Would it kill ye to show a little gratitude? 'Twas for your sake I did it, you know."

"Aye, but...oh, Gavin, at what cost?"

"Oh, whist, now, don't be troubling yourself over such nonsense, lass. 'Tis a very small cost to be sure." Opening his eyes again, he smiled at her tenderly. "I've taken far worse hurts than this, you know. Sure and I'll be right as rain in a few days time." Then he glanced down at his ruined hand, noticing for the first time the extent of his injuries. His eyes grew wide. "Yerra, or maybe I won't. That-that does not look so good."

"Nay." A strange sound broke from Aislinn's lips then, something close to a sob, as she said, "'Tis very badly hurt you are, my love."

He lifted his eyes to her face. "But...I don't feel any pain from it."

"Oh, Gavin! Forsooth, with such an injury, how would ye now? Why, there's naught enough flesh left on your bones for to pain thee."

"Am I done for then?' The idea surprised him so much he could not quite wrap his mind around it.

"Done for?" Aislinn tossed her head. "Ridiculous man. What sort of talk is this? Nay. Of course you are not. Never think it."

Gavin scowled at her. "Did I give up my soul, then, just so you could tell stories to me? I'm not a child, Aislinn.

Tell it to me plain. Am I dead?"

"I'm fae," she replied, her voice flat, her expression bitter. "Sure and you know well enough that my kind cannot lie. Did you not say so yourself—on more than one occasion?"

"Aye." He smiled sadly. "And yet, methinks you've just done so, lass."

Aislinn swallowed hard then shook her head again. "Nay. 'Tis nonsense, I tell you. For, have I not explained it to ye? No one is truly dead if there's even one person left alive to remember them. And, Gavin O'Malley...if you don't yet know it...I shall be remembering thee until the end of time." She'd turned her head away as she spoke, but he could see that the tears were falling freely now, down her cheeks.

"Now, now, don't cry so, *a stóirín*," he whispered. "'Twill be all right, you know. 'Tis the way of the world, it is. Don't cry." But he knew she would. He knew she had to. And he was content with the knowledge of all that implied.

The room grew steadily darker and more cold and though Gavin knew the fire was burning low, he also knew it could not be going out as quickly as all that. "I wonder what 'twill be like to die?" he asked rousing himself a little, feeling, at last, a little trepidation at the thought.

Aislinn sat up straighter then. She brushed her hand across her cheeks. A small smile played about her lips. "Well, *mo chroí,* some do say 'tis no more than a falling asleep. Which, after all, is something you do every night without thinking anything of it, is it not? Only this time, Gavin, 'twould be into such a beautiful dream that you'd be falling that sure and you'll decide it's never again you want to wake from it."

Gavin thought about that and felt a little more cold steal over him. He shook his head. "I don't believe I'd fancy that sort of thing, lass. There be dreams enough here for me and I've already lost too much time whilst sleeping."

Aislinn closed her eyes tight for a moment. When she opened them again, it was to smile even more brightly at him. "But, then again, you know, there are those who say 'tis no such thing at all. That 'tis more like waking up, in fact, after a very long and pleasant sleep. And 'tis only because the dreams you've been having still seem so sweet that it pains you to leave them."

"Aye," Gavin replied faintly. "It *is* a sweet dream, is it not? But, it's taken me long enough to see her for what she is and I'd rather not be leaving her just yet."

"Ah, but the day you'd be waking up to would be sweeter still—sweeter than any you've ever yet known. 'Twill be like...well, like Spring and Summer and your Christmas Day all rolled up together, I imagine. And altogether fairer and warmer—as well as everlasting; don't you be forgetting that now. For that, or so they tell me, is the very best part."

"Nicer, that." Gavin smiled to hear her tell it, for the voices of the fae can oftentimes have that effect on mortal men. "But, still, I fear it will not please me. For, nicer still would be a shorter day that had you in it."

Aislinn stared at him, her eyes filling suddenly with hope. "It-it could be so," she murmured softly, so softly he barely heard. "If 'twas truly what you wished. If I were to take your soul back with me now, to my own realm, it could be just like that, for a while."

"Could it now?"

"B-b-but...ah, Gavin, are you sure that's what you're wanting now? For, 'twould not be Heaven," she cautioned him. "I fear you would lose that, my love, and all that your Faith has promised ye, and you could ne'er get it back again, an you changed your mind and came to rue the choice you made today. And 'twould not last forever either—only 'til the end of this world and then you and I would be no more."

"'Tis time enough, I should think," the blacksmith murmured, his voice failing. "And it was ne'er very sure I was that I'd be seeing Heaven anyway, you know. But, tell me, is it very far, this realm of yours? Might I not grow old or tired before I get there, or lose myself somewhere along the way?"

"Nay," Aislinn croaked, her voice harsh now, as though all the magic were gone from it, shaking her head so fiercely that the tears flew wide, the drops sparkling like diamonds in the fading light. "Nay, my love, never think it. 'Twill take no time at all, I swear it. 'Twill be like walking through a door, from one room to the next. And you'll feel no change, other than your wounds will be healed and your hand restored. And I'll be there beside thee, Gavin, always, to make sure you are not ever lost. If you come with me now, my love, I promise I will never leave your side again."

"Aislinn," he said softly. "My own true love."

"And the room we'll be walking into, ah, it's like no room you've ever known here. A room filled with delights such as your kind can never even imagine. And treasure, Gavin. Treasure beyond counting."

Gavin chuckled weakly. "Ah, Fae, sure and now I *know* 'tis just more stories you're telling me." He met her eyes, smiled at the stricken, uncertain look that filled them and, using his last bit of energy, reached his hand toward her still bright face. "For do ye not know I've already found my treasure? Right here in this very room as 'twere. And all the delights this man could ever want. *Is tú mo ghrá*, Aislinn. *A ghrá geal mo chroí...*"

*****

And that's how they found the smith the next morning. Dead. His ruined hand stretched out, as though reaching toward the cold embers of his forge. His face wreathed in such a smile, "As though he'd caught a glimpse o' paradise aforetime," so Auld John said. "Or mayhap he'd seen the face of the angel who'd come for his soul."

But Doctor Butler insisted it was shock and a loss of blood, together with a punctured lung, that had killed the smith; and suggested that, perhaps, he'd been smiling in disbelief at all the damage he'd somehow managed to do to himself. Privately, however, the doctor thought it was more likely a grimace that had twisted Gavin's face, and not a smile at all, for the doctor was one who feared death and thought of it only as an adversary.

Father Cullen, too, said little; and it was only when he made his own confession that he admitted his doubts as to whether or not the blacksmith's soul had been bound for Heaven. Still, he prayed for Gavin's soul, that it might be saved, and asked for God's forgiveness on his own if he had done anything wrong in allowing the smith to be buried in the churchyard with his wife and his child.

With Gavin's passing, the O'Malley line came to an end in Kilbanning, as rarely happens in Ireland today but was much more common back then, what with so many of the young folk emigrating, never to return. And the Kilbanning forge stood cold and dead and silent for many long years. Until, eventually, with the passage of time, the wild roses grew over it and all manner of songbird came and nested in the rafters. Though not, of course, the nightingales who are never to be found anywhere within Ireland's green shores; but of whom 'tis said they sing the sweetest when they are dying, pierced through the heart with a thorn...

Epilogue

Gavin closed the book with a satisfied sigh. "It seems a sad sort of story," he observed as he placed it gently on the bedside table. Soft summer sunlight spilled down around them and the drowsy sound of bees drifted along on the gentle breeze. The sweet scent of flowers filled the air within the leafy green bower in which they reclined and somewhere, he thought, a harper was playing. "Quite thrilling in places, that I will say, but all the same..."

"Aye," Aislinn agreed, her lips compressing as though the bitterness of the tale was something she could taste. "Sad. As are most of the stories your kind insists on telling. And why it is you are all so fond of such melancholy things is beyond all rational understanding."

Gavin laughed as he reached for her, pulling her down to lie beside him. "Sure and it's obvious why we're so partial to them, is it not? For there's naught can be sweeter than the love and the laughter that comes after the tears."

"I'm not so certain of that," Aislinn said, tracing a finger down his cheek. "The sorrow...you can never quite forget it, can you?"

Gavin nuzzled at her neck. "Nay, but then again, why ever would you wish to?" He slipped his hand into the neck of her gown, smiling as he felt her tremble at his touch. "Such sweet, sweet sorrow, it seems at times. You know, he was quite a poet, that Shakespeare, for an Englishman. Besides," he murmured as he swept the fabric aside to bare one breast. "Have I not explained to ye yet, lass, the way it is with my sort? Along with the pleasure there must come a wee bit o' pain." And, so saying, he bent his head, took one berry-like nipple between his teeth, and bit gently down upon it. Aislinn cried out softly and arched against him, her fingers clutching at his arms, to hold him to her.

After a moment, Gavin released the tender nub and laved it with his tongue. "Well?" he asked, raising his head to meet her gaze once again. "Did I not speak truly? Is it not better so?"

"Yes, love," she murmured breathlessly. "'Tis just as you say. But stop now. The children will be coming in soon. Would you have them find us so?"

"What's this?" Gavin gazed at her in surprise. "Why, Fae, are you saying you can no longer weave time to your liking? Will you not fashion us a little more yet for ourselves?"

Aislinn smiled. "I could do so, perhaps, if it's true you no longer find such magic too distasteful for your sensibilities to allow. And how little is this time you'd be wanting then?"

"Oh, just an hour or so, I think," Gavin replied biting softly at her neck. "'Twould be enough for now."

"One hour?" She laughed mockingly. "Why, Gavin O'Malley, for shame, are you saying you'd tire of me so quickly then?"

He shook his head. "Nay, *a muirnín*. Forever would be too short for that."

"We've all the time in this world, my love," Aislinn replied, eyes gleaming with love as she gazed at him, as time bent and shifted around them once again. "Beyond that I can make you no promise."

"Aye." Gavin nodded in answer. "We'd best be quick then."

About the Author

PG Forte inhabits a world only slightly less strange than the ones she creates. Filled with serendipity, coincidence, love at first sight and dreams come true…it also bears an uncanny resemblance to Berkeley, California.

She wrote her first serialized story when she was still in her teens. The sexy, ongoing adventure tales were very popular at her oh-so-proper, all girls, Catholic High School, where they helped to liven up otherwise dull classes. Even if her teachers didn't always think so.

Originally a Jersey girl, PG now resides on the extreme left coast where she writes rule bending, genre blending erotic romance and paranormal stories.

It's a tough job, but someone's got to do it.

Links to reach PG Forte:

www.PGForte.com
Facebook.com/AuthorPGForte
Twitter.com/PGForte